Warwickshire County Council

~~Myst~~			
LiL 6/19			

This item is to be returned or renewed before the latest date above. It may be borrowed for a further period if not in demand. **To renew your books:**

- **Phone the 24/7 Renewal Line 01926 499273 or**
- **Visit www.warwickshire.gov.uk/libraries**

Discover ● Imagine ● Learn ● *with libraries*

Working for Warwickshire

and geopolitics, is a genuine tour de force, and
an exciting literary debut'
Seattle Times

'A great wrenching beautiful book'
Laline Paull, author of *The Bees*

0141564749

'As electric a novel as I've ever read'
Esquire

'Sunil Yapa is a writer of great compassion'
NPR

'In the contemporary tradition of Aleksandar Hemon
and Philipp Meyer, with echoes of Michael Ondaatje and
Arundhati Roy, Yapa strides forward with a literary Molotov
cocktail to light up the dark ... A symphony of a novel'
Colum McCann, author of *Let the Great World Spin*

'A stunningly orchestrated work of narrative power.
This novel marshals all the vital forces of our existence —
from the domestic to the political — and offers them to the
reader with equal doses of compassion and beauty'
Dinaw Mengestu, author of *All Our Names*

'Its heart beats and bleeds on every page ...
This book is delightfully, forcefully alive, and I feel
more alive for having read it'
Eleanor Henderson, author of *Ten Thousand Saints*

'A full-throated chorus of voices on all sides ...
Sunil Yapa has achieved something special,
a story that is as tragic as it is relevant, as
unflinching as it is humane. Watch out'
Smith Henderson, author of *Fourth of July Creek*

YOUR
HEART
IS A
MUSCLE
THE
SIZE OF
A FIST

SUNIL YAPA

ABACUS

First published in the United States in 2016 by Little, Brown and Company
First published in Great Britain in 2016 by Little, Brown
This paperback edition published in 2016 by Abacus

1 3 5 7 9 10 8 6 4 2

A CIP catalogue record for this book
is available from the British Library.

ISBN 978-0-349-14142-8

Printed and bound in Great Britain by
Clays Ltd, St Ives plc

Papers used by Little, Brown are from well-managed forests
and other responsible sources.

MIX
Paper from
responsible sources
FSC
www.fsc.org   FSC® C104740

Abacus
An imprint of
Little, Brown Book Group
Carmelite House
50 Victoria Embankment
London EC4Y 0DZ

An Hachette UK Company
www.hachette.co.uk

www.littlebrown.co.uk

This is a work of fiction. Although for authenticity I have referred to
real events, the characters in the book and their actions are entirely fictional, and
any similarity to real people or organisations is entirely coincidental.

For my parents:
My father, who taught me how to see the world;
My mother, who showed me how one might love it

1

The match struck and sputtered. Victor tried again. He put match head to phosphate strip with the gentle pressure of one long finger and the thing sparked and caught and for the briefest of moments he held a yellow flame. Victor—curled into himself like a question mark, a joint hanging from his mouth; Victor with his hair natural in two thick braids, a red bandanna folded and knotted to hold them back; Victor—with his dark eyes and his thin shoulders and his *cafecito con leche* skin, wearing a pair of classic Air Jordans, the leather so white it glowed—imagine him how you will because he hardly knew how to see himself. He was nineteen years old and should have felt as sweet as a bluebird in the dew, but in the awful damp of the early morning, after another night of sleeping on cold concrete—or not sleeping—he moved like an old man, grumbling like the world was out to get him, had in fact perhaps already gotten him, struck him down without mercy or care or intent as if it hadn't even seen him standing there, he had just been in the way.

He knelt and made a cup of his two brown hands. Look at him bowing his head to this fragile light, joint pinched between his lips, wearing a puffy down jacket, olive green and so ragged he might have found it abandoned on the beach. Listen to the quiet

1

rhythm of his breath. This is his morning ritual, the closest this boy comes to prayer. Skinny Victor, who believed in his heart of hearts that most everything was bullshit, for three years he had tramped the world and still he had no idea just how it worked, how people managed daily life on this blue-green planet of slums and smog, the easy knife, the lazy blade.

The traffic on the freeway thundered over his head, the sound of the big trucks hitting the joints of the highway a muted clacking like a pair of spoons. Beyond the cave of the underpass, beyond the water and the warehouses, out in the city where the streets climbed from the docks to the downtown core, the sound of the chanting crowd was a distant buzzing—fifty thousand desperate flies knocking against fifty thousand closed windows. Victor had heard talk of it for weeks. At the shelter. Bumming smokes from the tourists on the pier. At the coffee shop nursing a tea and swiping scraps from the empty plates. And now, here they were, thousands in the streets and the way their voices rose and fell, sliding down the hill, ringing off the renovated lofts, the brick apartments, the cars parked nose to tail along the oil-black street—it was like an alarm bell sounding in his chest. It was the million-voiced ocean roar of Calcutta or Caracas booming from their angry mouths, echoing in the canyons of smoked glass and steel.

An alarm ringing in his chest saying, Go, go, go.

He had been camped in a cheap tent beneath the underpass for three months now and he had put his mind to the matter, rolled it around in that big old brain, and he knew this much—he needed to get the fuck out.

Victor, he was onto some higher math.

The calculus of kind bud, the physics of dispersal, the geometry of escape.

He had more sticky, stinky, purple-haired marijuana on his

person than ever before in his short life, and the glory of it, the mind-fucking enormity of the possibilities, had him whirling.

Because weed equaled cash and cash equaled a ticket on the airline of his choice to the destination of his choice. He was going to ignore how he scored the weed because escape velocity was the dope necessary to break free from the gravity of home's heavy hold. Lord, let us fly. Yeah, get the feet moving at a pleasant cruising speed of five hundred miles per hour to some dark and lovely corner of the globe. Let pilot and copilot read the dials and mark the birds; Victor only wanted to recline his seat and watch the border recede below him like a line of marching ants following a trail of sugar to its source.

He lowered his head to the flame, mindful of his braids. But in the windiest spot he could have chosen, his hands proved an insufficient home. His little cardboard match, his little paper flame, she bent horizontal and made her exit, disappeared before she had done what work he required.

He gave up. Dropped joint and matchbook in the breast pocket of his down jacket and retired to his tent, where he ducked inside and gathered his sleeping bag in his arms and stuffed it into its sack. He rolled his mat and tied it with a length of cord. He sat on the roll of foam and slid off his shoes and removed an old toothbrush from the pocket of his jacket and began polishing the white leather, the brush kept strictly for this purpose. The shoes he hadn't seen in years. A gift from his father, long ago. So long ago it seemed like another life. He had kept them boxed for years—preserved in the clean antiseptic air of an anger so large and old and familiar he had no name for it. His father.

In the morning when he woke and at night before turning in and during the odd windblown moments of the day when the boredom or regret or homesickness were so heavy he felt them like a knot in the pit of his stomach—he swept and tidied. He put things in their place. Joint in his pocket, braids behind his ears. Memory and longing a black gunpowder he tamped down the wide-bore barrel of his neck. Even here, living beneath an underpass with the rumbling traffic overhead and bits of metal, he didn't know what, slivers of brake pad, oil-flecked grit, drifting down and settling in his hair, grinding between his teeth and covering his tent in a fine film of filth—even here, yes, he cleaned and swept.

Because that was what you did to keep the loneliness at bay, to keep at arm's length the sense that you may have made a vital mistake somewhere, or perhaps it was your parents, or maybe it was just the world in general that had fucked everything up. Thoughts like these could not enter the swept half-moon he carved thrice daily in front of his tent. Thoughts like these had a certain regard for cleanliness, for industrious energy and purpose. Doing something, he had discovered, anything, however small, that contributed to your meaningfulness of self and surroundings—well, that was the trick. That was the trick to not feel like shit.

Victor heard his stomach growling and back behind him, where his camp sat in the gravel spread beneath the highway, the thick-throated rumble of the daily commute. Farther off, in the distance over the hill, that roar of voices faded and grew, came rolling through the slotted streets to rest in the salty air of the pier. It had a rhythm to it. Sounded like ocean swells crashing on a beach, volleys of cannon fire destroying some corporate citadel and, hearing that, man, he bent and laced his shoes, grinning like the devil.

His heart of hearts—it was a thing he sometimes imagined, when high, as a moon circling a lifeless planet; a satellite waiting transmission from the once bright surface where billions had lived and died, the history of their ruin written in twisted steel; ash drifting against the homes like a wet, blinding snow.

If he was being honest, or if he had been perhaps a little less tired, he could have said his heart was laced with anger, holey as Swiss cheese. His heart of hearts poisoned by a bitter, wounded hatred, a sickness of the soul. But he was too tired for that. Too tired to believe in any of that—the heart or the soul. Too tired to hate or care or rage, because how could you hate if you didn't care, and he had cared too long already. He was burned out on it. He didn't have a name for it—this feeling out beyond the orbit of the tiresome rage—and he didn't have the time. His feet were growing restless. He'd already been here too long. Time to go; to go; to go.

He zipped his tent tight and dropped a little lock on the zip and then he was hoofing it up the hill in his white Jordans, his olive green jacket with the ruff-lined hood keeping him warm. Sludgy Seattle light painting the buildings around him gray-gold, reflecting bright off the broken windows of the warehouses to the east, the gray project towers to the north with laundry flapping on the balconies like flags of a tenement nation. But what was this? This street was dead. The shops shuttered, plywood boards nailed over their windows. He shook his head and bent and humped the pack up the hill.

By the time he turned the corner and hit the crowd he was sweating, and the sheer human multitude, the force of the compressed humanity, nearly knocked him over. There were people hollering from every corner, marching people of all shapes and sizes, all body types and hairdos, an assortment of clothing choices and fashion accessories to express their personalities, and goddamn, fuck the protests? No, no, no. His brown eyes blazed bright. God *bless* the protesters. How many were here? He didn't know, but yeah, they were the revolutionary souls who were going to buy his weed. They were his ticket out. He did a little clap with the chant, nodding his head to catch the rhythm of the thing, and watched them spinning delirious in the street. Hippies in their

Gore-Tex, punks in their sweaty denim, and holy crap, it seemed to Victor as he joined the surging crowd that they were popping out from every hole and door, waves of protesters sloshing in the streets, bright-eyed thousands appearing as if summoned. Pierced kids in army jackets squatting on a bench to pass a clove cigarette. Dreadlocked djinns dangling from the lampposts, cameras around their necks. And the entire motley crowd chanting, chanting and now singing, old and young, their voices raised to the cloudy sky as if song were the very root of being.

He didn't know whether to stand or sit, to go streaking through the city with his hands on his head or to collapse in the street in openmouthed wonder. Because here they came, stomping into the dawn from their suburban warrens, from their gorgeous mansions that glittered fat on the Sound. Civil rights lawyers wearing combat boots. Radical teachers in sheepskin-lined jackets. He saw them come rising into the morning air, a chant on their lips:

WHAT DO WE WANT???
JUSTICE!!!
WHEN DO WE WANT IT???
NOW!!!

What did that mean? Justice?

He looked at a blond girl in overalls, an African-type shawl looped atop her head. He looked at her angry blue eyes, her perfect white teeth, her gym-sculpted arm, naked to the cold, and he didn't know what justice meant to her, to him, to anybody in this country. He saw them come rising from North Face tents gone swampy with sex; from the paint-splattered warehouse where they gathered to gossip and train; from the cellar of the church where they had sat in foldout chairs discussing what they knew of what

6

they called the Third World and there was a look on their faces—all their sweet, round, high-fructose faces—that was hoping everything was more or less okay with the world, even though they knew it wasn't, and Victor, looking at that look, he didn't know whether to laugh or cry.

Because here came the defenders of democracy, riding the ferry in from the islands. Climbing down from the haze of an interstate bus. Crossing the bridge in their Subarus, their aging Toyotas, their cheap American rolling junk, and Victor, bestowed with the unenviable gift of geography and sight, saw their merino wool scarves twisted at the neck, their T-shirts and flannels and fleeces, their backpacks and jeans, and he thought of the factories he had seen along the border in Mexico, the lines of women waiting for work to begin, the razor-wire fences behind which the things of the world were made, the smoke curling into the sky like a pencil drawing of a drowned woman's hair.

How do you protest this?

Three topless girls went by crying "Death to the police state," their breasts bouncing in the cold air, duct tape across their nipples. Victor almost expected to see families lining the sidewalks, mothers and fathers set up in beach chairs and blankets, children hoisted onto shoulders, crying "Daddy, Daddy, here come the beasts." It was a painted carnival for the end of days, and on an impulse, just the weird out-of-body feeling of it, Victor turned to the guy next to him, a hefty guy in a blue jacket, and said, "Hey, man. You need any weed?"

"Do I need any what?"

On closer inspection, the guy seemed to be a union man, the bulk and size of him, the rusty air of his moonscape face, one of the guys who worked down at the docks or something. His face folded like an old jacket.

7

"Any weed. You need any weed?"

The guy looked to see was Victor kidding. He was walking and holding hands with his union buddies, or whatever, a great long line of them, bowling league buddies holding hands, which Victor thought was kind of weird.

"Trust me," Victor said more loudly. "It's great shit."

The guy looking at him like he might be contagious.

"Kid," the big man said.

"What?"

"Get the fuck out of here."

Victor slid his bandanna from his forehead, shook his damp braids, and felt the stuffy weight of their bodies shuffling by, their signs, their hope, their smell, not entirely unpleasant, of incense and baked-in sweat, and he was remembering and living and thinking and dying more or less all at the same time. It was 1999 in America, he had traveled the world for three years, looking for what he didn't know, and now here he found himself: absolutely allergic to belief, nineteen years old, and totally alone.

8

2

John Henry stood in the crowd inhaling them through every pore, perfectly at rest, perfectly at peace. My people. They smelled of onion and cigarette and sex, the human animal musk of sixty beautiful human bodies beneath their beautiful blue tarps and he raised his arms to the sky and breathed them deep. Around him they marched and they danced; they chanted and they sang. He felt their voices buzzing in his chest. People linking arms with strangers they had never met, hand in hand with people whose homes they had never seen, and he closed his eyes and felt the power of what they were doing coiling around him, some force inexorably gathering around them here at the edge of the millennium, one month from the end of the American century.

Look at him there, this forty-four-year-old man in a handwoven cowboy hat and chunky black Medicare glasses, his red beard long and wiry like some mountain monk's. This was a man with the days stitched into his skin. This was a man you could imagine in a dream of the Himalaya, high above the clouds where the granite falls away like glass and you turn a corner and there he is, spinning a prayer wheel. Not from the Himalaya, but from Detroit, Michigan. Holy man of the Rust Belt. Sacrament of iron and steel; blessed be these assembly lines; blessed be these tired hands. Look at his pierced ears and his crooked teeth. Look at his eyes shining behind those busted-up glasses, the frames more duct tape than plastic, but the repairs neatly done. Check him there among the densely packed bodies, feeling the heat and the human smell of them, a humid funk to spark the morning air, and know that if there was one place in the great, glorious dying world he wanted to be, this was it.

My people.

John Henry had at one time been a churchman, a storefront preacher, and, inevitably it now seemed, he had lost the church, but not the need, and here he was in the middle of it all, heart a broken clockspring in his chest, leading a chant.

AIN'T NO POWER LIKE
THE POWER OF THE PEOPLE
AND THE POWER OF THE PEOPLE
DON'T STOP.
SAY WHAT!?!

Their voices together a roaring wave careening down the alleys, cascading off the cordon of metro buses parked around the convention center and up through air vents of the Sheraton, voices reaching for the delegates hiding in their rooms on the upper floors. John Henry could see some of them gathered in the lobby of the Sheraton, two floors above the street, shadowed forms pressed to the floor-to-ceiling windows, hands on either side of their faces like kids at the aquarium watching the sharks make their dumb circles in the tank.

He saw the South Korean delegation with matching flags on their matching shoulder bags paused on the low wide steps of the Sheraton, standing there with newspapers over their heads for the rain and polite, puzzled smiles as if someone had just told them a joke that didn't quite translate.

Here came a European-looking delegate in tasseled loafers. His hair was curly and white. His suit was gray and he was making notes in a leather-bound notebook, nodding and smiling as though he recognized something in the cityscape, like there was a shop that sold his favorite sweet, an indulgence he kept secret from his wife. An aide running after him with an opened umbrella.

AIN'T NO POWER LIKE
THE POWER OF THE PEOPLE
AND THE POWER OF THE PEOPLE
DON'T STOP.

"Say what?!" cried John Henry.

The American dream was dead. All those promises now just cold ashes between his people's chanting teeth, sitting heavy on their tongues.

Instead they said, "Sustainable agriculture."

They said, "Global solidarity."

They said, "How beautiful is a seed, a tender green stalk of life."

They wore hooded sweatshirts peopled with homemade patches. They wore bandannas slashed outlaw-style across the mouth, a triangle from nose to chin, knotted at the neck. They ate bread and cabbage looted from dumpsters because it was a form of political protest and he loved each one of them enough to die for them, if it came to that, which it would not.

He stroked his beard and heard them say, "People are more important than profits."

"People," they said, "are more important than profits."

"*People.* Are more important than profits."

11

Their words had the quality of midnight prayer, deep from the depths of another sleepless night, as if the right words might call forth a future where they need march no more.

They said, "We're going to shut those corporate motherfuckers down."

John Henry heard their voices and knew this was no ordinary protest, this congregation in the streets. No, this was the new American religion. This desire which leapt continents. The longing of the heart to embrace a stranger and be unashamed.

They said, "A global nonviolent revolution."

They said, "How beautiful and brave when a people rise for what is right."

Six a.m. and he watched them swarming the streets of his city in a gauzy mausoleum light, a people's army climbing from basement mattresses and garage apartments, the skyline of the city black-crowned and spooky at their back.

In their hooded sweatshirts and shin-high boots they looked like end-of-the-world penitents stretching into the dawn. Hip to the world's saddest sins.

They said, "The future belongs to us."

And maybe it did, but they looked so young, so young and fragile, and when the time came would they have courage—would they have the discipline to make it so?

Look with him at his people. This man who once preached from a pulpit, John Henry, who was wound up and weary with too much love, too much joy, too much rage. How many shelter cots that barely registered the man's weight so light he was, the soft pillow of how many stone steps had cradled his head? John Henry, who had lost his church, look with him at his people. Look at his god made manifest in every form and shape of the broken world. Look with him at how they exit the church in an orderly fashion and tip their chins to the sky. Look at how they come from the darkness of their homes, backs stiff, stretching and tying the bandannas tight, checking one another's faces for an idea of what violence this day might bring. Look with him at these wet American faces, ordinary and beautiful, and tell me you don't feel more than a little bit afraid.

They wanted to tear down the borders, to make a leap into a kind of love that would be like living inside a new human skin, wanted to dream themselves into a life they did not yet know.

He heard them in the streets saying, "Another world is possible," and beneath his ribs broken and healed and twice broken and healed and thrice broken and healed, he shuddered and thought, God help us. We are mad with hope. Here we come.

3

Officer Timothy Park knocked his riot stick against the stiff polycarbonate of his armored leg, producing a hefty sort of clack and
whack, which, right this second, he found immensely satisfying as
he sucked a black coffee spiked with fifteen sugars and watched the
way they walked, heads high, arms swinging, and thought: Why
in holy hell do these people look so happy?

Surely they knew they were going to lose?

Welders greeting plumbers with flung-open arms; scrawny
old guys with crooked backs and the kind of crappy cardigan his
dad used to wear while raking leaves, they were shaking hands
with society ladies strung with pearls, and Park grimaced as they
hugged and helloed, threw their arms around one another's necks,
a grainy mist falling. Hugging? Why were they hugging? The last
time Park had hugged someone had been at a funeral.

Park was standing beside the department's armored vehicle—
affectionately known as the PeaceKeeper—with his sometime
riding buddy, Julia. The PeaceKeeper was some civilian version
of an armored Humvee—a great metal duck painted matte black
with tiny rectangles for the driver's windows like the slits in hilltop
bunkers and down below four fat tires which meant they could roll
wherever they pleased. There were two swinging doors on the back,

a hatch to pop your head from the top, and running boards on each side, and look at Ju there kind of lazing around like it was a cover shoot on some tropical isle, one hand resting idly on the butt of her department-issue pepper spray, the other resting against the side of the vehicle where the letters were painted huge and white:

SEATTLE POLICE DEPARTMENT

Call her Miss July, even though it was, in fact, November and a probable riot situation. But Park didn't mind the riot gear, didn't mind watching Ju's body absorb the rough vibration of the idling truck. Call her Miss November Riots if you wanted—she was as lovely as a parade rifle that the kids spin and twirl—and watching her was his reward for the frustration of having to police a protest march. Protecting an anarchist parade, that was the kind of world we had come to, but Ju was beautiful and tough and what was the word? Willowy? Park didn't mind the show at all. She was like a video game knockout is what she was and ever since he'd moved to Seattle and joined the SPD he'd been trying to get her out for a drink. The guys in the precinct all laughed—everyone wanted to sleep with Ju; that Mayan, almost Asian look she had going with her bronze skin and dark almond-shaped eyes, that razor-sharp tongue that could cut you a new one in *two* languages, the long hair tucked high in a ponytail the color of coal-black tar. The thing Park liked was her eyes. He thought she had brown eyes so bright they could have been used as lights in some kind of emergency operating situation. If the need arose.

When Park told his buddy Baker about his crush, Baker looked at him crosswise. "That one?" he said. "She looks at you and you feel like a bug waiting for the shoe, but, you know, like, pleased about the situation."

16

"Yeah, I know," Park said, "but ... "

"Like happy you're gonna get squashed," Baker said, laughing and walking to the vending machine. "Like you think it's going to feel *so good* to get stomped."

Park watched a group of young people taking over the intersection in front of him. They were a part of the crowd, and yet separate from it in a way he couldn't define. One minute it seemed an undifferentiated mass, and then these young people materialized out of the chaos of bodies.

To his eye they were wearing stained and greasy jeans like some kind of junkie army risen from their mothers' pullout couches, but there was an urgency to their movements, shuffling quickly like they were loonies five minutes escaped from the Harborview nuthouse on Ninth, and he sipped his coffee and laughed. There was a calm camaraderie, too, a sort of ease he recognized. As though they were an elite military unit—saying little, communicating instead out of seasoned memory, the easy gait of shared purpose.

He set his coffee on the 'Keeper and watched in total stunned astonishment as they sat down in a circle and then began locking themselves together with chains and PVC pipe.

Maybe as an officer of the law he should be doing something about that?

He turned to Julia and nodded toward the kids.

"I mean what's going on here, Ju. Are they protesting the world?"

Julia—Ju—she looked at him in that way she had of looking at him. As if a thousand miles stood between her body and yours. Or so she wished. Aristocratic, was that the word?

"Are they protesting the world?" she said flatly. "That's what you want to know?"

"Yeah."

17

"Which one, Park?"

"Which one what?"

"Which world, *pendejo*? Yours or theirs?"

He turned away. The PeaceKeeper was parked in the zebra lines of the south crosswalk at Sixth and Union, its ass with the double doors pointing west toward a bank, its headlights and flat hood pointing toward a coffee shop, which was wisely, Park thought, closed and shuttered for the day. On the other side of the intersection, perpendicular to the wide side of the 'Keeper, beyond that mess of kids and hippies, a series of low wide steps fanned upward, creating a wedge-shaped plaza with the wooden benches at the bottom as the crust, which was funny, Park thought, because the plaza was not public, but private, narrowing and climbing as it approached the entrance, ending among potted ferns and the glass doors of the Sheraton lobby. Above the lobby, ivy-covered beige walls. Above that, gray glass rose a neck-craning thirty-five floors above the street. Pretty much your typical pretentious downtown bullcrap in the opinion of Park, who was feeling pretty irritated because he hadn't eaten anything besides a banana and a power shake this morning and whose stomach was already growling despite that being only about two hours ago, when he woke at four a.m. to do abdominal crunches in the dust of the bare floor beside his bed.

A young mother in a thousand-dollar mountaineering jacket was circulating behind the PeaceKeeper. She was on the south side of Sixth, behind their lines, and Park saw her over the top of the PeaceKeeper distributing coffee and cupcakes from a tray. She seemed suburban and pleasant. Park noticed she had parked a baby stroller in the cedar chips of a municipal tree for which he could cite her if he chose, which he did not currently feel like doing, but as he reminded himself, he could if he wanted, which was the point. He stepped around the front of the PeaceKeeper and was pleased when Julia stepped down and followed him.

The lady approached them where they stood beside the PeaceKeeper.

She offered them the tray of fresh coffees and the paper-wrapped cupcakes, nodding toward the protesters chanting behind Park and Ju.

Her voice pitched conspiratorially, she said, "Aren't they a pain? I mean, gosh, I thought the sixties were *over*." She released a bright laugh as if a little surprised at her own naughtiness.

"All those banners and shouting," the lady said. "What are they doing? It's almost Christmas!"

She was sort of whining now and Park, his back to the 'Keeper, asked her to please step away from the vehicle. The lady continued forward as if she hadn't heard, offering the tray to them as if she were in her living room entertaining guests.

Park put on his gloves and flexed his fingers until the fit was tight.

"I just don't know what they hope to *accomplish* sitting in the street like that," she said.

"I asked you to step away from the vehicle," Park said. And then he paused and added, "What's the matter with you?"

The woman smiled in a neighborly way as if these were just morning pleasantries, as if a smile were enough because, after all, they were on the same side—the cops and a friendly patriotic young mother offering coffees—they were on the same side here, right?

"I just don't know what they hope to accomplish," she said again, a little less brightly.

And just like that, Park's baton was in the air and quivering just above the tray of coffees, pointing to her throat.

19

The smile plastered to the lady's face like a light someone forgot to turn off.

"Park," Ju said.

Some of the other cops had stopped what they were doing and were watching good-naturedly even as they unwrapped the lady's cupcakes and gnawed at the edges.

Ju stepped in front of him. Normally he would never have allowed another officer to intercede in his arrest, his encounter. But Christ, it was Ju. She placed her hand on the baton. He lowered it gently to his side.

Ju looked him in the face. The acknowledgment passing there. There would be other, better moments. He nodded, said to the woman, "Thank you for the coffee." Then, gesturing with his chin at the stroller, he said, "But why don't you get your kid out of here? You know?"

The woman's smile hadn't faltered. Her eyes had gone wide, face pink as a plastic doll, and still she went on smiling like a thousand-kilowatt idiot in her mountain-climbing jacket and her stroller parked next to a goddamn armored police vehicle.

She stumbled backward away from Ju, away from Park. The tray crashed to the ground. Cupcakes and coffee spilled across the concrete steps and a general groan of misfortune went up from the assembled troops.

Didn't matter. The lady was already halfway down the street, stroller smooth and gliding before her.

The cops returned to their conversations.

Park racked his baton. "Ju," he said.

"What?"

"Don't ever freaking do that again."

"Chief said we should take it easy, Park. Chief said they're nonviolent."

"Nonviolent. Is that right?"

"Yes."

Surgical, that was the word. Her eyes looked bright enough to be surgeon's tools and Park sometimes liked to dream himself under the knife.

"Well, not for nothing, Julia," he said, "but what does the Chief know? The Chief is as soft as butter on a picnic plate."

4

Reports were coming in from all over the downtown, crackling through the radio clipped to his belt, and Chief Bishop knew he should be paying attention, but he felt distracted, a kind of tectonic drift of soul, as if something fundamental were loose inside, an oceanic plate going molten beneath the continent's weight.

Tom-four-two.

This is Command. Go ahead.

Approximately seven thousand southbound. We see chanting and signs. Over.

Bishop listening to the radio chatter on his belt and looking over the growing crowd from a spot twenty feet above their heads in a cherry picker requisitioned from Seattle City Light. He felt a fondness for these people, a kind of love-struck nostalgia for his city. Americans marching in the rain. Their faces, failed and flawed—they were the faces of a part of American life that was passing away, if not already gone, the belief that the world could be changed by marching in the streets. Bishop perched like a bird on a wire watching the crowd from the cherry picker. He extended the crane to get above the bare branches of November trees, thinking he had protected these people for thirty years—first as a beat cop, and then as a captain going to the community meetings twice a week, which was where not incidentally he had met his wife, on and on up through the ranks, working the job, investing himself, practicing the profession of policing as he best knew, and now here he was their Chief, their leader—and, now, why now did they see the need to come marching like lambs to the slaughter?

Four-one-three to Command.

Go ahead, Four-one-three.

Anarchist seen headed south.

Can you describe the anarchist?

Black hooded youth. Over.

Bishop in the bucket at the end of a crane wearing his Chief's blues with the five stars on the lapel. He kept himself fit, but he wasn't a gym rat. He preferred to be outside—fishing, camping, diving—and after a summer spent diving alone in Mexico, hiking alone in the Cascades, he had a deep tan, a healthy glow about him that had absolutely nothing to do with his mental state or inner condition of the soul. His hair was sandy brown, going gray at the temples, his eyes a watery blue behind his out-of-fashion overly large glasses, and he held a radio in one hand and a megaphone in the other. He brought the megaphone to his mouth and clicked it on:

HEY YOU. YOU CAN'T PEE THERE. YES YOU. MOVE IT.

Bishop knew his son was out there somewhere in the ragged crowd. His sweet skinny ebony son, missing since August 1996. Three years. His son who had graduated from high school at age sixteen, part of an accelerated program where they jumped you grades because of your high IQ, and when you finished early you jumped your home because of your asshole dad. Or so Bishop supposed. Who knew.

His son left when he was just sixteen, disappeared into the world, and some part of Bishop's memory still insisted on remembering him as that skinny sixteen-year-old sitting on his bed with his Jordan posters hanging on the walls.

"Electricity," his son said, gesturing around his room, books stacked in piles on every available surface. "Do you ever think about what electricity means?"

And Bishop, thumbing idly through the odd titles, said, "Sure I do, son."

"I flip the switch and the lights come on."

"Son, go to college," Bishop said, putting the book down. "We can afford it. Join a group. Hand out flyers."

"I flip the switch and the lights go off. Where does it all come from?"

Bishop and Suzanne's only son. Suzanne's son, in fact, whom Bishop had inherited when they married eight years ago, so, not his son by biology or birth, but did that make the loss, the crush of longing, any less dense? He felt like he was sixty meters below and falling still.

"Go to classes," Bishop said. "Meet a girl."

His son—missing since August 1996, a little less than a year after Suzanne's death—saying, "Water. I twist the handle and it comes streaming out. No buckets, no pails, no trudging to the well in the ashy light of dawn. Anytime I want it . . . boom! There it is."

And Bishop saying, "The ashy what? Listen, college is the key. We can afford it."

"Water in the kitchen. Water in the bathroom. Water in the garden hose."

"Go to college. Meet a girl. Get a job."

"Dad, are you even listening to me? Water. I twist a gold handle and it comes leaping out as if it had spent its whole life waiting for my sweet touch."

Bishop paused. He saw them there in his mind's eye, two men, blue-eyed father and brown-eyed son, breathing and talking in the son's room, and him so blind, so alive and blind to the intensity of his son, of what it meant to live as a brown man, a black man. And which was his son, he didn't entirely know. They had never really talked about it, one among a million things, and why should we, he is my son and I am his father and he, a black man or brown man, but a young man and me, his father, a grown man, and I love my boy. Me, a man who only wanted somehow to protect this younger, more vulnerable version of himself. Tell me what else is there to it?

"Son," Bishop said, "suffering is everywhere. I see it every day. And if you wear your heart on your sleeve, the world will just kill you cold."

"What's that mean?"

"Stop caring so goddamn much."

And if you were counting, Bishop thought, go ahead and add this conversation, which occurred one blistering summer afternoon exactly two weeks before his son took off, to the long list of his failings as a flawed human being, his failure as a father. Because, truthfully, Bishop had recognized the thing in his adopted son for what it really was—the fever of grief. It was a brokenhearted rage that he, too, felt slamming around his chest. Suzanne. Yes, the boy missed his mother and what did Bishop want to say? He wanted to say, Life's a cruel thing, son. Give it enough time and it will take back everything you have ever loved.

Three years his son had been gone. Suzanne—it seemed she had left just yesterday.

Four-one-three to Command.

Go ahead, Four-one-three.

We are a soft platoon here, Command. Permission to go hats and bats?

26

The Chief brought the megaphone to his mouth and then lowered it. What had he missed in the world that had brought these people into the streets? He watched them pass and felt a dip in his mood, the familiar phlegmy despair, because what kind of revolutionaries were these? They didn't wire themselves with explosives, strap ball bearings and nails to their ribs. They didn't detonate themselves in a crowded marketplace at noon.

No.

These were children who put their bodies in the street, who chained their bodies together and waited for the cops to come—his cops with their batons and their tear gas and their pepper spray.

Eighth and Seneca we see—

Three-five-one to Command. Over.

Bottle in a brown paper bag. Be advised.

He had scheduled nine hundred on-duty officers. Now they were looking at upward of fifty thousand protesters in the street and four hundred delegates—four hundred delegates from one hundred and thirty-five countries who may or may not speak English—to safely shepherd from the Sheraton Hotel to their meetings at the convention center.

Nine hundred on-duty cops. Fifty thousand demonstrators, maybe more. It was only three blocks up Sixth Ave, and yet these streets were impassable. They might as well have built a wall in the intersection. He would have to clear the whole damn thing to get those delegates through to the other side. And how the hell was he going to do that? These streets were shut down.

Bishop watching the crowd, watching his line of officers and thinking about his son, when a voice cut through the noise. It sounded irritated, harried, on the verge of out of control.

Bishop, this is MACC, do you copy?

Chief Bishop recognized the voice as belonging to the Mayor

and he imagined the Mayor there at the Multi-Agency Command Center, surrounded by FBI, by State Patrol, Secret Service, by all the agency men. The Mayor in a suit, talking tough and waving a cigar. Even though, to Bishop's knowledge, the man did not smoke.

Anarchist seen headed south with flammable accelerant. Advise. Over.

Please stay off the

Is Bishop. Repeat.

Not under control. We need

This is MACC. Bishop, what is your situation? Over.

Repeat Bishop, what is your situation at the Sheraton?

The MACC was the new two-story complex halfway up the hill, the nerve center and brain trust for the officers in the street. The central control room was lined with monitors relaying information back from the more than two hundred cameras installed all over the city and where Bishop himself, as chief of police, probably should have been, but he wanted to be out here in the street. Where police belonged.

Bishop brought his radio to his mouth. What the hell was the Mayor doing at the MACC? He wasn't a tactical director. He was a politician. A fucking PR man with wingtips and a firm handshake.

Mr. Mayor, sir. Our situation at the Sheraton is stable. I am seeing three to four thousand protesters in our area. But they are peaceful. Repeat they are peaceful. Over.

Bishop, the delegates. They need to be at the convention center. Where are the delegates? I got Secret Service breathing—

Bishop keyed his radio.

Mr. Mayor, the delegates are safe. I have instructed them to stay inside the hotel.

Sixth and Seneca. Over.

Please stay off the command.

Bishop, I need that street clear for the opening ceremonies. We need to get the delegates to the convention center. Do you copy?

Seattle Command, this is Three-five-one. 11-40 at Eighth and Seneca.

Bishop's radio hung in front of his mouth like a forgotten forkful of supper. 11-40. That was a request for an ambulance. And then the Mayor's voice was so clear a shiver went spilling dark and cold down the Chief's spine.

Bishop.

Sir?

I don't care what you do to get it done.

Sir?

Bishop, clear that fucking street.

5

Victor marched and moved with the crush, nodding his head to the syncopated beat. He checked out the hippie chicks in rain-soaked fairy wings, the punk chicks with pierced lips, and he laughed and did a sort of high-necked slouch strutting and bouncing down the street. His jeans were belted around his skinny waist and the extra loop of leather wagged loose from the buckle like a tongue.

He was high as shit.

For three years he had wandered the world and he remembered seeing burning cars on the streets of Managua; he remembered a man in India who would not eat; he remembered a line of women in their bowler hats and long skirts standing atop a hill on the high border between Bolivia and Peru, each with a stone in their hand silently waiting for the police. Protest. Globalization. Victor carried the two lines deep within him. He saw the secret and not-so-secret threads that connected his body in the here and now to worlds three continents away.

The dark sky above him like the dark sky above Shanghai where he had hardly seen the sun, people walking with surgical masks as if that would protect them from the fleets of particulate matter flying their skies like endless flocks of blackbirds bound for the rich nations of the West.

Victor pierced by clues and impressions gathered from the wind like pollen. It was like a radio dial between stations, the way they chanted and cried. The overlapping voices like whispers of other realms—come in, London, come in, New York, come in, Paris, France. Yes? Give China back her sun.

Doing the strut past Banana Republic, past Old Navy and the Gap. Beneath Niketown he stopped. The lights were on and people were in the stores doing their holiday shopping. People were drifting leisurely through the aisles, comparing prices. What were they doing behind that glass? Buying *pants*? He hammered against the window with a closed fist. A woman who was placing folded garments in a bag looked at him with a face like murder.

Whatever.

Trying to sell to a union man—that had been stupid.

He was smarter than that.

Since then Victor had made three more attempts. He tried a girl in a sundress who, when he offered, looked at him like he was diseased.

He tried an old man banging a goatskin drum. The old man closed his eyes, hands going full tilt, lost in the rhythm of his own making, and the way he smiled Victor figured he was already stoned.

He tried a kid in black boots and suspenders wearing a Rage Against the Machine shirt. The kid showed him a large X razored into the back of his hand. Victor had said, "Okay, but what about the weed," and the kid just shook his head and told him to go fuck himself, he was straight-edge. Victor almost threw the weed at him, bounced it off his ugly fucking mug, but then he thought better of it and moved off, shaking his head, sliding the weed back into his zippered pack.

If only someone would buy a goddamn bag. At least an *eighth*.

People were looking at him funny, and he knew why. The pair of loose-tongued Nikes. Yeah, white Nikes with a red silhouette of a black man who could fly. Go ahead and look. He wanted that, he needed that, the edge, the distance, the fuck you. Wearing a pair of sweatshop shoes to a sweatshop protest—well, he wanted to say, what the fuck do you think you're wearing? I wear my Nikes and they remind me I am small and the world is large and who are you to judge me for a thing like that? The world is large and I am small. The first thing he thought when he woke up. The thing he had thought at her grave just two days ago. Four years to the date. The last thing he thought every night when he went to bed in his tent with the waves bellowing and the cars chugging like ships passing through the port, every night since he had returned to Seattle three months ago, returned to his father's house on the hill, busted the latch he had always busted, crawled in the basement window he had always crawled into (or out of), and retrieved the shoes in their box from the closet of his room.

So hell yeah, go ahead and look, people. They're my lucky sneaks.

And then he saw them. The perfect boomer couple. Victor decided to go for the woman, she was wearing gold earrings in some Native design, attractive and kind of hip-looking in a funky hat. She was with her husband and a little girl who was stuffing carrots in her mouth.

Victor sidled up and went into a monologue, improvised on the spot, about marching for Native rights.

The woman's eyes lit up. She began nodding enthusiastically, wisps of brown hair lifting in the breeze. "We're marching with the Nature Conservancy," she announced, something mildly apologetic in her voice. "Working on the turtles."

"Freedom Riders in '64," the husband said.

"Wow," Victor said, "far-out."

The note of pride in the guy's voice contained something Victor suspected he was supposed to relate to, being a brown man with two thick braids, but he couldn't guess what.

"Listen," Victor said, trying to read their faces, feeling this might be his last and only shot at making some cash.

"You guys are some pretty cool heads," he said. "Should I call you Mary Jane?"

Blank looks all around. He searched desperately for the perfect word.

"Reefer. Do you guys puff the reefer?"

"Wait a second," the man said. "What are you trying to do?"

"Grass? Dope?"

"Are you trying to—?"

"Skunk? Dank? Pack a pipe of the kind bud?"

"Are you trying to sell me marijuana?" the man said.

Victor smiling huge, clapped once, glad they could finally connect. "That's right," he said. "That's it, exactly."

"Jesus Christ," the man said.

The lady picked up her little girl and put her on her hip like a sack of groceries.

The husband was suddenly not so friendly. He was irate. Righteous-looking. "They put stoned Indians in jail is where they put you," he said. "You know that?"

"Yeah, yeah," Victor said, "I read something about that once." He back-stepped into the heat of the crowd, looking at the little girl still shoveling carrot sticks into her mouth like trees into a mill. He wanted to tell her: Don't grow up. Nothing but assholes.

They were mad and happy and Victor, he felt suddenly tired. Flat-out exhausted. He climbed a bench and sat with his feet on

34

the seat, letting the people flow around him, feeling low, the self-pity and bile building in his throat. Fucking protest march.

Was that what you called this shit anyway?

A protest march?

When you take to the street to chant the chants, to stomp your feet and rhyme the rhymes?

And all the energy you spend, all the outrage and disgust, is not for you, no, not some sort of personal draining of the pus-filled guilt, but an expression of your compassion for a sad desperate people in a country far away?

Some expression of your compassion for that war-torn country whose citizens are just skin and bones, and who, you imagine, weep long into the night cursing God for a scrap of bread?

A protest march—that's what we call this, right?

Or maybe they're crying because their children make T-shirts in an export-zone sweatshop and yesterday there was an accident— the place burned to the ground and no one had the technology on hand to identify one pile of human ash from another.

Or maybe their son was shot in the head and dumped in a muddy hole and floured with lime and buried beneath a shallow mound of bulldozed earth.

Maybe it was HIV and they couldn't afford the drugs.

Wasn't that what it was called? When you called some friends and made a sign with colored paper and scissors and glue to express your solidarity with the charred bodies of children?

A protest march?

"Sometimes," Victor said to nobody in particular, "I feel like I'm living on the fucking moon."

"I know. I mean that's why we're here, right?"

He turned to find a girl sitting next to him.

She took his hand nonchalantly as if they were brother and

35

sister, Christmas morning, circa 1989, waiting for the orgy of paper and presents. "Can't you feel it? All these people out here together, marching for, you know, justice?"

Victor nodded. He was sort of noticing her hair. Noticing the way she was sitting next to him on the bench. She was pretty in a sophomore year of college kind of way with a button nose and a pink bandanna knotted peasant-style in her corn-silk hair.

She noticed him noticing.

"Don't you have one?"

She touched her hair. Apparently she thought he was checking out her bandanna. When he didn't say anything, she undid the knot. She unwound the bandanna, shook her hair free, and offered it to him.

"That's all right," he said, and touched his forehead where his own bandanna held back his braids. She smiled and shrugged and together they sat and watched the crowd.

On an impulse, just the good feeling of it, he leaned into her ear.

"Let's get high."

Victor felt an immediate ice. She was still sitting there, but it was a certain thing you could sense, a withdrawing into the self as if a switch had been flipped.

"It's good shit," he said, and reached for the half a joint in the pocket of his down jacket.

She actually stepped off the bench.

He bent and lit the roach. Made his body a cave in which a match could flame, and by god it did. He nearly cheered. He shook the match and took a great gasping drag. He held it in his lungs a beat, and then exhaled sweet smoke that zipped across the heads of the crowd like a little runaway train careening off a bridge.

The girl was just standing there looking at him. People were passing in the carnival behind her.

"You can't do that here," she said.

He offered it to her. "Don't worry about the cops," he said.

"No. Look, you don't understand. This is a drug-free area."

He took another drag and laughed smoke. "This is a protest march."

"Where'd you hear that?" she said. "This isn't a protest march. This is a direct action."

"Whatever," he said. He hit the roach again. "What's the difference?"

She stepped forward, put one foot onto the bench, plucked the joint from his lips, and then flicked it to the ground and crushed it into the pavement with her boot.

"Fucking seriously, dude."

In the beam of that cool knowingness he suddenly felt less sure of himself. How could he ever have mistaken her for nothing more than a sexy undergrad? She was a radical, a revolutionary, and he suddenly wanted to be as far away from her as humanly possible.

Her bandanna. The pink flap of cotton which had been holding back her hair. She pressed it into his hand and closed his fist around it.

"Trust me," she said, beginning to move off, "you'll want it later."

Victor, frozen to the bench, dumbfounded, watched her go, the bodies moving past him, sat there mute and scared, letting the noise wash over him in waves.

He wanted to call out to her. He wanted to apologize, to throw away his weed forever and call her back.

He looked at the pink bandanna in his hand. He wanted to call out, "I'll need it for what later?"

Which is when he heard the man's voice. The pissed-off Freedom Rider husband saying loudly, "That's him, Officer. That's him, right there."

Victor turned. The husband was talking to a cop on a horse. The cop was sitting tall. Following the husband's finger pointing Victor's way. There was something wrong with his face. A seriously nasty burn running along the right side of his jaw. And the look on the cop's messed-up face? God bless him if he didn't look like he'd just won the lottery.

6

Her name was Kingfisher, but her friends just called her King. She liked King, the small bite of irony, this twenty-seven-year-old white woman with dreads to the small of her back. She was tall, olive-skinned, vaguely Mediterranean if Mediterranean meant you were trash from coal mining country who could catch a tan easy. Her mother, when drinking, claimed some Cherokee blood way back in their family tree and that was just fine with King. She was muscled, thin, and tough. This woman with ambiguously light brown skin, with green eyes as bright as any sea, who at one time ran a sort of illegal animal shelter behind her off-the-grid house on an unnamed island beyond the city, who journeyed here with four friends in an Econoline van, the four of them eating sandwiches of sprouts and beans, this pretty girl in laced black boots who wore black jeans and a loose white shirt, the sleeves rolled to the shoulder like some kind of back-alley tough—she had the kindest of smiles, a smile which creased her mouth and lit those green eyes and which you could see were she not currently wearing a full-face black gas mask.

She turned to her friends and motioned them into the intersection, looking totally comfortable, a military person of some kind in her gas mask and jeans tucked into her boots, dreads bound with a loop of twine.

Her friends came running around the corner, heading for the intersection.

The police were standing on the southern side of the intersection, between a Niketown and a bank. King noted with amusement that the cops were on the wrong side. Like always. They were standing with their backs to the sloping streets, the streets dropping away behind them five blocks to the water. The convention center where the meetings were to be held was on the *uphill* side of the intersection, two blocks up Union, behind her, where her friends were now setting up their barricades in front of the Sheraton Hotel.

Look at them there. The line of cops in their riot gear. Standing still as statues thirty feet away while behind her, the crowd danced and sang. Here in the front they were calm, a row of seated protesters three souls deep, their arms linked at the elbow. The cops' front line was calm, too. A solid wall of storm trooper flesh and King thought that said it all. They were humans after all, doing a job, and the need to move, the need to shuffle and shift in their heavy gear, was innate. But there they were standing still, not moving a muscle, staring straight ahead like they were those red-coated guards at Buckingham Palace.

An old man in a union jacket was yelling at the police.

"Fucking pigs! You fucking pigs! You make me sick. Look at you! Tools of the corporations. Puppets of your corporate masters. Pigs! Tools! Fucking dirt! Huh? Think you're tough now? Fucking capitalist tools."

The cops stared straight ahead. They didn't move a muscle. Not a flicker of an eyelid or the flexing of a fist.

"Bunch of kids! Jesus, what's the matter with you?!"

Were they trained to react like that? To go faceless, not lift a foot while the crowd built and they waited for their orders?

To King their shocked stillness said it all: like any cops in any American city, they were used to patrolling streets that they controlled. They owned the streets, and they enforced their laws. This was something else, and they knew it, and they were afraid. How to handle it? Their stillness said it all.

The cops were standing stiff and silent, all the tools of pain hanging at their waists—but what were they protecting? Nothing. They were on the wrong side of the intersection and plain and simple the police had fucked up. King couldn't help smiling. The morning hadn't even begun and already she and her friends—the various affinity groups scattered strategically throughout the city—had won the most important battle. They had all the territory they wanted, and the cops had none.

Had she thought yet about whether the police would allow that situation to remain as it was? How they might want to retake that intersection? What violence might lie in store?

Sure. But right now they owned the intersection and she had other things on her mind. Right now King was watching a mounted cop in the front line halfway down the block where things were a little looser. There was something about him which had caught her attention. He was a medium-sized white man, maybe thirty, unremarkable save for the birthmark (or burn?) ascending pink and smooth from the left side of his mouth, over his cheek, and into the whiteness of his hair beneath the riot helmet. Goddamn. Looked like a slab of raw steak. Visible from fifty feet away and King felt momentarily heartsick. She had a flash of recognition, a moment's transportation to her childhood in western Pennsylvania, when she had been what, thirteen? fourteen? and her stepfather, who'd worked for a while as a short-order cook, because he didn't have the temperament for coal, couldn't stand the cage or the drop or the dust (least of all the darkness), and what else was there to do for money after the mills closed their doors and your education consisted mostly of knowing the difference between pounders and ponies. Well, this guy, her mom's new husband or boyfriend or whatever, he had some sort of accident at the restaurant, something had happened when he was changing the oil in the deep-fryer, and he deep-fried his face.

When the gauze came off however many months later, the left side of his head looked like it had been pressed to a sheet of hot steel. His left ear reduced to a lump of melted wax.

A thirteen-year-old girl, what did she think about that? She didn't think anything about that. She knew he deserved it.

This cop's face looked nothing as bad as that but he was messing with a kid, a protester, and for King, really, the feeling was the same.

The kid in question—a young light-skinned black man with two braids and a badly mistreated olive green puffy jacket—was playing tug-of-war with the cop on the horse. A sort of middle-class-looking couple stood on the corner pointing to him. The backpack seemed to be the object in question, the point of dispute, and although the couple was angry—red-faced and gesturing— and the cop was clearly on their side, demanding the backpack, the kid hadn't given it up, and hadn't, it appeared to King from where she stood, given in to panic. His manner was both calm and strong and King admired that. He looked clear-eyed and intelligent, cloaked in a defiant sort of loneliness, which was nothing new to King, and she liked him in a way she didn't need to define or articulate.

He looked totally alone out there, and now this cop was messing with him and King didn't like that. She didn't like that at all. She pulled the gas mask from around her neck and slung it underhand to Edie. Edie caught it by the strap and winked.

"Go get him, girl," she said.

King crossed into the thirty-foot strip of pavement that separated the front line of the cops from the heaving surging crowd behind her. Into the no-man's-land and down the street, heading for the cop. She looked for the officer who seemed in charge, a tanned older man in glasses who had been up in a cherry picker making unintelligible pronouncements on a megaphone: I don't want to hurt you this . . . I don't want to hurt you that . . . King saw the cherry picker parked down the street, behind some buses, its crane folded, but she didn't see the Chief anywhere around.

The cops all watched her coming, all, that is, except the mounted asshole on the horse. He didn't even notice her until she was beside his horse and the boy. Her body so close to the horse she could feel the heat coming off his heaving sides, the horse, and, ridiculous, yes she knew, she longed to reach out and stroke the soft hair, to comfort the animal with her touch.

"Hi!" she said loudly, neck craned backward to see the man's mangled face.

Up close it was even worse, the skin angry and red, glistening in the drizzle as if it were made of plastic.

Suddenly his riot baton was out of its holster and pointed at her chest.

"Miss," he said, "please return to your people."

"Hey, that's a little aggressive," King said, still smiling, trying to keep her voice bright, "swiping at me like that. I just want to talk."

But what she really wanted to do was touch that horse.

"Miss, return to your people."

"Why don't you leave this kid alone," King said. "This is a peaceful protest."

"Miss, I am not going to warn you again. Step back."

43

She felt the other cops watching with interest and she took one more step forward reaching for the horse's flank with one hand and with the other taking gentle hold of the backpack. The horse shied from her hand, lifting its feet high and moving a foot or two away. The cop let go of the backpack and suddenly she was staggering with the weight of the pack and feeling the first flush of triumph running hot in her veins.

"Hey!" His voice suddenly beyond angry. "I said that's enough. Now step back."

King knew she was antagonizing him. She should never have touched the horse. But she was beginning to feel a little amped—the familiar current of voltage as she got her first real taste of action. Once that juice got going in your veins, it was tough to stop. She should know. She was a student of conflict. She had been trained in the tactics, techniques, and philosophy of nonviolence. She was a trainer herself and she knew how to engage with police, with security officers, with enraged people of every stripe. When she had lived in the city, she used to go into the federal prisons—the maximum security blocks where the prisoners were on lockdown twenty-two hours out of twenty-four, the murderers and rapists, the friendly demented men who had taken a hammer to their neighbor's skull in an argument over a dented car door.

She went into the federal prisons, this green-eyed woman with dreads to the small of her back, and they respected her. They talked to her.

No, ma'am.

Yes, ma'am.

No, ma'am, I should not have hit him with the hammer, ma'am.

It was a delicate art, conversation with incarcerated men, men who had killed. You had to push to get to the real. And you had to *be* real—you couldn't go in and ask these guys to share their life stories and not share your own. That would be straight chicken-shit. And that wasn't her. So she shared her own stories. She wasn't proud, if anything she was often ashamed of her own temper—the way she sometimes lost control. But she told them about it none-theless; shared her fury and violence there in the concrete-floored room with wooden benches and a guard doing a crossword with his chair leaned on two legs against the locked door.

Mexico? Did she tell them about Mexico? No, she did not. She wanted to break through, yes, to dissolve momentarily the prison walls, but she didn't want to end up living inside them. No thanks. So no, she did not share her stories about Mexico. About her disaster on the border.

Her heart tripped over itself every time she entered the prison—no matter how many times she went, she never got used to that electric buzz and rattle as the double sliding electronic doors rolled shut behind her. But it wasn't that she was frightened of the men. No, it was that she was frightened *for* them. Because anger expressed in prison —well, who would really be the one to suffer? This was why a prison employed guards, was it not? In the corralling of all the unaccountable emotions?

Yes, Alfred Framingham, a man convicted of killing his wife and both of his children (and a UPS man who had the unfortunate timing to arrive at the door just as Alfred was putting the shotgun to his wife's head), had once put a sharpened spoon to the soft hollow of her throat. Great big Alfred whose hands were so lashed with scar tissue it looked as if he scrubbed them every morning with shredded razors—King had suggested one morning that maybe Alfred killed his wife because he was scared of her.

That had been very stupid. The result of her blind impulse to get at the truth of a man. She had spent years trying to tame it.

But that was the thing with anger. That was the tricky thing about pain. Sometimes it was hiding around a corner just waiting to slice you from stomach to throat.

She studied the mounted cop. There was something loose and frantic in his eyes and she imagined the nightmare scenarios pounding in his brain—Molotov cocktails, blown out storefronts, the city descending into explosions and flame.

"Miss," he said, "step away from the horse."

She knew instinctively that she needed to de-escalate the situation. She needed to find some way to relate, some way to empathize. And where the fuck was John Henry? John Henry could talk to cops. John Henry would help her calm down. Because the problem, she was discovering, was that she didn't want to de-escalate the situation. She didn't want to fucking *empathize*.

"Miss," he said, and there was no mistaking the tremor of impending violence in his voice, "step back now. I don't want to hurt you."

King leaned forward. She laid her hand along the horse's neck and then, pitching her voice low and kind of sexy, said with a smile, "You want to hurt me, darling? I'd *sure* like to see you try."

7

Julia was Guatemalan, originally, as they said, by way of L.A., city of angels, and as she watched Park on his horse messing with a protester she found herself thinking of her rookie year cruising MacArthur Park, L.A.'s Central American ghetto for Guatemalans, Salvadorans, all the economic refugees who had made the journey north to send their money south. There was a lake in MacArthur Park—a little piss pond with a fountain covered in fading tags that they called Gun Lake because it was filled with so many weapons discarded after jumps and murders and jackings. No matter. Talking with the men on the stoops, the 'bangers that owned the corners, the old men who fanned themselves with their mesh hats and ate whole-kernel corn roasted on a stick—she felt at home down there. Relaxed.

But then in April '92, the Rodney King verdict came down, all five officers acquitted, and Ju wasn't joking with anybody on any stoop because the city had lost its collective mind and was trying to burn itself to the ground.

On Crenshaw Boulevard they were looting. Down in South Central, Korean shop owners were building their own private armies, scared clerks firing into crowds with shaking shotguns.

Ju had caught one woman climbing out of the shattered glass

of a pharmacy, not like she was the only one, just the only one Ju had caught because the others took off and this woman here was a good four hundred and fifty pounds if she was one. The woman stood there holding her loot, face devoid of expression. In her hands she held two packages of Pampers, a can of roach spray, and a Pepsi.

"They be climbing over the baby when he asleep," the woman said by way of explanation. "The cockroaches, I mean."

Ju took the Pampers and the roach killer. Then she cuffed the lady and put her in the van with the others.

Because that was the job.

Front-cuffed her on account of the soda because sometimes you had to break the rules to hold true to a higher law. Even if it was just a woman's need to drink a stolen Pepsi on her way to jail.

Because, in Julia's opinion, then and now, that was the job, too.

"You know what I see?" Park had said before mounting his horse. "All this racket and complaining?"

"You see someone getting me some decent coffee? What's the matter, you get some for yourself, you don't get any for your pal?"

"Soviets in blue jeans. Rooskie revolutionaries with their stale black bread and their crappy weak tea."

Park was fresh from Oklahoma, early thirties with the long lean muscle of the compulsive triathlete. Ju thought he had a decent smile and a thin sort of nuclear skull and he might have been good-looking were it not for that patch of scar tissue occupying the lower left side of his face—from the chin running back along the jawline and then up across his cheek and disappearing into the shorn field of dust that was his ash-colored hair.

Nuclear. The guy was as radioactive as a blast survivor. Like someone who lifts their head from the dirt where they fell and their face is as white as the flash and their eyes radded little pin

48

dots flattened by memory. A ghost looking up at you and hoping you are the salvation they were promised so long ago.

That was the sense she got, at least, from, you know, looking at the guy. And she was not his salvation. Standing day after day in the 4-by-6 of his private space. Ju got the sense the nutjob had mined his personal bunker, booby-trapped it against intruders, and she thought it was burn tissue from the color, a mottled pink you might see beneath the skin of a peach that's been violently slammed against a wall. And you might think that a disaster that difficult to hide, something that visible and out there and sort of heartbreaking in its ugliness, would change a person's demeanor. Perhaps make him shy, or awkward or silent. But no. Not Park. His head-on collision with the howling shitstorm of life hadn't broken him in the least. It had made him outgoing and goofy and weird, cast out forever with a radish-colored head and a private smile and a hair-trigger temper that could go off, it seemed, at any moment.

And yet. And yet, despite all the reasons not to, there was something about him that she liked. The secrecy. The scar. The weird, private laugh. His aura of utter and total self-reliance in the teeth of the world—it appealed to her. Because this is a man, let's say you're on a date and some guy comes out of the alley with a knife and a rapey kind of vibe. You think this ruined, grinning beast, this nutjob freaking cop who once drunkenly half-bragged to Ju about pulling burned bodies from the rubble of a building, saving them, that is (he shut up when he realized what he was talking about, and the next day she did not mention it or even forget to mention it), tell me, this is a man that hands over your purse? This is a man who begs for his life? No. This is a man who cuts monsters into little pieces and eats them like the weird pieces of vegetable in an MRE.

He kept inviting her to his Wednesday night youth-league basketball games of which he was the volunteer coach—the counselor of troubled juveniles or maybe just their broken-toothed leader, she wasn't quite sure which. And can you imagine, I mean, asking her to a hot, smelly gym to watch sweaty delinquents pound up and down a basketball court? I mean, the fucking *cojones*, right? One of these nights she was thinking of going. Maybe.

"Commies writing in their diaries about the pretty girls." He had mounted his horse now and was looking down at her with that weird little smile. "Because really that's what all this revolutionary stuff is about. Deep down, you know. The evil system that steals the pretty girls."

Ju made a sound through her teeth that was something like a laugh.

"I mean where did they go?" he said. "Those pretty little girls we used to play with in the grass?"

On the second day of the Rodney King riots, half-cracked on lack of sleep, Julia and four male officers had stopped a wild-haired Latino man coming out of a charred and smoking store with a package of Oreos and a gallon of milk in a yellow jug. The smell of gasoline hung heavy in the air. The man got aggressive, dropping his cookies and pushing Ju in the chest in an attempt to get away, or maybe, more precisely, he dropped his milk and screamed bloody murder when she circled her hand around his wrist like one half of a pair of handcuffs and then they all five beat him like he was a dog they didn't like and left him bloody in the street for somebody else, someone who cared about things broken by the world. One cop removed the man's watch and held it to the light.

"Stop screaming," he said. "You sound like a girl."

She watched as Park out in the crowd now turned his horse in a circle. She tapped her face shield with one short lacquered nail. If you disregarded the scar maybe he was kind of cute. Broad in the shoulder. Eager to please.

But how could you disregard the scar?

Five days of lunacy. A city burning itself to the ground. On the TV in the precinct when she went back to refresh her supply of plastic cuffs, she had watched live as a mob, mostly black, pulled a white truck driver from his cab and beat him over the head with a cinderblock.

She read later in the papers that a man, watching the same live footage at home, raced down there *on a bicycle*. An unarmed black man. He kept the mob at bay somehow and pulled the unconscious white man back into the cab of his truck and drove him to the hospital.

Ju cried when she read that, and she knew if she ever had a son, just what she would name him.

Bobby Green Jr.

The name of that man on a bicycle who had saved the truck driver's life.

She cried when she read that, drinking her bitter coffee sitting alone at a kitchen table that could have been hers, and was, or could have belonged to any one of a thousand other people who had misplaced their lives like it was something you could lose among the folds of the newspaper or the litter in the street and she didn't know why exactly she cried reading that because she hadn't misplaced her life like some sad homeless nobody. What she had done is she had lived through the L.A. riots, lived through the mayhem and rage, do you understand, the pain of the destruction of a city, and when you are police and do you understand, when you are *police* and you live through something like that, you have only three choices: you can quit, you can start making change, or you can suck it up and ask someone for a favor. Ju knew someone in the Seattle Police Department. And she knew, too, even then, that she was police for life. And she surely wasn't made for political hearings, so six months after the riots, she put in her papers and made the call to Seattle.

Imagine that man seeing something on his TV and standing from his couch to go down there to stop them from beating that truck driver as if what happened on the TV and what happened in the world were somehow related, as if he believed them to be the same.

Crying alone there in her kitchen, the coffee going cold in her hand because what exactly? Ju staring into the middle distance and the sound of her own weeping competing with the old refrigerator because what kind of courage makes a man. What kind of thing in a man watching it on TV makes him jump off the couch and go racing down there on a bicycle? Was it courage or something else entirely, she didn't know, really, but god she felt it in her chest like a certain heat, had seen it how many thousands of times on the faces of the men and women she worked with, had felt it how many hundreds of times herself. Had seen it on the face of this walking landmine of a cop, who was out there in the crowd right now harassing protesters with his horse. The what? The willingness to carry the burden of protecting other people from themselves? Well, yes, except that sounded like some *mierda* to her, except mostly not when it came down to it, it sounded exactly right, so let's just agree to never talk about it again. Because why else would she be here, dressed head to toe in riot gear and willing to risk her bodily safety, if she didn't love being police in the greatest goddamn country in the world?

Something was happening in the street. She saw a woman standing next to Park's horse. Saw her touching the horse. Saw Park's baton begin to rise.

His eyes were the color of blue marbles, his arms long and muscular, but how did you ignore the scar, that was really the question, wasn't it? She didn't know. With a final-sounding sort of click, she flipped down her face shield, turned her back on Park, and made busy watching the marchers marching toward wherever.

Willing to protect people from their own stupidity. Willing to be the bad guy. Knowing when to look and when to look away. That was the job, too.

8

There was a time, perhaps, when it could have been said King was in love with violent revolution. At eighteen she carried Che Guevara on a key chain. She read *Live from Death Row* and quoted Mumia Abu-Jamal to her growing circle of activist friends.

It started as a simple infatuation. A New York City girl, a Brooklyn transplant, rising from the cinders of the dead hamlet where she had been born, she read FBI surveillance reports on John Lennon. She studied the details of CIA assassinations in Colombia, in Congo; in Guatemala and El Salvador; in Iran and Angola and Greece.

At age nineteen she went to her first protest. The School of the Americas in Fort Benning, Georgia, where the American military taught Central and South American leaders how to torture their own people. One night camped in a muddy field, she slept with a towheaded gangly boy with a Southern drawl who was not her first, technically, but the sex wasn't bad and the conversation was better. She discovered to her surprise, it was sort of thrilling to fuck someone who believed what you believe.

At the age of twenty-two she learned how to hop freights and headed west. Her confidence grew. She made friends and in the high-altitude forests of Colorado they studied revolution. She read the books they gave her: *Manufacturing Consent, If They Come in the Morning*, copies of the journal *Earth First!* Her friends and her books gave voice to what had been inarticulate; they gave shape and mission to what had been a formless longing. She practiced climbing and spiking. On the western slopes of the Continental Divide, she tore distributor caps from twelve-ton Cats. She sugared tanks and hammered sharpened steel rebar into logging roads. She went camping and torched a ski resort.

The cascading whump of ignition a pleasure she felt from the flat muscles of her belly all the way to the crown of her head.

She changed her name to King and did a little hideout time in Humboldt County where she slept with a woman who called herself simply—and accurately—Red. Together they started a 'zine and distributed the anonymous black-and-white sheets of text and drawings, folded at the break, all over town. They wore gloves to keep the ink off their fingers and their fingerprints off the paper. At night they leafed through federal manuals on covert operations in Chile, hearts leaping in their chests. Together they made love among the mimeographed pages of their 'zine and the ink stained their bodies with letters and strange hieroglyph tattoos which they examined together in the moonlight drifting through the window, laughing.

When it seemed safe again—the Vail thing over and the FBI with no idea who had done it or how—she went to Portland to protest a toxic incinerator. There she fell in love with a Greenpeace guy and decided to stay awhile. Wide-eyed and cursing and slapping her knee, she listened to his tales of high heroics on the North Sea. Then one night he had tried to rape her while she slept, had come home drunk and tried to fuck her, had continued even after she woke and said no. King broke two of his fingers. One in the confused struggle. The other, afterward, in the quiet of his weeping.

Colorado and California and Oregon, finally she drifted north. At the age of twenty-six she arrived on the Olympic Peninsula, the rough and wild coast where she did tree-sits in the Olympics and slept with no one save the warm solitude of a mummy bag bivouacked eighty feet high in the trees and the sheltering morning light of liquid gold that gathered in her lap and warmed her face.

And for the first time in her life, among the quiet of the massive moss-bearded trees and the curled booming of the salt-whipped waves, she felt like she could finally hear herself *think*.

Yes, there had been a time when it could be said that King felt the burning glow of violence, but no longer. Now she believed in the transformative power of militant nonviolence. Now she suffered to see so many thrown in the fire.

Which was why King could not believe that here she was fucking with a police.

This was *not* how you de-escalated. This was not nonviolence as it was practiced or preached. She saw the cop's blue eyes go hot and then his riot baton wasn't poking or prodding, it was rising and immediately King regretted what she had done, regretted not the baton which was about to come crashing down on her head, regretted not her anger which had pushed her to humiliate this man. No, she *wanted* that. Big man on his horse—she wanted to make him feel confused and small; she wanted to fill him with helplessness and the need to hurt. Yes, let him feel that electricity for a minute. Lord knows she had felt it often enough—that sad frustrated rage lighting up her brain for years now.

No, what she regretted was that her involvement in the day's direct action was about to end before it had even started.

With both hands and arms, she covered her head. She knew it would not save her. She had fucked up. She had lost control of herself, of the situation, of her own tightly wound bitterness. She waited for the heavy wooden baton to fall across her arms and head.

Royally was the word. She had fucked up royally.

But it didn't happen.

She risked a glance upward.

The commanding officer had stepped forward. The commanding officer who had earlier been calming the crowd over a megaphone, who had been pacing and calming his own agitated line. His hand was on the flank of the horse. And the look on the cop's mangled face—it was so classic she wanted to take a snapshot. He looked like a little boy whose mom just told him not to spit on the sidewalk; he knew he was caught; he looked, in fact, not unlike her mother's boyfriend the day King had slammed the trailer door while he stood there with his dick in his hand.

The Chief's hand patted the horse. "What seems to be the problem?" he said.

"Sir?" the cop said. "This woman, this citizen here, was directly—"

The Chief wasn't really looking at the cop. He was looking at King with a cool appraising glance. He wasn't smiling, but something ironic shone behind his glasses. He clearly did not like this officer as much as King had decided she didn't like him.

"Park, I want you to report to MACC."

"Chief Bishop, sir?"

"I said I want you to report back to Command. We are not going to start beating our own citizens," the Chief said. "Not on my watch. Now get your ass back to the MACC."

The cop seemed about to say something, but then decided against it. "Yes, sir. Back to the MACC."

He clicked from the side of his mouth, turning the horse.

"Hey," the Chief said mildly. He patted the horse's rump with affection.

"Sir?"

"Did you hear me say take the horse?"

Cops all down the line were coughing into their fists, trying not to laugh.

The Chief pointed at Park and then pointed to the ground.

"But this is my *horse.*"

"You walk, my friend," the Chief said.

His humiliation complete, Park climbed down from the saddle. The Chief wrapped the reins in his fist.

King couldn't help it. She was smiling so wide her grin could have powered a thousand cities for a thousand years. Her cheeks hurt. It just confirmed everything she believed—the Chief showing up like this. The power of love. The transformative power of nonviolence. The indisputable fact that the universe itself was on their side.

Two cops stepped aside, pointedly gazing out at the crowd, and Park stepped through the hole they had made in the line. He looked back once, marking her face, King knew, for all eternity.

She put her lips to her palm and blew him a kiss.

Bye, asshole.

As he disappeared back into the sea of black-suited riot gear, just one more anonymous storm trooper among hundreds, the crowd behind her suddenly erupted in a roar. She turned. People were applauding. Folks who had watched the whole scene play out now jumping and clapping and hooting. She waved, feeling a little queasy. This wasn't about embarrassing the cops. This wasn't about the cops at all. This was about shutting down the meetings. *Peacefully.*

"Are you all right?" the Chief said. He was studying her with some care, fingers idling along the horse's mane. He seemed amused.

Now that it was over, her adrenaline was running an even race with her shame—shame starting to pull ahead, and she couldn't remember what she had come up here in the first place to do. She could hear her heart beating in her ears. Breathe, she commanded herself, and took a deep gasping breath, all the way down to the pit of her stomach. She let it out with a long sigh. She shook her head.

"Sir, all due respect, but we don't intend to provoke you or put your officers in harm's way. We are not here to riot."

"Good," he said.

They stood for a beat just looking at each other. This was one of those moments. The calm, the sudden sharp sense of ease. The tension was still there but different, somehow transformed into a kind of high-wire clarity King recognized from her time working with the inmates.

"Chief, I want you to know—"

King breathing steady now. They had passed out of the moment of confrontation and into a moment of human dialogue. She wasn't sure how she had accomplished it, but she was here now, exactly where she wanted to be.

"I just want to say again, this is a peaceful protest. We have trained for months. We are disciplined. We are here to shut down the meetings. *Peacefully.* I can promise you there will be no violence."

Chief Bishop with his hand on the horse. He seemed relaxed, the Chief next to this huge animal, rubbing its neck.

"Good. I'm glad we understand each other. Because I'm going to need you to clear this intersection in fifteen minutes."

It was like a punch to the stomach.

"What?"

The Chief waited.

"Didn't you hear what I just said? We don't want there to be any violence," she said. "We aren't here to riot. We're here to shut down the meetings."

"Yes, I heard you the first time. And I'm saying I need you people to clear this intersection."

"Okay, I understand you want us to clear the intersection," King said. "But I'm not in charge. There are tens of thousands of people here."

"Look," the Chief said, baring his teeth in something between a grimace and a smile, "either clear it yourself, or we will do it for you. You seem like nice enough folks, but there are larger forces at work here. We *will* bring those delegates through."

King—for once she had nothing to say. How could that have gone so wrong so quickly? And where the fuck was John Henry?

"Don't make me hurt you people," the Chief said. "I don't want that. Don't make me do it. This is *my* city. And I'm telling you we will bring those delegates safely through. They will make the convention center and they will have their meetings. The thing to understand is this is *my city*, not yours. Clear those intersections."

He nodded as if they had agreed on something and gathered the reins to walk the horse back through his line of officers.

"I'll give you fifteen minutes to get it done. Then we're coming through."

She stared dumbly at his retreating form. The horse's rump swung past and she took two blind steps to be clear of its hooves. She stumbled over something, almost ready to believe the lunatic cop with the fucked-up face hadn't really left, but had circled back and was now ready to give King the punishment she deserved. She looked down and discovered it was just the kid's backpack.

61

King blinked. She had forgotten completely about the kid. The young black guy with two braids and a red bandanna that she had decided on the spot she liked so much. And where the fuck was *he*? She looked up. He was halfway back to the crowd. Moving fast. Had he hidden behind the horse?

"Kid!" she called out. "Hey wait up. Your backpack!"

Which is when it hit her. The stinky reek of weed.

9

Later in the day, a rumor would circulate about a lone protester who locked himself to the door of the East Precinct of the Seattle Police Department. He was a radical in his seventies, old-man-skinny with wild white hair, the kind of guy that used whatever he had on hand at home, in this case a U-shaped bicycle lock. He slid the U around his neck, then ran the bar through the handles of the double doors and locked it tight. He leaned his head against the doors, wispy hair pressed against the glass, and then he dropped the key down the front of his pants, and grinned deeply at the cops from his wrinkles, as if to say, Now what?

John Henry could vouch for the rumor because he was there and he watched it happen, and it looked like the old guy hadn't seen this much fun since Chicago '68. John Henry admired his courage, the man's earnest recklessness, but as brave as it might have been, it accomplished nothing. The police knocked the old guy in the legs with their batons. They beat him repeatedly about the shoulders and arms. They leaned down and slapped him in the face until finally, cursing, crying out in pain, he agreed to unlock himself.

In the end, the old man slowed traffic entering and exiting the police station for less than fifteen minutes. John Henry saw one kid with a digital handheld recorder, but he asked himself what would the kid do with it? Who would ever see it and what did it mean? It was a forgotten second of history, one more story among a thousand such stories today. The man reached into his saggy underwear, sobbing and swearing, and unlocked himself. The world went on its way.

John Henry knew this one-man action meant nearly nothing, but in his heart, he thought that it was beautiful in its way. In a single act, the distillation of fifty years of American protest.

You sit at the counter. You order a cheese and mayo sandwich.

They say, "We don't serve niggers here."

You look them in the eye anyway.

Maybe they look away.

You sit at the counter and wait for the malted milk that isn't going to come. Your ass occupies the seat. Your ass controls the territory of the plastic spinning seat as you wait for your cherry soda or your BLT or some white boy's grinning fist.

And fifty, a hundred, five hundred of your friends waiting behind you, waiting just beyond the frosted glass doors, five hundred strong souls just waiting to take your place.

That was the old man's mistake. The thing he had forgotten. You don't do it alone.

John Henry wished he had known about the gutted warehouse at 420 Denny Way. The old man. The white-haired radical. They would have helped him, trained him, joined him, and loved him and fought for him, wild as feral cats. The warehouse with its cathedral ceilings and dusty high windows which was church and workshop and meeting hall—their point of convergence, where all their forces came together in a humming disjointed harmony. It was a square squat building with high walls and a paint-splattered concrete floor where they did their work—voices calling back and forth, echoing beneath the high ceiling like voices in a stone vault, young people shuttling back and forth, building and laughing, full of the high energy of community and purpose.

It was there in the burnt-out warehouse that they built their giant puppets. Caricatures of heads of state. Devils and villains and sharp-horned tricksters. It was there among those concrete walls in the dust-laden light from the high windows that they handcuffed each other and laughed, learned the meaning of civil disobedience, learned how to nonviolently accept arrest. There where they discovered the true nature of struggle. How to do it together. How to coordinate a direct action. There where they learned that courage is not the ability to face your fear, heroically, once, but is the strength to do it day after day. Night after night. Faith without end. Love without border.

It was here, too, where they first spoke the names that would carry them through the fire. Where they first felt the stories issuing forth from their lips. Where they gathered to build the family that would survive.

When he had first looked at the maps, some six months ago, he almost didn't believe it—the geography of the city was an ally they had never expected. Any other city and it would probably have been just a protest. But here in downtown Seattle, thirteen intersections formed a triangle around the convention center. The center where the World Trade Organization planned to hold their auction of the Third World. The World Trade Organization whose opening ceremonies began, John Henry checked his watch, in three hours.

Shut down those intersections and you would own the city.

A chokehold that would trap the delegates and the diplomats and the experts in their fancy hotels eating smoked salmon and Brie or whatever it is they do when they are not busy buying and selling things they have no right on earth to claim as their own.

These veterans of the anti-nuclear demonstrations of the 1980s. Tree-sits in the high Sierra and on the Redwood Coast. Who had arrest sheets that read like a timeline of American protests: Seabrook, Rocky Flats, the Nevada Test Site, who trained for months on a farm in Arlington rented by none other than himself. My people. He was lit up. They had been fighting corporate Goliaths for so long their tactics had become streamlined and beautiful and efficient.

The first wave, they lock themselves together—a lockdown at the center of each of those thirteen intersections. They would be the immovable core of the block. Surrounding them and protecting them was the second wave—standing groups to clog the streets, a buffer of faces and voices and flesh to stand between the locked-down bodies and the cops.

Surround that with a street party—the flags and the trumpets and the beating drums—and let the cops just try to figure out what was going on, let alone clear the streets.

Lockdown. Each person sat cross-legged on the pavement with both arms locked into PVC pipe, each arm locked from the inside with a chain to the person on either side. Only the person locked down could release the chain.

The pipe itself, to break the locked circle, had to be cut with a diamond-tipped saw, very carefully or you were likely to slice off an arm. The cops hated the lock-boxes. They hated having to cut so carefully. They hated that they could not force you to release.

John Henry loved the lock-box because it said everything. One PVC pipe was not enough. It was only working in concert that the lock-box became something special. Eight people in a circle; eight people with each of their arms in one of the prepared pipes. Eight people willing to lock themselves together in an unbroken circle, to sit on cold pavement, totally immobile and vulnerable, waiting for the loggers to come to reclaim their tree, for the cops to come to reclaim their city.

John Henry himself wanted to be in lockdown because it was neither *their* tree nor *their* city. But they had agreed to come as medics. That was the plan at least. Less risk for King with the Vail thing hanging over her head, although he thought that a needless worry on her part. Still, man, just standing there in the warehouse earlier this morning in the gray light of half-dawn watching those women in their cuts-offs and boots and T-shirts, watching those strong women slinging chain and preparing the pipes, he felt the nervous excitement thrumming in his blood. He felt a growing icy thrill in the pit of his stomach that was the beginning of his body's preparation for the confrontation with the police—the hours of sitting, the facing of his own fears and doubts. He had watched the girls and his heart was singing. His soul felt coiled like a spring. They needed to be medics. Fine. But John Henry, he was a man that when the spirit came a-calling, he answered. Whatever the language. Whatever the price. The words of Mahatma Gandhi inked blue-black across his chest for how many years now:

> *Rivers of blood may have to flow*
> *before we gain our freedom,*
> *but it must be our blood.*

10

Victor watching the woman who had saved his ass—King she was called—saying, "Okay, people, the cops want us to move. Are we going to move?"

"Hell no!"

"The cops have asked me to clear the street. They would like to bring their delegates through this intersection. Are we going to let those delegates make it to the convention center?"

"Hell no!"

"Are we going to clear this intersection?"

"Hell no!"

"What *are* we going to do?"

"Shut the motherfucker down!" they said in unison. Everyone laughing.

Victor drifting and listening to the beautiful girl with olive skin and green eyes and the muscles of a rock climber. After stashing his backpack in the nearest dumpster and telling him he could come back for it later, but first she wanted him to meet some people, she'd brought him to the group. And the way she looked at him, he knew he didn't have a choice. He marked the dumpster in his mind and then followed her. King introduced him all around and he raised a hand in a half-enthusiastic greeting. The guy they called the Doctor had pulled him in a wide-armed hug and pressed him tight, saying, "Welcome, brother!" but really what he was thinking of wasn't the hello, or this new strange group, what he was drifting and thinking of was the moment he'd seen the cop approaching, not the cop with the fucked-up face, but the other one, the Chief of Police, which was when he had given up on the backpack and put the horse between himself and the man. What he was thinking is that when the Chief started talking it was the first time in three years that he had heard his father's voice.

Five feet on the other side of a fucking horse saying, "I need you to clear this intersection."

Saying, "I don't want to hurt you."

His father close enough to extend a hand. Almost close enough to kick.

"Okay, people," King was saying, "here's the situation. The Portland Liberation Front is one short for lockdown and they've asked for our help. Is anyone willing to join their lockdown?"

The others were looking at each other.

"There's a good chance you'll be arrested," King said.

"King, we're here as medics," one of the guys said. A guy with a red stringy beard and chunky black glasses, a pinched cowboy hat perched on his head. "Shouldn't we stick to the plan?"

Victor broke in. "How do you know you're only going to get arrested?" he said. "They look ready for war."

"You'll have to trust me," King said.

"I wouldn't trust those cops as far as I could spit. How can you be so sure they're not just going to beat everyone senseless. That's all I'm asking."

"Because," King said, "John Henry met with the police and negotiated a mass arrest."

Then Victor was turning with an incredulous look on his face to the red-haired fucker with the long beard. "You met with the cops? Wow. It must be nice to be white."

There was a stunned sort of silence.

"Look, Victor," John Henry said, pulling on that beard, "we're all glad you're here, we're glad you care. But that is not how we go about this. If you want to be a part of this, then you need to learn there are some rules. We don't interrupt. We don't swear. We don't—"

"If I want to be part of what?" Victor said, interrupting again. "Getting my ass whupped?" He was laughing good-naturedly now. He didn't need a fucking lecture from this guy. "And who said I care?"

King looked at her friends laughing and talking on the cold concrete, laughing in the shadow of the hotel, talking while the cops nervously fingered their tear gas, sitting and laughing in a small circle that contained all the love you could ever hope to contain among four people sitting cross-legged at the corner of an intersection in a dying city, and she was surprised to feel a hitch in her throat.

Here they were, one short for lockdown, and which one would it be?

The youngest of them, the nineteen-year-old they called the Doctor, who lived on a garlic farm and went around everywhere barefoot.

"A thousand years from now," the Doctor was fond of saying (ecological apocalypse being one of his favorite subjects), "we'll all be walking barefoot. All of us. Walking barefoot through the wreckage; barefoot through the swishing grass."

Grinning while he spoke, the Doctor in overalls, with his blond hair the color of cornstalks hanging neat to his OshKosh buttons, he was serious and self-mocking and there wasn't much in the world that could make her laugh like one of the Doctor's rants. They were exaggerated and informed and passionate and a joke and she believed it and half-believed it—ecological apocalypse—she wouldn't be here if she didn't feel it looming, and yet weirdly that was what made her laugh.

Six months ago, the Doctor and a team of climbers had scaled the Golden Gate Bridge. They had climbed forty stories in the whipping wind while the cops watched and swore below. The fire department tried to reach them with their longest ladder trucks, but they were far too high for that, clinging to the cables. Finally they revealed the purpose of their climb. They dropped a sixty-foot banner for the cops and the firemen and Bay Area commuters to quickly read. For the news helicopters to linger on. The words of Subcomandante Marcos, the leader of the Zapatistas. It showed him in his black ski mask with his signature pipe protruding from the mouth hole. It read:

WE SEEK A WORLD IN WHICH THERE IS ROOM
FOR MANY WORLDS

Not the Doctor. He might be a bad-ass climber, but he wouldn't make it in lockdown.

Edie? Could it be Edie? Edie who didn't make King laugh—she made her believe it might all be possible. Another world. Another way to live.

Edie, whose gray hair shone damply, rain running across her deeply lined face, so much worrying, so much thinking and talking and planning, the mark of all those years engaged in the struggle, and yet they seemed not to make her old, but to light her from within, to saturate every word she spoke. Edie, who had been an AIDS activist back when people still thought you caught it from toilet seats.

And what about John Henry? John Henry, her first trainer in

nonviolence. John Henry who first gave her the courage to go into nonviolent lockdown when King had still been a red-eyed revolutionary living ten to a house out in West Seattle.

John Henry who taught her the necessity of patience and struggle.

John Henry who taught her how people changed their world—small brave groups willing to risk everything. Willing to sacrifice everything. John Henry who taught her the meaning of ordinary daily courage.

No, not John Henry and his windy mattress in whatever abandoned building he had most recently decided to claim as home. Not John Henry and his political hands, his political beard, his political mouth that kissed her hips gently as if asking is this okay, even as he sucked and slurped hungrily in the cool clear light of another activist squat.

The Doctor saying now, "You're entitled to believe what you want to believe. But for me walking among those trees, the smell of wet earth, the light filtering down through the canopy, the branches bearded with moss? It was so quiet and peaceful you could hear individual raindrops dripping. Say what you want. For me that place was as close as I come to believing in a god. That place, among those trees, it was a holy place. It was sacred."

"But our fight isn't with the loggers," Edie said.

"Or the cops," John Henry said.

"If you bring class into the equation," Edie said, "then they're victims of the same political-economic system. If we want this to be a truly democratic revolution, we need to understand our fight is not with the working class at all."

King nodded. She believed in the power of love. Love was the animating force that filled her body. She let it move her arms, her legs, her lungs. It was love that governed the workings of her mouth, the words called forth from her larynx. And yet it was a weight on her heart, pressing down, because while she knew any one of these folks would joyfully join their brothers and sisters in lockdown, to let the force of their community confront face-to-face the force of the police, King herself was less eager. She knew what could happen. She was not afraid to take the gas—it was just that in some way her love for these people made her want it to not be so goddamn necessary.

For the country to change, did blood always have to be spilled? One short for lockdown. And who would it be?

76

12

When the Doctor had started talking about holy places, a memory
had stolen unbidden into Victor's mind. A memory of his mother
and father's basement. A memory of his mother who died when
he was still a boy. She absconded for better climes, set sail for the
never-never—but he didn't, truthfully, harbor any grudge against
the shitball world for taking her. Nor her for letting it. Because
when Mom jumped ship and left a half-orphaned brown boy at
sea, the other thing she left behind balanced the scales in Victor's
mind. Boxes and boxes of books. Cardboard boxes of books stacked
floor to ceiling in the darkest, dustiest corner of the basement.

Victor's mother had been an activist, an unrepentant hippie, a
teacher and an artist, a black woman who had a child with a white
man, and when he left, years on she married a different white man.
Whatever any of that meant she had been a woman who had a
heart which could not turn away any stray, any of the bad-luck
bodies the world kicked around, and for that Victor loved her
and did not worry once about the first father who never was. His
mother was father and mother both. A tremendous force that even
he recognized. She was also a painter and there in her studio, in the
girdered half-light beneath the underpass, his mother had painted
abstract acrylics, huge canvases of a shimmering gray which she

then defaced with a stub of charcoal, the first thing that found her hand. Victor had never known quite what to make of his mother's art, but he loved her for it, loved watching as she scrawled collapsed apartment blocks and smoldering cars, McDonald's crushed beneath the rubble, trees growing from the craters. Working fast, she drew stick-figure dogs eating garbage in the rain, except the dogs were maybe people.

She painted a canvas gray and then sketched great sailing ships; drew dark outlines of exploded city buses, charred bodies climbing from the windows, throngs of black charcoal people in piles of slashes and lines, wide gaping charcoal mouths, black charcoal X's for the sightless eyes of the dead.

Victor had decided when he was about ten that the dogs eating garbage were definitely people.

His mother, the woman who had raised him and taught him, holding her stub of charcoal and thinking, wiping her chin with one ash-stained wrist, the woman whose blood ran in his veins, physically present on some other continent of being and emotion while gulls dive-bombed from the darkness of the underpass, falling wing-tucked toward the water. And Victor on a paint-splattered couch eating a crust of bread and reading and watching and loving her.

And this was why he had traveled; this was the disappointment he felt when he looked in the guidebook and trooped off with his pack to see another crumbling ruin, blurry-headed in the noonday sun. He traveled, in some way, to discover who he was, to recognize himself in the world because, a half-black brown boy, not-quite-white, he did not see it. But what he found was the inside of some empty ruin, cool and dim, and outside in the sun, ragged human shapes littered along the path like leaves.

The year she died Victor did serious time among the books.

He schooled himself from the boxes. He liked to read. He liked crashing down there in the basement with the smell of concrete and earth, liked reading his mother's old books, liked the idea that he had inherited more than his dark skin and dark hair from the woman who disappeared.

Fanon, Freire, Guevara. James Baldwin and bell hooks. There was poetry by Ernesto Cardenal and Oscar Romero. John Berger. A set of strange novels called *Memory of Fire*—part journalism, part fiction, part mystic trance—by a Uruguayan writer named Eduardo Galeano.

Sometimes, late into the night, he could swear he felt something like his mother's presence among the books—some sense of her touch in the smell of ink and paper, the stained pages, the occasional fingerprint smudged with paint. It was almost as if she had never left.

Victor, of course, never failed to fire a monster joint on these underground missions. And there he would sit, reading. He liked how those books made him feel, the books and the weed, his brain humming with knowledge, an odd and lovely sort of expansion feeling these threads of words that stretched across continents and decades, a sort of feeling that he, too, was stretched and flattened, his brain spread like a map across the world as if sending tendrils of connection creeping out to places and people far removed.

He felt somehow close to his mother in these moments. As if she were the one speaking to him. And for a moment the loneliness that was always with him left him alone. It was a feeling of indeterminate shape, sometimes resembling a faucet that would not stop and the drain which caught the water, other times a boat made of newspaper folds turning slowly in a rain-soaked gutter, but that strange new knowledge of the world brought home by the boxes and the books pushed it a step back. Gave him some room

79

to breathe. After all, what could be better, Victor thought in his basement lair, than the words of dead or distant teachers for a boy with a dead mother?

That is, until the day his father (he never once, not until this day, thought of him as his stepfather, or his adopted father) descended the stairs and found him with the boxes open and a bong smoking in his lap. He lifted his head, and smiled, red-eyed and raw.

His father, great leader that he was, had smashed the bong against the concrete floor. Shards of purple glass everywhere. He had nearly broken Victor's arm, so forcefully had he twisted it behind his back and marched him up the stairs. And later that night, Victor in his room had watched through the window as his father—his sweet dear daddy—had dragged the boxes of books into the backyard, made a pyramid as tall as a man, doused them in gasoline, sloshing and cursing, and had his dad been crying as he cursed and stumbled, Victor didn't know. His father lit a match and threw it toward the pile, and the books went up in flame, the light playing orange and yellow against the house, against his father's swaying body, against Victor's thin face as it hung in the window like some strange reflection of the moon in a mud puddle, his father seeing his face there, saying, shouting up to the window, "This, this, this. This is what happens when you care too much."

"The blindness of the heart which capitalism demands," John Henry was saying.

"Alienation," Edie said. "This is our enemy."

Victor nodded. "Sure," he said. "Me, too."

Then he looked at King. "I'll do it."

"You'll do what?"

"Lockdown," he said. "I'll be the one."

13

Bishop gathered his troops behind the PeaceKeeper. Massed them on the south side of Sixth and Union. On the north side, on the east and the west, thousands of protesters were bunched and surging. He needed to get the delegates north through that mess.

From the back of the 'Keeper they were putting on the riot gear, the hats and bats. An officer was handing out the tear gas guns—military-style weapons that reminded Bishop of Apache attack helicopters.

"Let's go over it again. I don't want any screwups."

He surveyed the assembled troops, saw one about to speak and raised his hand, palm forward. "Wait until I'm done."

This tanned widower in spectacles who had summited Mount Rainier this summer, one year before his sixtieth birthday. Chief Bishop. Who believed in community policing, who despite the Mayor's weak protests led the efforts to rid the department of the racism in their rank and file, who, six months ago, on a warm summer's day marched in solidarity in Seattle's Gay Pride Parade, who had a heart full of loss and a head full of doom.

This man, the Chief, he said, "We are going to clear this intersection."

He paused, collected the stray scraps of attention with his strongest look.

"But ladies and gentlemen, I want restraint and I want strength. We are the law and we are proud and we are peaceful. Any questions?"

A voice from the back. "Yeah. We going to have to pay for parking?"

The assembled fell into laughter. Bishop frowned. "Lieutenant?"

"Yes, sir, I'm just curious if we're going to have to pay for parking while we're being proud and peaceable."

"Yeah. Cuz I had to put my Caddy in a garage and that's like twenty-five for the day."

The cops putting on their gear and chuckling—the helmet and mask, the belt and spray.

Bishop adjusted his glasses.

"Gentlemen, I'm sorry about the parking. That's a question for the Mayor when all this is over. For now let's focus. Anything else?"

"What'd I hear about some city buses?"

Bishop's eyes went bright. The buses had been his idea.

"There will be ten to twelve metro buses parked at the corner of Eighth and Seneca," he said. "The buses will be both a barrier and a temporary detention facility. You need to make an arrest? You cuff them; you put them on the bus."

"And do the buses have to pay for parking?"

They erupted into laughter. Bishop waited patiently for it to die down. They were just blowing off some steam and he understood it and he let them, because he felt some element in the air. Something that wasn't there before they saw the crowds. Something that wasn't there in the days and weeks and months they had been preparing. He was confident, but there was something in the street, some rogue undercurrent in the way they muttered and shifted and adjusted their gear, the bitterness of their joking that wasn't exactly joking. He thought his boys and girls might be afraid.

82

Bishop cleared his throat and collected them in his gaze.

He had about one hundred and fifty delegates stashed in the lobby of the Sheraton. The Mayor himself was with them, had left his sheltered spot in the MACC and was waiting for the signal. The all-clear that would mean Bishop had done his job.

"Ladies and gentlemen, let's get something straight. We are police in the greatest nation in the world. We are professional and we are prepared. There are five thousand protesters just across that intersection. But we are going to clear this intersection, and then we are going to clear the next, and then the third one after that, and we are going to get those delegates to the convention center. Is that understood?"

A chorus all around. "Yes, sir!"

They were in their gear now, smacking the armor and feeling good.

Then another hand raised.

Bishop sighed. "Yes, Sergeant?"

"Sir, some of these protesters. I don't think they want to go."

A few chuckles.

"Sir."

"Sergeant?"

"If they don't want to go . . . ?"

Behind his troops he saw a caramel-colored kid weaving his way through the crowd on a unicycle. He had to shake his head. No, that is not your son, you fool. Three years his son had been missing. His beautiful, brilliant, mixed-up son. But missing wasn't exactly the word, was it, because his son who had run away three years ago, who had disappeared into the gaping maw of the world at the age of sixteen—he wrote his dad postcards. Nothing periodic, mind you, six months could pass easily before his son deemed him worthy of a missive, and nothing indicating his whereabouts besides a postmark, or his safety, as if that were even possible to indicate. And yet, how could he, the Chief of Police, notify anybody, let alone file a missing person report? Hadn't his sixteen-year-old son left with a dislocated shoulder and an arm black and blue with fingermarks? That would have required filing an altogether different report. And so, Bishop had let him go without a word.

Postcards. For three fucking years. The last one had featured a black man without a shirt sitting cross-legged in an intersection. A black man skinnier than any man Bishop had ever seen. A postcard of a black man on a hunger strike, his ribs protruding, his chest so narrow it was nearly concave. His skin dusty from the street, his face gaunt. Straw somehow caught up in his hair. He was a portrait of cheekbone and eye socket and dirty beard, his eyes two brilliantly bright watch dials marking the time. On the back Vic had written: *Dad, does this man love the world?*

And he had wanted to say, Son, stop caring about people you don't know and have never met. Just stop caring. It hurts too much. For three years his son had been gone and nothing more than postcards. It made Bishop, frankly, want to strangle the kid. Where had he gotten a postcard of a hunger strike anyway? Who made something like that?

"Sergeant," Bishop said, "these are our streets. Don't ever forget that."

"But what if they don't clear the street when we tell them to?"

"Sergeant." Bishop grimaced. "You are holding a tear gas dispenser. If those protesters don't want to move . . . "

"Yes, sir?"

Bishop leaned forward to gather their attention, but he didn't need to. Everybody was listening.

"Then, Sergeant, you fucking light them up."

84

14

The sound of the chain against the plastic was a hollow kind of knocking like the sound of Victor's heart whomping in his chest.

The Chief was striding back and forth through no-man's-land, a megaphone to his mouth. A line of police at his back and the mostly seated crowd before him. Thirty feet of black pavement between them. The Chief—Victor watched him through the forest of people between himself and the front line. He looked at the Chief's polished helmet which reflected the passing clouds, white streams of smoke growing long and then disappearing over the curve. Victor lost sight of him as the crowd milled and yelled.

And then saw him again. He looked at his round glasses and remembered the ring of keys that hung from his belt. Looked at the line of black-suited cops standing behind him like a SWAT team preparing a home invasion and he thought, Dad, what are you doing? Dad, don't do it.

"Citizens," his father said through his megaphone, "it is time to clear this street."

Behind him the cops were sliding on their beetle-masks. They were loading their guns with tear gas and locking them tight.

"Citizens," he said, "I don't want to hurt you."

Victor breathing and trying to will himself into whatever transcendent state it was that would ease his pounding heart.

His father spoke slowly and carefully. He wasn't wearing riot gear—no polycarbonate faceplate, no chest protector, no elbow pads, no knee protectors, no riot shield—just the stiff blue shirt, the creased pants, the stars climbing his lapel.

"Citizens, if you do not disperse within two minutes," he said, "we will deliver pain and chemical compliance."

Victor thinking, Chemical what? Chemical *compliance*? Is *that* what he said?

"Citizens," his father said, "don't make me start now."

A chant began among the seated and the standing. It was a simple call and response.

Whose cops? a voice asked.

OUR COPS!!! the crowd roared back.

Whose cops?

OUR COPS!!!

John Henry sat to Victor's left, a girl he didn't know sat to his right, both with their arms locked in PVC pipe perpendicular to their bodies and connected to Victor's own. Both with their faces raised to the rain. Both chanting their damn hearts out. And Victor thought If I could chant. If I could just chant maybe I wouldn't be so shit-scared.

He studied his sneaks. Not so lucky anymore. The light rain fell on his downturned head, gathered in his braids, ran in streams down his face. They were locked together in a circle at the corner of Sixth and Pine. Eight of them sat in a circle, facing out, locked on the pavement in front of the Sheraton. He could feel the locking mechanism above his hand in each pipe. He felt the chain running through the pipe. He felt the ache beginning deep in his shoulders as he held the pipes aloft. Above him the traffic signal turned red. Beneath his down jacket, his shirt was soaked in a cold sweat.

WHOSE COPS?
OUR COPS!!!
WHOSE COPS?
OUR COPS!!!

Victor closed his eyes and listened to the howling, heard the voices bouncing off the buildings, the discordant symphony of a thousand voices chanting and shouting and he thought, Shit, man, what did I *do*? *Our cops?* Did they really *believe* that? The police protect money and power. They protect the few from the violence of the many. Do you have to be black or brown to know this? No. Maybe it helps. Shit, our cops? The police, they pickle the world, preserve it the way it is. They are guard dogs keeping us afraid and obedient. They—

John Henry's voice interrupted Victor's panicked train of thought.

"Victor, how you doing? You feel all right?"

Victor nodded. Took a breath. What had he been saying?

"Because you're looking a little pale."

Victor smiled. Forced himself to speak, willing his voice not to tremble.

"I'm good."

John Henry studied him as if he were a talking exhibit in the Museum of Bullshit.

"It's all right," he said.

"What's all right?"

"It's all right to be scared."

"I'm not scared."

"You'd be crazy to not be scared."

Victor looked down.

"Try chanting," John Henry said. "The chanting helps."

Victor listened. He closed his eyes and listened. A thousand voices hoarse with fear and rage. A thousand voices joined in rhythm. It was a primal sound, a roar like a waterfall, a thousand voices becoming for the briefest of moments one voice, one roar, threaded through with frustration and yearning, their desperation to break through to another plane. One where the city belonged to them and they had no reason to be afraid.

He listened. He even moved his mouth. But he couldn't do it.

"Victor, listen. That is the power of the human voice at its most profound. This is Ayahuasca chanting in the Amazon. This is incantation. This is the power of the spirit as formed and shaped by the human voice. Do you hear it, man? Do you feel it? You got to chant, buddy. It'll make you feel better. It's the communal ritual of the thing. The tie-back to older times. The chanting is the thread that links us to every people's movement in this country that ever rose up for what was and for what is and for what will come. They chanted, Victor. That's what they did. They chanted. I mean wow."

"I hear it."

"Look at the cops, Victor. They *hate* the chanting. Look at them there squirming. You think they fidget like that in their squad cars? No. They feel the power of our chanting in their boneless limbs. Ten thousand voices. They feel the power of it in their sparrow hearts. Look at them dancing in their jackboots, Victor."

And what was it? Chanting with your friends on the cold concrete, chanting in the face of a line of pissed-off cops. Chanting in the street and waiting for those cops to come break open your stupid head like an overripe melon. What was it Victor heard in John Henry's voice, what impish spark that suggested in some not-so-secret part of his heart John Henry thought this the purest fun known to man?

"Try to feel it, Victor. I know you didn't get trained. But I'm here with you. We're all here with you. You got to chant, buddy. Try a little one. This is the human music. This is how we shape the fear; it's how we possess it and make it ours. The chanting, Victor. It's how we hold the fear in our mouths and transform it into gold."

"I told you I'm not afraid."

"Victor."

"Seriously."

"Victor."

"I told you I'm not fucking afraid."

John Henry just shaking his head and turning away from him.

There were white Christmas lights strung in the trees.

There were thousands sitting in the drizzle and mist.

There was the Chief of Police with the megaphone, his father's amplified voice echoing over the sea of bobbing heads.

"If you do not clear this intersection, you will be the subject of pain and chemical compliance."

And Victor saying under his breath, "Don't do it, Dad. Don't do it."

There was the crowd, the thousands of bodies packed between the buildings, some standing, some sitting, some, like Victor and John Henry, in lockdown in the center of the intersection.

And there was the cold fear crawling up his spine; his hands trembling in the chains. If he could only chant. Join their shaking roar.

"Head down, won't you, brother?"

A woman in black jeans and a white T-shirt with a gas mask around her neck was kneeling before him.

"It's easier if your head is down, Victor."

He lowered his head, realizing in the same moment that it was King. The sudden sight of her made him want to cry. He had the overwhelming urge to say something, to do something, but what? To ask her for a hug?

She leaned over and soaked Victor's pink bandanna—the one he'd gotten from the girl—in apple cider vinegar, and then lifted it to his nose and fixed it tight.

"King," he said, his voice muffled. The smell of vinegar burning through his nostrils.

She bent to John Henry.

"King," he said again.

On her knees in front of John Henry, did she hear him? Or did she just not care? She poured vinegar in the bandanna and then knotted it carefully around John Henry's nose and mouth. Neither of them looking Victor's way—in fact they were staring at each other, King and John Henry, lost in each other's gaze, something passing there between them, and for all it mattered, it was as if Victor, although only inches away, had ceased to exist.

"He shouldn't be here, King."

She laid her hand against the side of his face.

"He'll be fine."

"He's not trained and he's not chanting and he will not be fine."

And the crowd now chanting just one word, two syllables drawn out and forcefully expelled.

COURAGE
COURAGE
COURAGE

King turned back to Victor. She laid a hand upon his knee. He knew it was meant to be reassuring, but what he really wanted was her arms around him, pulling him tight, and it felt cold and perfunctory, the sort of nice little pat you give a stranger's crying child.

"He'll be fine," she said. "Won't you, Victor?"

He found himself dumbly nodding as if that were an answer to something. She watched him and then drew a pair of swimming goggles from a pocket. She slipped the band over his hair. Fastened the plastic fishbowls to his eyes.

"When the gas goes off," she said, "don't breathe too deep."

And then she was gone, disappeared back into the crowd, tilting her bottle of vinegar into bandannas and tying them around people's mouths and noses. Behind the Chief the cops were fondling their six-chambered tear gas launchers. Victor looked at his father there in front of the line taking a deep breath and he whispered beneath his bandanna, "Don't do it. Please don't do this."

There was a can of pepper spray passing back and forth between his father's hands and Victor wanted to ask him if he felt this same gaping emptiness opening beneath his throat, but he didn't speak to the man. Three years and not a word.

COURAGE
COURAGE
COURAGE

The police raised their tear gas guns like a line of archers. Black barrels angled skyward at forty-five degrees. Victor watched his father finally remove his glasses and pull a black gas mask down over his face. He was a hundred feet out, and yet Victor imagined his father's eyes were shiny behind the faceplate as if blinking back

91

tears and Victor's chest suddenly opening to a grief and loss he had never known existed.

Oh, Dad. How I've fucked things up.

COURAGE
COURAGE
COURAGE

Resonating in the cold morning damp, a chord composed of a thousand trembling voices rising and humming.

COURAGE
COURAGE
COURAGE

Then, with the solid kick of a bass drum, a thump that seemed to displace air, the cops fired. Above their heads the first cans rose in an arc and still he could not chant, could not even open his mouth. Just sat there and watched the canisters climb. They reached their zenith and began the descent, tumbling end over end like some strange satellites returning to Earth, trailing smoke. Falling straight toward him as if meant for him and him alone. Yes, Victor saw and he knew.

COURAGE
COURAGE
COURAGE

Here they came tumbling out of the sky with a message meant just for him, he could actually hear it, hear the voice in the smoke, in the canisters descending, the canisters that in about two seconds were going to reach their earthbound destination. About one second from now they would be landing in Victor's lap, and he heard the message the smoke wanted to tell him, heard it as clearly as if his father knelt there on the cold concrete beside him, whispering in his ear.

"Son," the smoke said, "care too much and the world will kill you cold."

DR. CHARLES WICKRAMSINGHE

Intermission I

Twelve Hours Until the Meeting

Dr. Charles Wickramsinghe stepped from the noise of the terminal into the quiet of the cabin. A tall man, he bowed slightly to clear the door, gave a small smile to the business-class stewards. He was shy at times with the luxuries of importance, and so carried only his usual briefcase and overcoat. Uncomfortable with the insulation his diplomatic status conferred upon him, he refused to travel with staff, not even an assistant. "When I get too old to carry my own cases," he had said five years ago when the negotiations began, "then it's time to surrender."

And yet, this year, turning seventy, the weight of the travel had begun to register somewhere beneath his skin, the negotiations softening the tough muscle of his heart, pulling on his bones with a whisper. Just once he would like to perform a miracle on a par with Gandhi's. He will swim the island's length and width, circumnavigate the coast, keep going until they all sign the bloody TRQs, the subsidy reductions, and then the final document itself. At a steady pace he will swim the sun down, he will swim the sun up, until they grant Sri Lanka's entry to the WTO.

A stewardess stood at his elbow.

"Welcome, Minister," she said. "Can I get you anything?"

"Just a cup of tea, please."

Of course he was fantasizing about the swim: Sri Lanka's coast was more than a thousand and a half kilometers. An island nation the size of Maine. He would not ever be swimming its length and breadth.

The stewardess took his overcoat and slid his briefcase into the closet. With the help of her outstretched arm, he lowered himself slowly to the seat.

"We'll be in the air soon, Minister."

Good. Still so much work to be done, even here so close to the final leg.

Five long years he had been at this, taking the meetings, slowly gathering the signatures. Forty countries in five years. Thirty-nine signatures. He wouldn't have believed it himself had he not been there to witness it. To live it. To survive it. The flights close to three times a week for five years straight; the memories still humming through his body like a running river. He felt sometimes as if he had lived enough in the intervening years to account for another life, a second go-round. At his age a small miracle. The world, it seemed, was full of them. His life included. From colonial subject to globe-trotting minister. The tall brown man with mahogany skin and snow-white hair—he was recognized and welcomed by presidents and prime ministers. Chirac, Yeltsin, Blair. Juan Carlos the King of Spain, and his prime minister, María Aznar. He knew their faces all too well. The food-flecked chins, the jowls, the tired eyes. Like a tribe of people capable of manufacturing charm at will. And their leader, the elder brother of the toothy clan—Clinton, who he was set to meet tomorrow afternoon in Seattle. President Clinton—the very last signature he needed.

But god he feared that "no." Export and trade. Making things to sell to the West. This was how Sri Lanka would feed its people in the new century, in the bright new age of the global economy.

They must open that door. Or I fear we will end up starving on its doorstep.

He sighed and warmed his hands on the tea the stewardess had brought him. He sipped from the cup and settled into the most recent batch of reports with a kind of tired, worried excitement: something about fuel oil tariffs from the Dutch. Another from the American State Department warning of possible protests. He scanned it and moved on, idly puzzling why anybody would want to protest the millennial meetings of the WTO.

* * *

Thirty thousand feet above the Pacific, finished with his reports for now, he was flipping the pages of a magazine, not really looking, just killing time, when he realized the woman he was looking at in the pages of the magazine was the same as the woman seated next to him.

He almost spilled his fourth cup of tea.

He couldn't look at her. He wouldn't look at her.

He looked at her.

She was asleep, or feigning sleep, beneath a blue blanket embossed with gold feathers and an eye mask of the same.

He tried to recline his seat, turn it into a bed of his own. He'd take a nap. Close his eyes and avoid the embarrassment. There was a panel of control buttons to his right, but he couldn't get the thing to go back even an inch. He fumbled. He didn't get where he was by being flummoxed by every beautiful woman that ever sat down next to him. Goddamn it, man, why won't this thing go back?!

He glanced again. Still asleep.

Don't make a bloody fool of yourself.

He could smell her.

He looked again at his magazine. Devouring the details. She was an actress, young but not in her first youth. A string of romantic comedies. A failed action flick. A failed marriage to a Hollywood star.

She stared at him from the pages with a clear-eyed gaze.

You are the Deputy Minister of Finance and Planning. Get ahold of yourself.

Then she was out of her own bed and leaning across him, blanket falling from her long cat's body, revealing a sari of all things. Stretched across him, pushing the proper button to make the seat recline.

"These things . . . " she said with a smile.

Stretched across him. God help him, were those her breasts pressed against his shoulder? Her famous breasts?

He looked at her in alarm as she returned to her bed and curled into it, legs tucked childlike beneath her.

"Thorry," she said, and removed a piece of plastic from her teeth. She wrapped the plastic thing in a napkin and set it in a plastic container beside her.

"I wear this retainer? For my teeth? Stupid, I know."

"No, no, no," he said.

"A grown woman. I mean where's my teddy bear? Where's my blankie?" Blankie. She said the word philosophically, slowly, as if throwing it out into the world to see what deeper meanings would come echoing back and he liked her immediately—her presence, her humor, the honesty with which she presented herself.

The stewardess passed back through the cabin with the tray of champagne glasses and she was stretched across him again, a pale

100

powdery flowery smell and was it necessary to stretch across him like this? She took the champagne flute and said to the stewardess, "And a little Chambord, too, please, if you have it."

He was fully reclined, staring straight at the molded ceiling. His spine rigid. He rolled his neck to and fro, caught her eye. She nodded at the tray, as if to say go on, and he reached and gently took a flute of his own.

"Cheers," she said.

"Cheers."

They lay talking in their seats, pleasantly fuzzed, drinking their Kir Royales, the name of which of course he had just learned. Lovely drink. How lovely to drink it in bed. Why had he never tried this? What part of him loved this? They were a world of two, and he was a grandfather and a diplomat, a widower alone with his work, at peace with his business, his solitude; he had three grown children, two girls and a son, and he had experienced domestic bliss, or something like it, the warm encumbrance of a happy home, but he had never experienced anything like this.

"So, Dr. Wickramsinghe. Is that right? Is that how you say it?"

"Call me Charley. Please."

He perhaps enjoyed the pleasures of the West a little too much. A good scotch. The tenderness of a filet, medium rare. Why was it a steak in Sri Lanka never quite tasted like a steak grilled in the States? And the women. He had always loved Western women, their beauty and ferocity, and yet they were a reminder of the foolish young man he once had been, when he had found fair skin to be more beautiful than brown. More beautiful than black. How strange.

"Charley. I hope you don't mind me asking, but where are you from? Originally, I mean."

"I was born in Sri Lanka."

A little happy shriek from her red mouth and heads in the business cabin were turning.

She stared back. Oh, the authority of a glance, he thought. The power of a famous face. The other passengers looked away.

"You've heard of it?" he said. "A small island in the Indian Ocean?"

"Heard of it?" She leaned over and squeezed his arm. "I love Sri Lanka. I was in Sri Lanka earlier this year. Oh, how lucky you are," she said. "What a paradise."

He nodded, and yet he didn't know what to say. He was thinking of 1983. The riots. The war which had been raging for sixteen years since with no sign of abating. He thought of his house in Colombo behind two lines of concrete wall and wire. Of the two armed guards who manned the gate, M16 rifles at the ready. He thought of his neighbors' homes which had burned in the rioting. Thought of his neighbors' daughters who had burned in the rioting. A paradise, she says. What kind of paradise was this where young girls burned?

She was looking at him intently, her hand on his arm, and he liked her attention. An intelligent woman. God knows she was beautiful, and powerful, too, her opinion mattered, her good opinion of Sri Lanka as valuable as any tourist brochure, but perhaps it was better to tell the truth. "It is an extraordinary country in many ways," he said. "We have much to be proud of. But paradise is not always what it seems."

She was silent for a moment. But then she nodded, saying, "I know I'm not an expert. I put on a shirt and the tag says: Made in Sri Lanka. I don't know. I'm sorry. I just put the shirt on and go on my way. I know where Sri Lanka is, of course, but do I know *what* it is?"

He nodded and under the spell of an intuition, placed a hand on her blanket above the ankle.

"I know you probably think I'm just another self-absorbed celebrity. But I'm not. I'm a human being. I have thoughts. I have feelings just like anybody else. I know what the world is."

He nodded and gently squeezed. She bent toward him, forgetting for the moment perhaps that she was wearing a sari. A shawl of blue and gold silk wrapped around her shoulders and across the chest, which left her stomach exposed. She moved her hand to brush hair from her face, and the effect was not so much erotic as evocative, the soft swish of the silk was a light whisper in his mind, a long echoing memory, and the years dropped away, and he was once again a boy in a musty schoolroom shaded by spindly palms, chalk dust in the air, and his schoolteacher, a nun from England, pondering aloud, upon seeing his mother and the other ladies waiting for their children outside the schoolyard gate. The nun clucking her tongue disapprovingly and saying, "Look at those bellies. Tell me, children. Have your mothers no shame?"

And the star student, the brilliant child understanding for the first time what the nun might mean. Feeling for the first time the shame of those exposed stomachs, the ridiculousness of how his mother dressed. What had they been trying to accomplish, those nuns, those English bureaucrats and their sprawling empire of oranges and tobacco? Two decades of education. Forever molded to be English, and yet not English at all because that was not possible. Like clay cast in an inferior mold, the products were forever breaking, forever found wanting. Forever cracked.

She pulled the blanket to her neck and smiled at him. She was more beautiful still, vulnerable and raw, looking him full in the face, searching his eyes.

"Charley," she said, "2.9 billion people are going to make less than two dollars today. Do you know how much I made for my last movie?"

He held her gaze, her eyes two impossibly blue bowls of ice above the embroidered rim of the blanket.

"Millions, Charley, millions and millions of dollars. And today twenty-two thousand children will die from things as stupid as malaria, and starvation and whooping cough."

She paused. "Do you want to know why I was really in Sri Lanka, Charley?"

He waited silently.

"To adopt a child. I make millions of dollars pretending to be other people. I have a beautiful home in the hills. I have an ex-husband who is dating a twenty-three-year-old and what do I want? I want a child. So I fly to another country. What kind of world is this, Charley?"

And Charles sat there silent because he didn't know the answer. He wanted to answer her, but he didn't know how, and yet he couldn't look away. The cool humming of the circulated air enveloping them.

"Blankie," she said. "Whooping cough."

He pulled his hand away from her ankle, wishing he had a report to read.

"An adopted child to hug and hold," she said. "That is what I want."

15

Rising above the mist-shrouded city, the sound of the rotor thumping above them, Seattle's downtown geography spread beneath him like the emptying half of an hourglass, wide at the top, tapering to a narrow valve in the south—Chief Bishop was taking a ride with the Mayor in *Guardian One.*

Downtown was bounded by the water to the west, the interstate to the east. The early morning traffic on I-5 snaking south and north, he saw people in their cars on their way to work, and he imagined them listening to the radio, drinking coffee with the day's first cigarette, applying lip liner and mascara and rouge. Did they still use rouge? He watched the glitter of brake lights from on high and thought of his son and salmon and death.

"What do you estimate, Chief?" The Mayor's voice scratchy in his ear.

They were talking on the headsets.

Bishop made the crowd at thirty to forty thousand and he felt a migraine coming on. A blinding headache that would require cool towel and empty room from whose darkness he did not dare stir. He had scheduled nine hundred officers. He had turned down offers of reinforcements and help from the FBI, the Secret Service, the Washington State Patrol, and the King County Sheriff's Office.

Why?

Because it was his city. And he would protect it. Look at it there turning slowly beneath him as the helicopter banked in another slow sweeping arc. In the southern section of downtown the towers of black glass reflecting gray sky like a city rising directly from the water. Like a city climbing hand over hand from the dark depths of the Sound. The tallest towers of a labyrinthine city whose work was buried deep beneath the waves, a society too complicated and brutal to exist in the light.

What was he talking about?

He had noticed this in himself. The drifting thoughts. Of late, a certain inattention.

When exactly did his city get so damn tall?

Where in the hell had he left his coffee this time?

There was the Space Needle standing alone. A structure Bishop had always loved despite himself. Erected for the '62 World's Fair, some architect's vision of the future, it looked like a plate balanced on two chopsticks, wavering improbably six hundred feet in the air, something beautiful but faintly ominous about the whole thing. Maybe he loved it because now here he was, a living breathing creature in the year 1999, an inhabitant of the future, and that future, the one they had imagined in 1962 when he had been a youngster dreaming, now seemed antiquated and quaint.

A relic that had once been relevant.

There was Elliott Bay to the west, shedding light off the waves—his love for this was uncomplicated: the dark water of the Sound where he had once taken his son fishing every fall while the whales moaned and sang.

"You see that clump, Chief? Ten o'clock." Christ. The Mayor again. "Looks like they're trying to block the freeway."

Spawning salmon climbing the river's ladders to breed and die.

Every year the same thing. Breed and die. Breed and die. Breed and die. Salmon were an interesting thing to think about.

Bishop saw them. He looked down through the bubble and saw the crowds massing. In the red square at the University of Washington; at Pine and Fourth; at the Seattle Community College on the northeastern corner; Pike Place Market to the west; a crowd numbering in the tens of thousands—all on the move.

Chief Bishop was scrunched into the jump seat, his knees around his chin, the laundry smell of his pressed duty blues tickling his nose. It was, quite frankly, too early for this horsecrap, and he was looking out the bubble and feeling his eyes start to pound.

Retirement. It had a sweet sort of ring to it.

The helicopter dipped and did another slow sweeping turn over the city.

"Chief, this is not under control," the Mayor said.

"It's under control."

"I'm calling the Governor. We're bringing in the National Guard."

Bishop rubbing his rough cheek and thinking that's what he would do: find his son, retire from this crapola, and set up shop on a ranch somewhere in Idaho. Not Idaho. Idaho was Aryan country, wasn't it? Montana, then. He would look into it. Was Montana friendly to persons of brown and black complexion? Could his son make a home there, quit all his wandering? Bishop almost laughed. It was friendly if you were a chief of police. If you were the kind of man capable of making rank and holding it. If you were the kind of man governed by the forces of compassion, strength, and the rare and strange ability to gather round you and somehow focus the dispersed chaos of personalities called a police department in a medium-sized American city. A man who was a natural leader. A man called Chief.

107

Then anywhere could rightly be called home because you took a place and made it yours.

Goddamn right.

Find his boy, then, and wrangle up a couple of horses, a herd of sheep. Sit on the porch with a can of pop in his hand like a silver dipper of ditch water and the two of them watching their herd come grazing over the hills like puffs of cotton.

Was that what you called them? A herd of sheep? No. A flock. A flock of sheep to shear come spring.

For a week the Chief had known his son was here. A routine sweep of the homeless in preparation for the various foreign dignitaries—really it was just for Clinton—had turned him up. They didn't arrest the boy. Just a discreet call placed quietly to his office. Yes, of course he had known Vic was here for a week, had even gone to find him. He had asked the officer who first called him, a beat cop who worked the neighborhood beneath the Alaskan Way Viaduct, to show him the encampment. He was a father, after all. He would bring his son home.

And so Bishop had found himself late one night after a shift following this young officer as he negotiated the blocky half-dark beneath the underpass. The blue tarps hung with clothesline, the crappy tents huddled in the grit with the trucks a constant pounding overhead like a galloping migraine. The cars green-bodied flies that whirred and buzzed above their heads. The concrete hollows lit by firelight and the blue hissing of the cookstoves. The low murmur of voices which disappeared beneath the sound of the nearby waves smashing against the seawall. He was frightened, and of course he said nothing, did not show this, how he was suddenly frightened of the dark, *this* dark, frightened by what might be out there and frightened by the sudden depth of the world and all he did not know. His son lived down here? In the darkness beneath however many tons of unstable concrete and rebar? He did not want this new knowledge of the world. He would stop at the first lighted corner and drop it in the nearest trash can. He would climb the hill and leave it on the street for someone to collect. Maybe as he walked it would simply fall from him as if this knowledge could be shed like dirt-stained clothes on the way to the shower.

The smile he wore like a clip-on tie because he wanted to give the appearance of friendliness, because these were his citizens, he was the people's police, and yet they were the homeless and the mentally ill and my son lives down here and the mentally disturbed who belong in asylums, but do we even have asylums in America anymore, weren't those for the fucked-up nations of the fucked-up world, weren't those for paranoia and schizophrenia, and don't show your fear because he wanted to know in which tent his son lived, but he did not want his officer to have to shoot anybody.

The beat cop stopped in front of a cheap-looking nylon tent which Bishop recognized immediately. It was his, purchased however many years ago and forgotten in some closet, except his son had not forgotten because here was where Victor was living: in his father's tent bought five years ago for a fishing trip they never made. He must have broken into the house and found it in a closet. When did he break into the house? He was in my house? Bishop removing his cap in a gesture almost of deference as though at a grave, at an accident, something equally real, equally incomprehensible, the emotions running across his face as he stood and looked, as he stood and thought and remembered. He was in the house. Victor. My son.

The tent was empty.

All around him, the encampment made its noises of the domestic. The settling in. The eating of dinner, the howling of a drunk, and the beat cop saying he was just going to go check on some folks and asking Bishop if he was cool for a minute.

The Chief of Police saying, "Yeah, I'm cool."

The tent as empty as the house as empty as Bishop now felt.

He gestured to the pilot. He had seen enough.

"Bring her down," he said.

"Bishop," the Mayor said. "I'm calling the Governor. We need the National Guard."

What a panicky little political machine, thought Bishop.

"Sir, you don't want to call them. You, sir, are the one that will take the blame. And I would be sorry to see such a promising political career cut short at the knees."

The Mayor looked at him and then turned away, a greenish cast to his face.

Bishop looking out the bubble at the massing crowds threatening to overwhelm his city. He heard the unmistakable ring of authority in his voice—it was how he led his troops, it was, in some ways, how he'd won Suzanne, it was, finally, he thought, how he recognized himself, when he sometimes became afraid.

16

The PeaceKeeper motored through the streets, climbing curbs.

Ju could feel the grumble of the diesel engine all the way up through her spine, the coughy asynchronous roar ascending like exhaust through the rubber soles of her booted feet, a trembling vibrato in the deep tissue of her thighs, and she held tight to the rail to avoid being thrown.

She ducked when they hit a trash can and cups and cardboard went flying.

A garble of static from her radio. Then,

South on Seneca. Anarchist seen headed south on Seneca in possession of a flamethrower device.

Four-one-three. Did not copy that. Repeat. Did you say . . . ? A flamethrower?

Repeat. A flamethrower. She appears to be using her mouth.

Ju looked at the radio and thought that was probably the stupidest thing she had heard in her eight years of policing. She shook her head. Finally, they stopped at the market. The engine wound down to an idle and Ju stood on the running board, feet planted wide, and began loading her six-shot semiautomatic projectile launcher, her GL6, or—in the words of the civilian crowd passing before her—her tear gas gun.

MACC had stationed the PeaceKeeper at Pike Place Market. They had called over the radio and said the crowd was rushing the market, arming themselves with fruit and other projectiles.

She only knew she was kitted up for civil war in the streets and people were freaking out.

But Ju? She was calm.

A man was building a pyramid of tomatoes under the overhang of the market. The neon lettering above him reflecting in the wet puddles along the walkway and she felt a tingling as she slid each round into its cylinder, locked it home, and spun to the next empty chamber, a tip-tap raindrop drumming on the canvas skin of her heart because what was a tear gas round but a genie in a bottle? Once free of her gun it would no longer be under her control, but captive to the vagaries of chaos, loose in the crowd— the milling, stamping crowd of feet and legs—and the gas—the powdered particulate—free to blow wherever the wind chose. Not in her control. Not under her domain.

Yes, violence was a genie in a bottle, even state-sanctioned, legal violence, because she knew the primal law, the lead-lined equation which was the foundation of all that happened on the street: if you want to carry a gun, you better be prepared to *pull* a gun; and if you pull a gun, you had better be prepared in heart, body, soul, and mind to fire a gun. To kill. Why else carry the freaking thing unless you were prepared for that? An empty threat was worse than none at all. And an officer unprepared or unwilling to kill? Just another walking target, another boob in blue and black.

PeaceKeeper idling. Ju loading her gun, foot astride the running board, feeling the vibrations running through her leg and up her hip. Concentrating and working carefully—perhaps working too closely, a little too fully absorbed in the task of round to

112

chamber, the lock and spin, because when Park appeared at her elbow she was taken completely by surprise.

"What you say, JuJu?"

His face was hooded, smiling a devilish little smile beneath his black poncho as if he knew he had caught her unawares.

"Park," she said.

"Sorry, didn't mean to spook you."

She gave him an up and down disdainfully as if clocking a staggering driver on Ventura Boulevard who stepped from his Porsche, breath so laden with bourbon it could be considered a flammable substance, to say, "Well, I might have had one drink with dinner."

"Only thing you're spooking in that getup," she said, "is your mother's memory of the sweet little boy you never were."

He grinned. "I was a good boy," he said. "Greatest boy ever, according to my mother's birthday cards."

"Hey, Park," she said, "where's your horse?"

He said nothing, but the look on his face was enough—he was a *boy*. A thirty-five-year-old boy with a fucked-up face. Something about him that was pure resentment. A pouting sulky little boy who had been wronged by the world.

"It's all over the radio," she said.

"What is?"

"How you harassed some kid with your horse. How the Chief intervened and busted you back to the MACC. That's what."

Park smiled and leaned in. "Ju," he said, "don't get too excited. You hear about the FBI report?"

Beneath the hood of the rain slicker he did not look right. Was he sick?

"Park, you're supposed to be back at the command center. I heard the order myself. So I say again, what are you doing here?"

"The FBI report, Ju. Did you read it?"

She looked down at the GL6 in her hands. She noticed she was nervously fiddling with the last of the tear gas rounds. She slid it home and locked it tight.

"I read it, yeah. The Feds put the risk at low to medium."

"Correct." He stepped forward and let his hand come to rest gently on her shoulder, behind the gun. "But the risk of *what*?"

"The crowd going violent."

"Is that what it said?"

"Yes, that's what it said."

"No. Incorrect."

"Park, what is the point of—"

He stopped her with a raised finger.

"The risk of a terrorist attack," he said. "Low to medium."

"You're freaking crazy."

He laid his hand now on the gun itself.

"Young lady, you should really read your assessments more carefully. The FBI estimates, minimum, four to five officer deaths."

He was close to her now, breathing in her face. Talking to her eyeballs basically, a trick her ex-husband sometimes liked to pull, sweet idiot.

"Officer deaths, Ju," he said. "Four to five. *Minimum*."

He was full of shit. He was so full of shit it was coming out of his ears. And yet, what was it, standing here on the PeaceKeeper, that caused her to shudder? What was this premonition she felt?

"*Minimum*," Park said. "Better believe. Somebody is going to catch a bullet."

A loneliness brought on by the rain? Some dim intuition of looming disaster? Perhaps some nameless form—thought to have drowned—rising from the deep wells of memory. The nightmare images from a war and a home she knew only through the fog of half-told stories barely begun before they disappeared like the people they were about. Guatemala. A place she both missed and did not miss. A place she both knew and did not know. A home she had never really had and yet longed for regardless.

"Four to five officer deaths," he said, counting them off on his fingers. "One. Two. Three. Four." He put his finger on Ju's left breast, laid it lightly against the bright brass plate that carried her name.

"Five," he said, pointer finger pressed delicately above her heart, thumb cocked in the shape of a trigger.

"Boom boom, Ju," he whispered, close enough now to kiss her. "Boom boom. Your family gathers in a dimly lit room."

17

Gooks. Slant-eyed motherfuckers. I can smell a gook-joint from two miles away. The vitriol, the way Park's father's face would crumple in bitterness as if fragile enough to shatter, the way he would suck his teeth and narrow his eyes, Park didn't understand that kind of hatred. How a person could live with that beating like a living thing inside him.

Park's pops had been a POW early on in the war, two years living in a hole eating white worms, blind scuttling bugs, whatever he could scrape from the mud, and Park supposed that entitled him. Who knew how the darkness had deformed him, what hunger and fear had done to his father's soul. It was odd though, because apart from the alcohol-fueled violence, only in this was his father so off, so strange. Gooks. His voice stretched thin as if traveling a wire which originated from the dampness of that dark hole and terminated somewhere in his trembling brain stem. Gooks, his voice so tortured and weird. Weird—that was the word because in moments like this it was as if his father were not his father, but would always remain that man alone in a hole looking for a bug to eat.

That and his laugh while sucking beers at the VFW and the subject of work came up. Eventually, it always did. What a weird laugh uttered from his father then. It was a laugh that said my job is not union. I am not allowed the privileges of the union because I work a crap detail as a security guard and we are not unionized. But it was a laugh that contained knowledge of what union meant—that his mother and father had both been union. That he would be union, sure, if he could, but that wasn't his job. But his job was his job and it paid the bills and he could hold his head up. It wasn't McDonald's for Christ's sake. But it was amused, too, a complicated irony because the laugh said this is the world, and I accept this fact, I am not the only one in tough times, I am not the only one working but still poor, which wouldn't be so terrible were it not for the indignity, for the shame, for being hungry, for the sheer fucking impossibility of surviving. A laugh which said, I used to be union, but the country has changed, hasn't it? That was the bitterness in the laugh. I used to have a union job, the laugh said, but the factory went ahead and moved, didn't it? South of the border, the laugh said. East of the sun, the laugh said. And we fought for what exactly? The laugh said, I ain't the only one, but that don't mean it ain't a crap deal neither. And who heard his father's laugh and understood? Well, anyone within earshot who was listening heard it and understood, except for the times there was only his son, only Timmy Park listening to his old man laugh and curse, which, truth be told, were many. Because Timmy loved his father and there were not many others on earth who could say the same of the man.

Park watched a woman in a lemon-colored slicker stoop to tie her shoe, thinking, in fact, there were a lot of people who couldn't stand his father's hateful guts.

"Hey Ju."

"Don't want to hear it, Park."

"Ju, what the fuck is with that car?"

He had his baton out and was tapping it against his knee.

"Are they filming us?"

"Park."

"Are they fucking *filming* us?"

He unclasped the holster of his pepper spray.

"I'm going to check them out. See who they are."

"Park, Chief said—"

"See who the fuck they are and why they're filming me."

"Park!"

He stopped.

"Take it easy," she said. "If you refuse to return to the MACC, at least just look from here. Chief said if there was nothing immediately threatening to take it easy."

Park looked at the car. He looked at Ju—telling him what to do for the second time today. It was all on account of the Chief busting him back like that in front of everybody. The Chief shouldn't have done it. It was a question of respect. The ultimate social law, the law of respect. In some ways a large offense done with respect was more easily overlooked than a small offense done with disrespect. Get busted smoking a blunt on the stoop of your building—an offense, sure, but one Park would probably let slide if you nodded when you saw him coming and put it out. Get busted smoking a blunt and lean back and let a big sweet reefer cloud go drifting over his head while *smirking*—that was taking your life into your hands. Not because of the blunt, but because you were disrespecting him, disrespecting the badge and uniform, disrespecting his authority. When you were on the street, respect was the currency by which you lived or died. Cops and criminals alike. And the more he thought about it, the angrier he got. Because who was Ju to tell him what to do?

"Wake the fuck up, Ju. We're on our own out here."

119

He pulled his arms free of his rain jacket and draped it over his shoulder, covering his badge number and name. So pretty when she was pissed at him, he wanted to what? He wanted to put ice cream in the angle of her hip and eat it with his teeth and tongue. He stepped into the street.

She grabbed her helmet from the top of the PeaceKeeper and hopped off the running board to follow him, saying, "This is crap, Park."

And Park, well, Ju following him. That almost made him feel better.

Almost.

He rapped the car window with his baton. Knock knock knock against the glass.

"Down," he said.

Two men sitting in the car. Caucasian. Age approximately fifty-five to sixty. Possible homosexuals. Not that it mattered. But everything mattered. Every stray scrap of information. You didn't know what was going to matter on a day like this. You had to pay attention. A late-model Honda Accord in robin's-egg blue, rust spots climbing from the wheel wells like mold. A handheld digital recorder was pressed against the glass of the closed window. What were they filming down here at Pike Place Market? This was about five blocks from anything going on. Maybe they were getting ready to film? Maybe they were set up here so far from the action because they were planning something? Sometimes you had to stop a thing from happening before it even happened.

Again the baton rapping against the glass.

"I said down."

The driver nodded. Professional-like. He passed the camera across the seat to his friend or whatever and rolled his window halfway down.

"Can I help you, Officer?" His voice was soft and smooth. As if he was used to talking to cops, as if he was used to conning dumb believing cops.

"You can't film here," he said.

"I'm sorry?"

"You will be."

"Sir?"

"The camera. Shut it down. You can't fucking film here."

He didn't even flinch, and it wasn't that it made him mad, but Park noticed. What kind of homosexual doesn't flinch when a cop says fuck in his face?

"Officer, how can we help you?" the man said.

"What the fuck are you filming?"

"We're Quaker witnesses. We have every—"

"Quaker what? What is that? Some kind of *religious* thing?"

"Officer, our lawyer specifically—"

"Step out of the car."

He was trying to appear calm, but feeling, in fact, the exact opposite of calm, whatever that was. The law of respect. Did this guy just say lawyer?

The man paused. Looked him dead in the face.

"No," he said. "We have every right to be here."

He took the camera back from his friend and pointed it in Park's face.

"Officer," he said, "why did you cover your badge number? That's illegal, you know."

Gooks, Timmy. No-good fucking gooks. That's how we ended up here.

18

Ju was halfway to the car, following Park, when he popped his pepper spray from his vest, leaned through the half-open window, and sprayed first the driver and then the passenger.

Ju frozen to the spot halfway in the street, halfway between the PeaceKeeper and the disaster unfolding before her eyes. Frozen in the street, which was against her training, yeah, and against her instinct, yeah, but she could not believe what she was seeing.

The interior of the car filling with mist.

Park turning away with a satisfied hitch to his belt as if to say job well done, congratulations, boy.

The doors opened and both men fell to the pavement on their hands and knees. Strangers rushing to help. The men howling with their hands all over their face and Ju knew, she took the pepper spray full-face once, an impromptu test at the academy devised by some asshole cadet who didn't like her high proficiency scores, and the pepper spray, it's just capsicum, like the pepper flakes you shake on your pizza, but man, about ten thousand times more concentrated, and when that spray hits, you feel the serious need to dig your eyes out with a spoon.

Park strolled over, wagging his baton happily.

"I told them they couldn't film."

"Park, what are you thinking? You need to get your butt back to MACC. Now."

"You got no rank on me, Ju."

"I'm calling it in," she said.

"Good idea."

He lifted his radio to Ju's face and twisted the volume. A garbled roar of static and shouting voices.

Krrrrrchhh.

NINJAS ON SIXTH.

Krrrrrchhh. Peat. Did you say KRRCCHH.

She knocked the radio out of her face.

"Ju. You pissed or something?"

"Right now, Park?"

"Yeah."

"Right now, I'm thinking about razor blades."

He smiled sideways. "Razor blades?"

"Yeah." She made a slashing movement across her face. Across where his scar would be. "Razor blades. Slice the offending flesh right off."

He was silent for a long while.

"I didn't want to hurt them," he finally said. "I told them they couldn't film, but they didn't listen. That's just the job."

"Sure, sometimes that's the job," she said. "I know that's the job." She keyed her own radio. The same mess of static and panic greeted her. "But you don't have to love it so fucking much."

124

19

Before she died, Victor and his mom had played an unusual game. Maybe you could say she practiced an unusually obsessed form of spirituality. But Victor thought it was just something that had developed between them, a sort of game they played around the breakfast table, mother and son. It started out more as a joke. She was eating a banana one morning at breakfast. She peeled the sticker off and stuck it on his nose.

She said, "You're a banana."

He said, "I grew in the low-lying regions of Costa Rica."

She leaned forward to investigate the sticker. "Peru, actually."

This was when they still lived on the farm. Before she married his father.

"Peru," he said. "I grew into a mature banana in the mountains of Peru. I am a banana from the Andes."

He waved his cereal spoon around in the air.

"Wait," he said, "do bananas grow in the mountains?"

"No. Potatoes grow in the mountains."

"Where did I grow?"

The phone was ringing.

She picked it up and put it down.

"Where do bananas grow in Peru?" he said.

"They grow on the wet slopes of the Andes. On the eastern side. They take out the rainforest and put in banana plantations."

He adjusted in his seat. Getting comfortable. It wasn't their farm, but they shared it, a sort of co-op, and he liked nothing more than digging in the dirt with his mom by his side. That year of happiness.

"I am a banana from the rainforests of Peru."

"Yes, the low-lying rainforests."

"The Amazon!"

"You are yellow and soft and moist to the bite," she said.

"I am not yellow and soft and moist to the bite. I am green and young and growing strong. I am hanging from a tree."

"Do you hear any birds?"

"It just rained. I can hear water dripping from the branches."

"The sun is breaking through the clouds."

"Yes, and there is a bird that sounds like a rusty gate opening. Another one that sounds like breaking glass."

"You are young and getting strong."

"I am hanging in a bunch. A bunch of banana friends hanging from a tree."

"Good food for a monkey."

"There are no monkeys!"

"Good food for a boy."

"Wait, wait, wait."

He adjusted in his seat, turned to face out into the room, sort of looking out in the small middle distance, the thinking distance, this was the way he sat when he wanted to think about something that required some stretching of the imagination, the attempt to inhabit a banana.

"There is a creaky rusting noise."

"Another bird?" she asked.

126

"No, there aren't many birds on this plantation. It's more like a factory. The trees are low and stretch as far as you can see. The ground is wet. There are ditches running between the trees. A percolation of milky blue water."

She was now holding the half-eaten banana, the peels flopping loosely on her wrist. "Where did you learn that word? Percolation?"

He shrugged like Who knows where one learns the word percolation, Mom, one just learns it.

"Okay," she said.

"The bananas are growing in blue plastic bags. They hang in blue plastic bags that contain the chemicals . . . "

" . . . the fungicide . . . "

" . . . the chemicals that kill the banana diseases or whatever."

"There was a creaky rusty noise?"

"Yes," he said. "There is a creaky rusting noise as the man comes to cut us from the tree. He carries a machete. There is a sound in the air. A kind of humming."

"Insects," she said.

"Machinery," he said.

"Okay," she said. "Here comes the man with the machete. He wears a blue mesh shirt for the heat. Who knows where he got it."

"One of those things you might expect a boxer to wear," he said.

"There is a complicated system to haul the bananas out."

"Not so complicated. An iron rail that runs through the trees like an elevated train track. The cart runs on a single wheel on the rail."

"The man pulls the cart along the rail."

"The machete is in the other hand," he said.

"*Swish, swish,*" she said. "The sound of a machete swiping at grass."

"*Thwack.* The sound of machete entering a tree trunk at lunch."

127

"Lunch is a small helping of beans and rice."

"*Thwack*," he said. "The sound of machete splitting a coconut."

"Not enough really, but it is what they have."

"*Thwack*. The sound of a machete splitting open the boss's head."

"Victor!"

"Sorry."

"The creaky rusty squeak of the wheel as the man pulls the cart along the rail, his machete in the other hand. You are ready to be cut."

"I'm ready to enter the world."

"The world awaits."

"I'm young," he said.

"And green," she said.

"And strong," he said.

"And you're ready to enter the world. The man stops his cart at the first row of trees."

"He is ready to cut me."

"Does he need a ladder?"

"No. He is extremely talented. He is the fastest cutter in the crew. The fastest worker on the whole plantation. Maybe in the whole of Peru," he said. "He works without a ladder."

"Young and strong."

"The best."

"His reward for his talent . . . "

"His reward . . . "

"His reward for his talent," his mother said, "is they tell him when the plane will fly over spraying pesticides."

"The others have to jump in the ditch," he said.

"While the plane buzzes them," she said.

"They put their hands over their heads and the plane buzzes

them and the chemicals kind of drift down over them like water from a sprinkler."

He paused, then said, "It doesn't help if they cover their heads though, does it, Mom?"

She looked at the banana. Flipped the peel back and forth.

"No," she said. "It doesn't."

20

Look at the tear gas falling like little pills. High-arcing moon shots which seemed to touch the sky. Gravity-bound cans which returned to Earth to tumble across the black asphalt, spitting steam. Look at the cops picking their way through the crowd like dancers, stepping daintily as though on ice.

And Victor's father saying, Son, have you ever asked yourself why Buddhist monasteries are built in remote mountains with walls thirty feet high? Love and compassion for the entire world, six billion selfish souls, Victor. Are you man enough? Know where you're going when you sign up, son.

Victor's mother who used to say, sitting in the kitchen, "In your dreams everyone is you."

Victor watched a woman on her knees being attended to by a medic. Her hands were clasped in prayer. He saw a mist of blood from a riot baton. Blood exiting in a fine spray from a man's shaved scalp.

The cops stepping like ballerinas. Testing the ground as if they might fall through.

Compassion for every living blade of grass, and yet walls thirty feet high, six feet thick from within which you meditate on the unity and beauty of all beings. Son, does this make my point?

There was a stiff wind blowing from the Sound. The smoke making pictographs in the street. Cuneiform letters of clay that drifted and cut. People moved around him like ships in a fog. He saw a shoulder, a swatch of neon jacket. The flash of a blue sneaker, then it was gone, sucked into the cloud. The wind shifted and the gas swirled and suddenly Victor was enveloped in a smoke so thick it was as if he'd been buried alive. He saw only gray, heard only the slap of running feet, the soft thump of batons striking flesh.

What terror does to your body and brain. Victor had discovered the threat of imminent pain had a way of focusing your attention. A week, a day, an hour—these were units of time no longer within Victor's ability to contemplate or feel. The day had shrunk to a morning. Then an hour of street battle. Then fifteen minutes of withering brutality.

Noon was like a foreign country.

Son, how easily an open heart can be poisoned, how quickly love becomes the seeds of rage. Life wrecks the living.

John Henry in his duct tape glasses and cowboy hat. He was chanting with the crowd, and Victor envied John Henry his belief. He wanted to believe in something. Wanted to get pulled down into it, absorbed and lost in the rhythm of the words.

If I could chant, maybe I wouldn't be so shit-scared.

But it was embarrassing to chant. It was embarrassing to believe.

Victor, who wandered the world, who had been wandering since he was sixteen years old, who now only wanted to be brave, to sit in strength and witness like his friends were doing—the more he saw the more it hurt. The more he felt the need to do something to ease the pressure building in his chest.

Victor, careful now, there are wisdoms of the East and practicalities of the West. Tibet, yes, the power of compassion, and what became of her? Son, there is a lesson to be learned in the case of Tibet.

A face loomed out of the fog, a woman wincing in the gas. She was running; panicked. She almost slammed into him, then reversed direction at the last moment and disappeared and Victor saw not a body, just a rag to a face, the hand-claw, arthritic then gone, the smoke clinging to her retreating feet cartoonishly as if her boots were on fire and leaking smoke.

At the age of seventeen, Victor had run into an American girl begging for change on the oil-stained concrete of a long-distance bus station in Bolivia. She'd been wearing a traditional poncho so cracked and bug-infested it might have been on loan from the Sundance Kid. She had a dog on a frayed piece of rope and a hand-lettered sign leaning against the dog's plastic bowl.

"Spare some change, brother?" she'd said in English. It was the dog that did it. Or the English. It made him want to kick her in the head. Or maybe it was her expression, eyes narrowed, lower lip protruding, some air about her that was both self-righteous and proud, this American girl with parents and bank accounts, who was begging for change on a bus station floor as if that somehow made her real.

This was in the El Alto bus terminal, the city above La Paz, coughing on the smoke of newspaper and trash, a drift of fine white ash coming to rest on your shoulder, and what was she doing up here and, more important, what the hell was she thinking?

He wanted to kick her in the damn head. But instead he knelt beside her and unzipped his pack. The dog barely lifted its snout. The dog could have been dead, and he looked at her and he looked at the dog and he read her sign.

TENGO HAMBRE

133

And it was because of the dog, or the sign. How pathetic and stupid and sad. That skinny pup lying dull-eyed at the end of its rope, panting in the exhaust. He took out his wallet and handed her the last of his money left in the world, a green twenty-dollar bill, seeing himself later that night looking out the window of his bus into the darkness asking himself why the fuck he did it even as he did it.

Son, in life there are winners and losers. Your choice is which side will you be on? Don't back the losers, son. They'll never let you go.

Victor breathed. He counted. He needed something, but what it was he didn't know. He was never going to survive.

John Henry said you had to believe. Sure, no problem.

But what were you supposed to believe?

DR. CHARLES WICKRAMSINGHE

Intermission II

Six Hours Until the Meeting

Nineteen eighty-three, when the war started, Charles was fifty-four years old and newly minted as the Assistant to the Deputy Director of Economic Research for the Central Bank. In July of that year, two months into his new post, a small band of Tamil rebels in the north attacked a police station. They killed thirteen Sinhala policemen.

The sweet Buddhist citizens of Colombo, so famous for their politeness and gentle ways, went completely mad.

These were people Charles knew. People he had once worked with at the university. His neighbors. The woman who mended his shirts. The man who brought fresh fish from the market. The toothless man who sold kites on Galle Face Green. They took to the streets in gallant mobs; they paraded in the night armed with carpentry hammers, simple boards with protruding nails, tins of petrol. The brave mobs burned the city. They tore Tamils from their homes. Tamils who had lived peacefully in the city for generations. Tamil businesses burned; Tamil homes burned; Tamil daughters raped and burned. The mobs stopped lorries on the street and demanded petrol. The petrol was placed in an empty tire. The tire was placed around a Tamil's neck. Someone lit a match and jumped back. They called it necklacing—that manifestation of human cruelty, mob madness.

Pinpricks of anxiety across his skin because now here he was how many years later, walking among a crowd of angry citizens.

He saw a father walking with his son, small steps so the boy could keep up. He saw a group of grandmothers carrying a cardboard coffin bobbing above their gray heads.

He heard drums and the chaotic piercing shriek of policemen's whistles, but of course the police were not blowing whistles, the half-naked people dancing in the streets were.

He thought of the actress on the plane. They had said their goodbyes on the concourse before Customs. She had offered him a ride into the city, but he politely declined, exercising his customary restraint.

"Thank you," he said. "You're very kind."

But then the moment of goodbye and he was at a loss. A handshake? Lean in for a kiss on the cheek?

He had extended his hand and she had looked at it and laughed and then threw her arms wide and pulled him into a fierce hug.

"Good luck, Charles," she said. "I hope you get what it is you want." And then she stepped back and placed her palms together and bowed ever so slightly.

"Yes, same to you," he said.

There seemed more to say, but what it was he didn't know.

He sometimes felt as if there were a wall between himself and the world. Not in the moments of negotiation, but outside, beyond the gates of the club or the Parliament or the palace. His status and power were the moat, the razor wire, and twenty miles of no-man's-land. Riding in a limo through the streets of London, D.C., Berlin, Mexico City, or Delhi, and the faceless crowds shuffling by like blobs of color, dark passing clouds of humanity drifting by the smoked-glass windows and he wanted to ask the driver to stop, wanted to step out of the car to speak to the people he saw, the shadows gathered under the trees, a million miles from his passing tires. But it always seemed there was not enough time, it was too dangerous, he didn't speak the language, he would never understand their lives anyway. Always something. Another report to read, another call to make—but this was his life, the duty he had chosen. Not to walk in the streets communing with the souls, but to ride in the limo, calling the PMs. To attend the conventions. To negotiate trade agreements. To build the nation through economic development. As much as he might like, his responsibility to his people did not allow him the luxury of time, of stopping to talk with them in their roadside huts.

He listened to the whistles and something like a bagpipe—could it be a bagpipe?—and he imagined Colombo, 1983, when those sticks were splitting open heads and he watched in absolute awe and a sort of admiration and disbelief as a line of cops stood on the opposite corner and watched the demonstrators peacefully pass. He heard their sweet angry American voices chanting and singing, saw their American bodies marching and dancing, and he was surprised to feel not fear, or anger, but a kind of happiness. A calm.

My god, man, he said to himself. This is America.

* * *

He worked his way into the crowd, a dampness of sweat gathering on his forehead, darkening the fabric of his Italian suit. He moved slowly, a slight limp to his step. The slowness of his gait, and the subsequent air of dignity, were partially the result of a broken foot which had never properly healed—broken during his time in Welikada Prison, years ago when he had been a leader of the opposition party, just a young man really. Ten years he had been jailed, and despite his warm manner, a certain solitude still clung to him. It was like the warmth of a tropical noon stretching into evening, a long-ago memory of suffering, forgotten, but still producing heat. The memory, he supposed, was like the broken foot improperly healed—the legacy of the injury stitched into the bone, nothing more.

He moved into the crowd, felt the familiar pleasant ache in his shoulders of fifty laps in the Mount Lavinia club pool. He needed the swimming even if he disliked the idea of belonging to a club—all the old British ways. The pretensions and condescensions of Sri Lankan high society. Behind the polite smile, the firm handshake and chuckle, he sometimes wanted to tear the bastards to pieces. Here they were born to wealth and comfort while their country threatened to slide into a chaos from which it might never return. Tiresome people, but he knew it was only human nature to believe it best to ignore suffering, to focus on your own good fortune. The human survival mechanism: to say your prayers, thank your gods, and hold your breath when you passed the slums. The sweet poison of privilege, wasn't it? To think blindness a preferable condition. And yet, there they were whether you wanted to see or not. The unwanted of the world. People begging on the street. People without enough to eat. People without the medicine and doctors to make them well. People without proper clothes or homes. Without clean water to bathe or drink. Did these self-congratulatory club members think their inherited wealth came from nowhere save their miraculous good luck? Did they not find a connection between their obscene wealth and the obscene poverty all around them? Perhaps it was too much to suggest the fault was theirs alone. The upper class was too goddamn stupid to be blamed, frankly. But how could they do nothing? How could they look upon their fellow creatures suffering and do absolutely nothing?

He didn't have an answer for that. He only knew he had his meeting with Clinton in six hours' time, and now here he was standing in a crowd, the streets were jammed, and three blocks down, rising black and lovely above the crowd, there was the object of his desire twinkling in the rain: the convention center.

He pushed aside a young kid with dreadlocks, another girl with a turtle puppet. He listened to their chants and he felt the energy of the crowd around him, and it began to occur to him that perhaps the crowd was not a crowd, but something else entirely. As he continued forward, moving more slowly yet, it began to dawn on him that this was not a formless shapeless mob without intent. No—it seemed increasingly possible that their intent might be to stop him from getting to his meetings.

Forty countries in five years.

Armenia, Aruba, Austria. Belgium and Bulgaria. Canada, Croatia, Cyprus, the Czech Republic. Denmark. Estonia. Finland and France. Germany and Greece. Grenada and Guyana. Some were easier than others. Haiti, Hungary, Iceland, Italy, and Japan. Latvia, Lithuania, Luxembourg. Malta. Sweden. Switzerland.

Perhaps it was excessive for a man his age, but he took a steady pace. He was a man of steady pace if nothing else. How else to do what he did? The Deputy Minister of Finance and Planning, specially appointed for Sri Lanka's entry to the WTO. To negotiate trade among the asymmetries of global wealth—it was a bit like navigating a coral reef in your bare feet. The bright darting bait. The razor's edge. The sharp-nosed predators lying back in their dark.

He visited the Four Tigers, and the Celtic Tiger and the BRICS. Tea with Mandela in a free South Africa. Can you believe it?

And, of course, last but not least, most visited, in fact, in the five years, the empire that had once ruled his own: the United

Kingdom. Leaden London, murky around the edges like a watercolor portrait of the Queen.

People were sneering at his suit and blocking his way. The crush of bodies pressing on him, buffeting him from all sides. Without much thought he pulled out his passport.

"Let me through!" he said, waving it above his head. "I am an international delegate!"

It had been quite a holiday. A five-year holiday with wine and photos and the ever-present threat of a massive heart attack because the stakes were nearly unbearable. Just one "no" vote from any of these men, or their representatives, would veto Sri Lanka's entry. One no. It was a kill shot. Like walking through the tall grass with forty long barrels trained on your soft parts. Forty bwanas waiting for the step that will reveal your heart. Christ. The patience required to placate these men and their oversized demands. The diplomacy. The charm and deep duty of international negotiations.

One more. One more signature. And who could it be but the Americans? Well, Clinton had agreed. All we need is his signature. Five years, five long years, and it's nearly done.

A soft glob of some human fluid arced from the crowd and landed warm on his cheek. He recoiled as if shot. He was finally beginning to see the individuals in the crowd—a rain-soaked woman, hair plastered to her forehead; a heavy man with a mouth like a fish, water beading on his glasses. A man filming the whole thing on a handheld video recorder the size of a small book. He was tall and pale with dark unwashed hair and a serious face, wearing a jean jacket and sandals with socks, and he turned and yelled into the crowd, "Don't spit on the delegates, you assholes."

"Thank you," Charles said. He replaced the passport and removed his pocket square and dabbed delicately at his cheek.

"Now, if you will excuse me, I must get through."

"I'm sorry, I can't let you do that, sir."

He replaced the pocket square.

"Thank you, but I have meetings which begin shortly."

"I know. We canceled your meetings."

"You did what?"

"We canceled them. Sir."

"You canceled what? My meetings? No, I don't think you understand."

But even as he said it he knew. It's you, Charles, that doesn't understand. He was seeing the scene, the motley assortment of faces, some angry, some listening, some formless and questioning; he was seeing the line of cops on the north side of the intersection in their leather and shields; seeing it all, but it was as if he were blind to some essential element. He knew suddenly that despite the apparently normal functioning of his eyes, he was seeing nothing at all.

"But you and I," he said, "all of you," he said, gesturing to the people, "we're on the same side."

The man laughed. "You're a delegate."

"Yes. Yes. I *am* a delegate. I am the delegate from Sri Lanka. That is *exactly* why I'm here."

"Oh shit." The young man in the denim jacket seemed very worried. He said, "Oh, fuck. I'm so sorry. Is that even the thing to say here? We're out here to protect countries like yours."

Charles nodded, thinking, Protect countries like mine? What did he imagine the Third World to be? This man with his denim jacket, his sandals and socks, his greasy brown hair. Did he picture a world without universities, without scientists and politicians, without writers and thinkers? What did he see there in his mind? A world of horses and hand-pulled carriages? Broken-limbed

143

beggars howling at every turn? Did he see a wasteland devoid of taxis and buses and the straight-backed men and women to stand and hail them?

As if every soul that had ever breathed the air of Sri Lanka—the Third World—had lived a miserable ill-begotten life. Died a nameless unremarked death. Charles looked around. It was a strange idea. Did these people imagine America to be a place lacking in sorrow? Suffering?

And yet, there was something distinctly American about it all, a fundamental difference in perspective and place—in how they saw themselves in the world. And this was what made it so American—not that they felt compassion for mistreated workers three continents away, workers they had never seen or known, whose world they could not begin to understand, not that they felt guilty about their privilege, no, not that either, but that they felt the need to *do* something about it. That they felt they had the *power* to do something about it. That was what made it so American. That they felt they had the power to do something—they assumed they had that power. They had been born with it—the ability to change the world—and had never questioned its existence, an assumption so massive as to remain completely unseen. The power and the responsibility to protect the people they imagined as powerless. The poor defenseless people of the Third World.

He felt a sudden queasy sadness. What if they knew what a real revolutionary was? How bloody is a real revolution. He looked around, suddenly feeling the need to sit, and saw nothing but their faces, their round wet faces staring back at him.

What a violence of the spirit to not know the world.

* * *

144

As a child Charles had known the geography of London as well as he knew the lanes of his own town. Piccadilly Circus. Waterloo Station. In his childhood dreams he had wandered Trafalgar Square, admiring the stone lions beneath Nelson's Column as though he were one accustomed to such sights. Easily, he had imagined himself walking along the Thames, the water sparkling in his imagination in a way it surely never had in reality. Buckingham Palace. The black-and-white photos of the Queen and her children—the Royal Family—published in the daily newspaper. He remembered running his fingers over the grainy photo until the tips were stained black with ink, touching the Queen's face, shattered somehow as only a child born in a colony can be by the unfathomable distance between himself and civilization.

Civilization. That faraway thing at the center of it all. That bright candle guttering in the boundless dark.

The young man in sandals and socks—Charley said to him and to the gathered crowd, "I'm not a rich man. I don't love money, I love my people and I want to change the system just as much as you do. But you have to change it from the inside. Will you let me do that? Will you let me through, so that I can go to work?"

The young man considered, while Charles waited with a small humble smile, his hands resting palms together. He was as surprised as anyone when the young man put down his camera and wrapped him in a clinching heartfelt hug.

They swayed in the rain.

And then the air exploded.

A series of deafening reports which blew apart the day. He instinctively hunched and covered his head. Flash memories of 1983. City buses flying to pieces. Air filled with ball bearings and nails. But this wasn't Colombo and this wasn't 1983 and this wasn't a civil war and this wasn't suicide bombs.

Was it?

He risked a glance at the police. They were pointing strange guns at the sky. He turned back to the crowd and saw blossoms of smoke sprouting from the ground. People with bandannas to their mouths, coat sleeves pressed to their faces, eyes and nose sunk into the crook of their elbows.

This was tear gas. It took more than a moment for him to realize it. He looked to the cops. Looked to the crowd. Looked back to the cops, the glass entrance of the convention center beckoning behind them, staff, janitors, and such, watching.

Blasts punctured the air. The police had not calculated the wind before they fired. And now it was gusting strongly from the west, was blowing the gas straight back into their ranks. Charles saw it not rising above the crowd, but moving low and fast, close to the ground, a roiling fog of gray smoke sailing through the crowd and past him, as if being sucked into the convention center by a vacuum, and still they were firing. Explosions tore at the air. Canisters crashed into the ground. He felt the poison drift collecting in his clothes. Tasted the grit of it on his teeth, his tongue. Away from the convention center. And even now he wanted to resist, wanted to stay.

Even now he thought he could still get in. He could still make the meetings.

His ears ringing, he bent and ran toward the line of cops. One of the skyward guns descended level with his chest.

"I Am. A. Delegate!"

Shouting in the roaring air like shouting in a train tunnel with the train passing over your face.

"I Don't. Give. A Fuck."

Charles pointing at the center, point, point, pointing, and waving his badge.

146

"I. Need. To Go. In. There."

Like trying to talk inside an airplane engine.

"You Are. Not. Going. In. There."

"I. Have. Meetings."

Like popping the door of a plane at thirty thousand feet and trying to conduct a conversation on the wing.

"Return. To. Your. Hotel."

And now the man's gun was at his side, and his baton was in his hand. He jabbed Charles in the gut, a beautiful shot to the solar plexus, perfectly aligned with button and tie.

Charles went to his knees. Sucking air and still trying to talk his way in.

"I. Have. Very. Important. Business."

And it seemed the cop, too, had very important business, because the baton which had poked him was now rising to strike him down. The convention center a mere twenty feet away, and yet impossible, closed to him and his desires. He turned from the glass then, from the steps and the police, his heart already plunging in his chest, his eyes watering, and he fell. Landed hard on cold pavement. Felt the shock through his knees. The rawness of his palms.

Someone took him by the elbow and helped him to his feet.

It was the young man in socks and sandals. The young man who seemed to think he was out here to save the Third World. He had Charles's hand and was leading him away from the police. First they walked. And then they ran.

Arm in arm. Hand in hand over the slippery streets.

And already, even as he ran, jacket flapping, hair wild, already he was thinking, Canceled? God help me, did this boy say my meetings are *canceled*?

21

Victor breathed and counted his breaths and focused on the rise
and fall of his chest. The low pounding of the chant was like a
blood beat in his temple. The gas an opaque cloud blanketing
the intersection, radiating weird light. His heart was racing,
each breath bursting from his mouth like a small explosion, the
hot shame like a stone held on his tongue because he was afraid.
Fear had taken over his being and he knew if he could chant he
wouldn't be so shit-scared, but he just couldn't do it.

Victor had been on the road for three years, had circled the
globe, east to west, and north to south. El D.F., Tegucigalpa, San
Salvador. Shanghai and Hong Kong. Bangkok and Delhi. He
trusted small signs, the ordinary language of everyday things. He
grew a beard and lost weight. His skin took on odd fragrances.
He ran out of money. He found a way back home where he could
earn in dollars: he worked potatoes; he worked apples, stretching
as tall atop an apple ladder as his skinny frame would allow. He
tried waiting tables and only lasted a week. Couldn't take it. He
liked to be outside where he could hear the birds and the banging trucks, watch the planes trailing overhead, sleep under a tree
during his lunch break if he wanted, the crunch of leaves beneath
his head reminding him that he was still just an animal on a

planet spinning through space. He liked to remember that. It was important to remember that. One fall he worked the wheat harvest, mucking and cleaning and moving north. Soon as he had enough money, he was off again.

He traveled because he knew he did not belong. The home where he had been born was not his home. Something was missing. From him or from his home, he didn't know, and so he wandered. He roamed and tramped and traveled, looking for what he didn't know. Tierra del Fuego to the Atacama and the Andes. From the Ganga to the high Himalaya. Victor remembered a meal of lentils and rice in Kathmandu overlooking a narrow lane where women gathered to sell nuts and buffalo milk. That was the day he saw the body burning on a pyre of six-foot logs, the white-hot flames licking at the arms and legs and head, the flakes of ash drifting like bits of leaf over the river.

He had wanted a knowledge born not from any school or teacher, but from his own eyes and ears. From his own brown body alone in the world. An experience and knowledge woven from every person he ever talked to, every bus station and hostel, every meal he had ever eaten squatting against a mud-stained wall, the hundreds of faces of the people he had met, the creased smiles, the yellow teeth, the bloodshot eyes. Where did he belong? To whom did he belong? He didn't know. He liked to walk. Sometimes he just wandered a city, trying to enjoy the feeling of being lost, the feeling as if he were a satellite thrown open to every channel.

The way a woman ate from a ceramic bowl sitting along the seawall in Havana. The way her hands moved as she argued with a friend.

Burning cars blocking the winding road which crossed the border between Peru and Bolivia—a protest against rising gas prices—and Victor opened his pack and sat and shared his crackers and talked with the young men, with the women in their bowler hats, and did they let him through because of his brown skin or because of his Spanish, bad as it was? Or did they just appreciate the talk, the crackers, the companionship and interest and salt.

Conversations wandering the back streets of cities so large he could have walked forever and never reached the end of every lane, seen the end of every shop.

An old man in pajama pants pushing his bicycle through the back lanes of Old Shanghai. Across the river, a young man working a backhoe in a new office park, sitting high and formal in the cab wearing a blue suit and tie.

People's fucking faces. He watched and lived and he felt a million distinct and separate truths beginning to accumulate within his chest like a murmuring crowd. It was an ache inside a need, a white-hot expansion of memory and intuition.

A blind girl begging change in Delhi, flies around the empty sockets of bunched flesh.

Further north, in a tiny mountain town, playing chess and drinking tea, while young guys stood around in sunglasses, watching the game beneath a movie poster, sharing a cigarette among them, lighting the next from the coal of the last.

In Chile, Victor for hours on a cliff, hours watching the endless succession of waves crashing against a continent's edge. Hours spent watching and waiting for what? It was so easy to forget what he had come for. And just a kid without a system, without a political framework, the more he saw, the less he understood. A million singular truths accreting inside him. A million strands. A needle moving so fast he couldn't see it, could only feel it, inking a new face, a new line, a new story. Just woke in the morning with a new tattoo he could never see, could never share. Just felt it deposited like crushed color beneath the skin.

Victor searched the crowd. Americans by the thousands, angry Americans in the rain, their faces round and wet. And he heard them chanting and he wanted to believe it was true. Yes, he envied them their belief and he wanted to feel it, whatever energy was passing back and forth between the seated chanting thousands.

But he couldn't.

He looked at John Henry next to him, searching for the source of his courage, but all he saw was his mouth working above those crooked teeth, his glasses misting and the way he held his head, the way he chanted as if those words held all his fear, all the lonely rain-soaked hope that brought him here to this spot, to this morning, to this 40-by-40 stretch of wet asphalt, chanting in the rain.

Victor knew suddenly that he couldn't do this. Knew it as deep as any knowing goes. And he felt like a coward, but he knew he couldn't do this. His heart was hammering triple-time and he knew. He had to get out.

The wind struggled and whipped. He saw shoes and jeans. Knees and legs and feet moving in a jerking fashion as if puppets on a smoky stage. Caught on a sudden updraft, the smoke rose and corkscrewed between the buildings and he saw the Doctor in his overalls and top hat out in the intersection motioning for people to sit, sit, sit as the canisters dropped and smoked. He was wearing a hand-lettered sign taped to his chest.

ONE HUMAN FOR HUMANITY

A nail of fear driven into his heart as he watched the cops identify the Doctor. They circled him like wolves and then knocked him on his ass. Victor winced as he watched one cop work a baton against the Doctor's upper body. The cop stood over the Doctor's fallen body, working that baton in long strokes from the shoulder like the Doctor's spine contained some stubborn rock he was trying to remove by pickax.

The Doctor in his overalls and flip-flops, still somehow narrating his beating from the ground.

"Police brutality. You are practicing police brutality."

One cop hitting him with the baton. Another cop knelt beside him on the pavement, punching him in the throat. *Thump. Thump. Thump.* A sound like a fish flopping in a boat that Victor would never forget, hard blows to shut him up, to close his windpipe, and still he went on.

"You do not need to use force. I am a peaceful protester, I am willing to be arrested."

The cops answered succinctly with their batons and fists.

Thump.

"You don't need to put your knee on my neck. I am not resisting arrest."

Thump. Thump. Thump.

Victor wanted to have the strength to watch, to witness the brutality and be strong enough to tell the world about it. He wanted to witness it and by witnessing make it real, unable to be forgotten; he wanted this horror seared into every pale pink fiber of his skull. But he was afraid. The batons rising and falling like pistons in an engine Victor didn't want to know about. Victor's arms were two pieces of wood shivering in the pipes. He counted; he breathed; but he didn't chant.

He watched as the Doctor lurched to his feet. Victor knew what was coming, but he wouldn't look away. He would witness this. The Doctor was turned around, disoriented for a moment, and in the mayhem he stumbled backward into a cop. The cop came low and fast with his baton. A sharp clip to the shin that crumpled the

Doctor's leg and sent him tumbling to the pavement, where the cop was already on him, tearing off the sign

ONE HUMAN FOR HUMANITY

and throwing it into the wind. The cop hit him across the face and the Doctor's hands flew to his teeth, still narrating, mumbling through the blood. "Police brutality. You are practicing police brutality."

Oh god, Victor was so scared.

In that other life, things made more sense. He ran out of money, he went home. He worked trucks in New Orleans. Graveyard shifts unloading sofa beds and plasma TVs. He saw a quarter on the oil-stained floor and he picked it up and put it in his pocket. Then he was gone again, looking for something he couldn't name, but which he felt inside like a saw blade spinning in the hollow space beneath his ribs.

"Lawyer," the Doctor slurred through his broken bloody mouth. "I want a lawyer, you fuckers."

The Doctor tried to cover up as the furious cop stood above him, thrashing him with the baton like he wanted to beat him back to a single-celled state.

The Doctor had stopped moving. His body lay motionless in the street not twenty feet from where Victor sat counting his breaths and sweating. One cop sat on the Doctor's neck; the other bound his wrists in plastic.

Lying there at night in his tent, thinking of all he had seen and known and not understood. Waking in the morning and shivering on the pier, feeling a weird black hole, a sort of hole inside a confusion inside a need, the immensity of the world, the unbelievable hugeness of it all, reduced to a scrap of newspaper a woman uses to wipe her mouth after a meal.

Sat there on the pier wrapped in his sleeping bag, shivering and watching the ships move from port to sea, carrying the things that fill a life: five-dollar umbrellas and paper towels and plastic chairs. Sitting there thinking of all he had seen, remembering the faces of all the people he had met, sat there feeling an ache inside a love inside a need, thinking of all the voices and complaints and smiles, all the stupid jokes and dreams. What did it all add up to? What did it mean?

Two cops dragged the Doctor away by his pretty blond hair. And here came other cops, swinging those fire extinguishers back and forth, letting the pepper spray soak the seated heads. Moving closer to where he and John Henry sat. Two minutes, Victor thought, and here he was, his arms locked in PVC pipe, totally immobile on the cold damp pavement, too scared to call it off, too scared to chant, asking himself what the hell he was doing even while he was doing it while the cops shuffled in a line, tap-tap-tapping their billy clubs.

Two minutes and here they'll be, he thought, the fear shaking his chest like thunder rattling windowpanes. Whether I believe or doubt or chant or die.

He had never felt so alone in his life.

22

King wading through the crowd—making her way toward where
Victor and John Henry sat in lockdown—watched four cops go
after a kid wrapped in an American flag. The kid—whoever he
was—was out front of the cop lines, right in their faces, flashing
them the peace sign. The cops came at him hard and knocked
him to the ground and he was lost in the black underwater shine
of their riot gear.

The scene in front of the Sheraton was chaos. Not what she had
expected. Not what any of them had wanted. The line of cops was
in tatters and she saw the hooded faceplated forms cutting wildly
through the crowd with their riot sticks. The mass surged and
collapsed. She watched as two cops kicked a young woman with
feathers braided into her hair. An Asian girl with glasses received a
blow to the knee. She felt sick. No one was fighting the cops. There
they sat, supplicant and chanting, a huddled mass at the center of
it all in lockdown, while the tear gas swirled around them like
incense around the shaved head of a monk. And yes, they were
practicing nonviolence, but how could you be nonviolent in the
face of this? The rules had changed and the cops appeared to have
gone temporarily insane. Or were these their orders? That was even
worse to imagine. That the Mayor, or the Governor, or Clinton

himself—whoever was in charge of this mess—had willingly let loose the dogs of war. Sent them armed and furious into a wall of peaceful protest.

She saw the kid trying to crawl out from between their legs. She watched as a baton came high from the circle of bodies and she thought of a small room in southern Mexico. Remote mountains where rebels and outlaws and a people's army went to hide. Chiapas. Her room, bigger than a cell, but perhaps the air of a quiet nun's corners. A place to cook. A place to read in the sun. A place to sleep in the cool nights. A place not without a sort of quiet hideout contentment. The outward reaches of the barrio where the neighborhood gave way to scrubland. Out there past the last of the buzzing sodium streetlamps, there was a quiet air of desolation, some twilight feeling of blue abandonment that seemed to cut her to the core.

Goddamn it, why had she not just stayed with John? Stayed in their off-the-grid paradise, their nation of two? Why had she gone to Mexico in a fit of anger?

Yes. She had been scared to go. Scared and yet angry enough with John Henry to sneak across the border under the radar in the guise of a tourist with her sunscreen and camera and her zip-off pants, safely using an old friend's driver's license for ID. Crossing from California into the loud clamorous wrack of Tijuana. Scared and angry enough to not fully consider just how she would get back home when and if the time came. It was never meant to be forever—nothing was—maybe a year or two, but then you get down there and how do you get back. Because going back, going north, it turned out, was nothing like being a fucking tourist. It was about as far away from being a tourist as you could get.

The cops charged and down the kid went again. King heard the scrape of riot boots on concrete and she looked at John Henry and Victor in lockdown. Two faces, two bodies in a circle of eight people sitting cross-legged, facing out into the intersection. Beneath them were pieces of cardboard, torn blankets, anything to protect their sitting butts from the coldness of the pavement. Their arms—their arms were the thing—held aloft and rigid, at right angles to their bodies. Their arms encased in white PVC piping. And helpers wiping their mouths, and helpers holding the pipes in the air. An unbroken circle. Yes, a circle of people sitting in an intersection locked together at the arms with PVC pipes and the cops rampaging on the other side of the crowd. How long before they made it to Victor and John Henry? And look at them. Totally vulnerable. Those cops would massacre them when they finally got here.

They had calls in to every newspaper and TV station and media outlet in the metro area, some national, too. Some of the reporters hung up. Some of the reporters apologized, saying it was not a story. And some of the reporters came down with their cameras and stood in front of protesters locked to each other with chains, and asked, "How do you feel?" "What brings you down here?" "Is this a revolution?"

Despite everything the media might say, and despite what her own wary weary heart might counsel, King knew that what they were doing was important and right. And she believed that if Americans saw what pain their way of life caused in the world they would respond. Americans were a good-hearted people.

So they sat in the street and they chanted and they made witness with their bodies.

Woman's body for bearing babies. Man's body for bearing loads.

American bodies no longer on the line. No longer employed in the so-called manufacturing sector. American bodies too expensive for work so they find cheaper bodies to feed the machine.

They were arranging their bodies in circles and lines. They were

159

linking arms. They were enduring overwhelming violence. They were making message with their bodies.

Wasn't it just a new kind of slavery? Was a cheap pair of socks really worth doing that to a child? People *had to* see that. The basic wrongness. They knew. But nobody was talking about it because it was hidden. They would have you believe it was the only way the world could be. And the WTO. The organization which makes it all legal and turns it to law? How legitimate could the WTO be if they are forced to beat innocent citizens in the street to protect their own meetings?

She watched and she wanted to believe that the cops would stop. Let it be enough.

She wanted to believe that the media—the reporters with their shaky mikes and gas masks—would pay attention and send this message to the world.

She wanted to believe the police wouldn't kill any one of the gentle strong people she had brought here.

But she did not.

Not for one beautiful fucking second.

Because how deep the darkness of the heart which longs for control.

Suddenly the kid was on his feet again. Somehow scrambling out from the circle of cops and stumbling away. He had lost his shirt and his American flag. King watched as he stood in the middle of the street, a skinny kid with a concave chest who seemed intent on personal destruction, and he had his fists up, though not to punch, pumping his fist and pumping his fist and pumping his fist, standing in the middle of the street pumping his balled fist, while the cops came charging after him with their batons and pepper spray.

Pumping his fist as if he had won something.

160

23

The Chief did not look good His sandy hair lying damp on his forehead and his glasses askew and his face gone pale beneath the tan. They were chanting and they were singing and they were sitting linked arm in arm and they were not clearing the street. So he grabbed one of the dispensers and let the pepper spray go streaming over their seated dripping bodies. He released the spray to drift down in a fine webby mist.

He pushed his way to the front where two of his men were trying to extricate a boy in an army jacket from the chain-link of arms.

He reached down between his men and removed the boy's bandanna in one easy motion. He hit him in the face with the pepper spray. His head was shaved. He wore loops of leather and beads around his neck. A purple crystal pendant on a silver chain.

The boy gagged and fell forward, still trying to chant. Bishop blasted him again.

"Sorry, kid," he said.

People packed between the buildings; people spilling from the sidewalks and up into the potted ferns and cedar chips. People dangling from lampposts and dancing in the crosswalks. He shot the spray hard into their faces, two spots of rough red spreading outward from his bright blue eyes, his thin-lipped mouth. This was the face of a man on the edge of cardiac arrest.

Screaming now. The boy was arm in arm with two girls on either side and now they were screaming and screaming and screaming and he couldn't believe how angry it made him as these kids sat unmoved in the mayhem and continued to chant.

Bishop laid his baton across the soft meat of the boy's back. Bishop himself had said in the MACC, he had said it again in the street, "Don't get out of control."

He wasn't out of control.

But he wanted very badly for this crowd to disperse. He wanted to clear a way through. He wanted to protect his city. He wanted the Mayor to quit shouting at him over the radio. He wanted his goddamn city back.

Bishop. KRRRCHHH

Anarchists seen headed north on Seneca.

KRRRCCCCCHH

Flammable liquids. Over

... soft platoon! Who can go hats and bats?

It seemed like everybody was talking on the same channel, and he felt a despondent anger, a helpless sort of rage as he keyed the radio and pressed it to his mouth.

Bishop here. Did not copy. Please repeat.

Chief! Chief! ... KRRRCHHH

Fourth and KRRCCCHH

BishKRRRCHH.

Bishop here. Did not copy. Please repeat.

Urine. Over.

Paper bags of crap. Over.

He stepped to the side. Kicked one of the girls in the leg, then stepped back and kicked the other one in her ribs. Kicked at their linked arms trying to break them apart.

"Sorry," he said. "I'm sorry."

People stumbling from the intersection, choking, heading north or east, away from the gas.

He had ordered his troops to fire on American citizens and they had fired and now he could not take it back no matter how much he might have wished it to be so.

BishopKRRRCHHH

Need assistance at Fifth and Pike.

Fifth and Union. Repeat please.

Volley after volley of gas until the intersection was so choked with gas he couldn't see the hotel on the other side. Couldn't see the streets behind him. They waded through the crowd, breaking apart bodies as if breaking ice in an icebound harbor. He wedged his heel between their arms and tried some sort of leverage. He smacked each girl with the back of his open hand.

They were screaming and crying and chanting.

They didn't understand—there were pressures, circumstances beyond his control.

"Sorry," he said. "I'm so so sorry."

He hit the boy with the baton, a half-swing with power, aimed for the fragile bend of his elbow.

He popped him in the pressure point of the throat. Knocked him behind the ear which was a mistake because then the blood started to flow.

"Sorry," he said. "I'm so very sorry."

Finally the kid fell away from the two girls on either side and his officers moved in and began to pull their bodies apart. The back of the kid's head was split open and his neck was smeared with blood. Bishop watched as his officers tried to carry the boy's body, neither of them wanting to get near the mess that was his face.

One officer was headed west with his arm; the other had one leg gripped by the foot and was moving east. The Chief watched in dumbfounded dismay. He thought for a moment he was going to be sick in his hat, but then the moment passed, and he turned and moved on to the next seated pair.

"I'm sorry," he said. "I'm so sorry."

24

King roamed the edges. She knelt among the fallen, feeling over-whelmed and lost. She lifted a face and poured Maalox and water into its upturned eyes and she dragged the wounded from the intersection and the entire time she was fighting the voice that wanted to tell her: This is your fault.

They talked until they agreed, it was that simple. They made decisions together, or not at all. Consensus was the political heart of what they did and who they were. It was the process by which they channeled their anger, used their sorrow and outrage, their deep sense of separateness, toward a higher purpose. And she loved it.

She loved the discipline, the community, the sense that they themselves had created an independent republic of eight hearts and minds governed by the purest expression of democracy that could be had. Conversations that went around and around until every point had been discussed and dissected and deconstructed. Years ago, if you had described this process to her she would have laughed. How did anything ever get done? It sounded like you'd still be debating, deeply mired in your democratic process, when the cops came to kick in your teeth. But now, in the thick of things, it was sometimes magical, as if joined by a common devotion to the process, they shared the same consciousness, eight solitary souls holding steady like one orange-tipped compass needle quivering at dead north.

So why did she let it happen? Why did she *make* it happen?

"I'll do it," Victor had said. "Lockdown. I'll be the one."

And she had swallowed hard, knowing it was wrong, but knowing, too, that the cops were coming and they needed to get people into lockdown if they were going to keep this intersection. So she ignored the lump in her throat and nodded, knowing it might be the move that saved them, that saved this intersection, but knowing in her heart it might also be the beginning of the unraveling of all they had built, all they believed and had fought for.

Even as she tried to remember the swirl of words from *The Black Cross Medical Field Guide*, the dark voice told her: Did you see that boy? That is your fault. All yours. The dark current that wanted to suck her under and never let go even as she touched and poured. Your fault.

A bottle with a squirt cap is ideal for the eye flush.

A man in a tan suit vomiting into his hands and when King reached him with the bottle he was blind and had no idea where to look.

"Here, I'm here," she said.

Before Mexico, she had told John Henry she wanted hard truths. There was something in the armed conflict of the Third World that drew her. A certain starkness, the solid reality of black-and-white lines that was unavailable to her in America.

She said this to John Henry, John Henry the alchemist, who had taught her how to transform her sadness and confusion into a strength as dependable as steel.

John Henry who said you must use your body. You must use your hands and spirit and mind. John Henry who taught her if you didn't do the work, then you wouldn't survive the work. You'd be left, in the end, with nothing but your own obsessed turbulence.

A solution of half Maalox (plain or mint) and half water works best to clear the eyes.

An older black man who had gone down to one knee and was holding his head to the sky.

King saying, "Don't touch your face," and reaching for her water bottle.

John Henry and King had lived in a box on top of a hill. The box was a recycled shipping container once corresponding to the ISO regulation size of 53 feet long, 20 feet wide, and 20 feet high. Together they designed windows and a rooftop garden, working by lamplight through the long summer evenings; later she cut the steel with an acetylene welding torch. From the top of the hill they could see the purple-black waters of the Sound. The dorsal fins of dolphins, orcas, breaking the surface. On a clear day they could see as far as the snow-covered slopes of Rainier. The perfect cinder cone volcano dormant over the city and valleys below.

A bandanna soaked in apple cider vinegar and tightly tied around the nose and mouth is far better than nothing, but still a last resort.

A middle-aged woman in a red rain slicker pawing at her face. King let the water run down her face like milk and held her while she sobbed.

King didn't know where she was most needed, where she could best help, and she looked at cops and the spiraling gas and felt a sort of frustration rising in her throat. She couldn't get to everybody. And she couldn't stop the cops from firing. She fought the urge to just turn and run. There were bodies lying everywhere, the police wading through the pileup, three or four cops walking with spray bottles that looked like small fire extinguishers, the spray looping over them in an arc. King kept her head down. She kept her hands clean as she tried to remember what John Henry had taught her.

The best protection is a gas mask. However, we can no longer recommend the Israeli gas mask as the lenses have been known to shatter on impact.

The canisters dropped and sputtered. Thick fumes smoldered in the air. People stumbled among the bodies, coughing and blind.

King saw a woman on her knees in the middle of the intersection. Her hands clasped in prayer, her face a mask of running blood.

Of course the locals thought they were crazy. But on their hill they had no neighbors. On a clear day, a hundred, two hundred miles of vision. Sight lines in every direction. No neighbors who could see like this.

And then came news of the first arrest. A man she had known as Billy the Kid. William Garrison, the paper said, eco-terrorist, conspiracy charges. Mastermind of an attack on the Vail ski resort in Colorado.

When she got in her truck and drove into town to check her email, the message boards were lit up with it. Billy—she still could not think of him as William—arrested in New York City, five years after the fact. It was unprecedented. The FBI had found other fugitives over the years, of course, but they had never pursued environmental activists with such vigor. Nor prosecuted them so hard.

Eco-terrorism.

It was a message and King heard it loud and clear.

Three more from Vail went down within the month. She began making plans for Mexico. She had friends there. It wasn't running or hiding out. It was a trip. It would be a productive time. Write some essays. Make a film. Take photos. She was so terribly frightened, but she didn't dare tell a soul.

A tremendously fat bald man who cried into King's shoulder as she worked to clean his face. The man repeating the words "thank you" as if they were a prayer, clutching her arm and then collapsing against her. Her arms around him as he shook.

She told John Henry she wanted to cross the border. Not forever. For a few months. A year. Just until things calmed down a little with the FBI. And she wanted John Henry to go with her. To be with her. To be together.

But John Henry, who believed that courage and compassion were everything, said he had no desire to go to Mexico. He said what you sacrificed in the struggle was nothing compared to what you got in return—a sort of blazing personal heat. You transcended your own history to become the person you needed to be. You stood apart. You transformed yourself. No more double life. It didn't matter the inconsistencies in your life, this is what John Henry dared to say to her—no more lies permitted in the sacred ground of your heart.

This was a man she loved to the point she would forsake all other men, forswear sex and violence. Be good. For him. Because he asked.

He said she was unduly worried. Said she needed to grow up. Almost said she was being hysterical, but caught himself and said instead their work was here, but still she saw the ugly accusation in his look.

She went to her knees before a gray-haired woman who had caught pepper spray in the face. The woman was on her knees on the pavement as the throngs swarmed and buzzed and people went running by, pursued by cops in flapping black. King held her eyes open with one hand and poured from the bottle with the other. The woman on her knees with her head tilted back, totally vulnerable and blind, mumbling and moaning as if awaiting execution while her hand played with the buttons of her coat.

King steadied her head. Her long fingers pulled at the woman's eyes. She poured the solution of water and Maalox and whispered words of reassurance as the woman's eyes searched back and forth in a panic, flashing helplessly in her head. She was trying to communicate some message but what it was King didn't know.

John Henry's mouth was a wound that leaked language—disclaimers and apologies. But she was tired of talking about how her work was nothing. Her worry was nothing. Tired of feeling judged. Days passed when she was all ease and control, as delicate as a perfumed wrist, as fragile as an armed bomb. She listened to him talk at her and she smiled and reached for his cigarettes, nodding.

The effects of pepper spray include: temporary blindness lasting 15 to 30 minutes.

But he would not budge. So she went alone.

Upper-body spasms lasting 15 to 20 minutes.

And at first it was glorious. In the evenings the first appearance of a darkening sky, swallows dipping and swooping above the desert floor. Jackrabbits daredeviling through the dust. A group of deer she spooked drinking from a trickle at the bottom of a dry creek. At first it was wonderful, yes, but how quickly it became lonely, and then she was lost in a nightmare of homesickness, of feeling foreign and utterly apart.

A burning sensation of the skin lasting 45 to 60 minutes.

One day, out of the blue, John Henry emailed and asked her to come back. Said they were planning a big one. It was going to be the direct action of the century. They were going to shut down the goddamn World Trade Organization and the whole world would be watching and he was sorry for being an ass, but now he needed her. They all needed her.

Direct close-range spray can cause serious and lasting eye damage. What is known as the needle effect.

170

She wrote back and agreed to come, still not understanding just how difficult it would be to make her way north, to sneak illegally back into her own country. She remembered Guadalajara. The twilight street, light spilling from the curtains which hung in the open doors. An open shop with the grille half-raised, people inside browsing American movies on pirated discs and she remembered her own feet like the feet of a stranger passing through white cones of light where the shadows of bats spun and fell across her boots as if her head were attached to a stranger's body, her ruck on some stranger's back. Two girls lounged against the wall, slogans painted behind them, movie posters glued to the wall, and she felt it with a suddenness she had not felt since she was a child—the strangeness of what she was doing, the vulnerability of who she was, a woman traveling alone through these half-deserted streets. She finally had to admit. She did not know what she was doing. Had no idea how she would actually cross the border.

So she bought a gun. And she found a guide, a man and his son, who were also going to make the attempt to cross illegally into the United States.

Opening the eyes will cause a temporary increase in pain, 30 to 45 minutes.

And then it all went wrong and she did what she did. And what she did was she shot a man on the border and watched him bleed just as she had once broken a man's pinky and ring finger and watched him weep.

Difficulty breathing or speaking: 5 to 15 minutes.

25

Park was leaning against the PeaceKeeper, on the opposite side as Julia, totally bored, looking around Pike Place Market. There was absolutely nothing happening here—except for the small knot of outraged people beginning to gather around the car where he had pepper-sprayed two Quakers or whatever—and he was beginning to think it was a knucklehead idea to join Ju on the 'Keeper in the first place.

"You know," Ju said, "we had a word for these kind of people back in L.A."

Neither of them had said a word in at least half an hour.

"Yeah?" Park said. He clocked silver pails of silver fish. Fish, blind and dead and wrapped in newsprint.

"Listen," she said, "I didn't mean anything by the razor blade thing. That was an unfortunate comment on my part."

He shrugged like what razor blade thing.

"No, really, I'm sorry, Park. I got carried away."

"What'd you call them?"

"What'd we call what?"

"These people, Ju," he said. "Back in L.A., what did you call them?"

"Hot dogs."

"Hot dogs I don't process."

"Yeah, hot dogs in a plastic pack. All feet and mouth and asshole."

And that was the thing someone said on the back lot, the thing that was so stupid and true and twisted it made you shake your head and spit a laugh into your Styrofoam cup and forget the human mess you were witness to.

And suddenly Park was shaking and laughing in his riot gear and grinning from every shiny corner of his fucked-up face.

"Assholes and lips," he said.

"Walking talking shit on a bun," Ju said.

"They had it tough?"

"Totally screwed," she said.

Both of them cracking up like a couple of maniacs.

"Hey, check this guy out," he said, feeling good.

"Who?"

"That smart-aleck protester in a suit."

"You think?"

"Heck yeah."

Park watched him coming down the rows of fish and fruits. Foreign-looking guy, sweating and something in the way he walked like he owned the city. Park just knew. Guy was bullcrap.

They stopped him in the market between the tomatoes and the fish. Asked him to raise his hands.

"I'm a delegate," the man said.

Ju spread his legs, patted his fancy suit. Park reaching for his plastic zip cuffs, noticed Ju touching the guy's soft suit, patting his legs and such. Why did she need to touch him so much? That wasn't necessary.

"What's in the briefcase?" Park said, taking it from the man and throwing it away.

"He's clean," Ju said.

And what was this, the Indian motherfucker freeing his arm and reaching into his jacket. Park and Ju. They reacted like a team, like they'd been partners for fifteen years, and Park, damn he was feeling good. Just the way they lifted the man by his arms, lifted him like a team, reacting instantly, hands in his armpits and lifting him away and up and then slamming him together into the table that held the tomatoes.

A team, reacting almost instantly, like they shared a brain, which felt amazing, to tell the truth, but the guy had gotten whatever it was he was reaching for and was now offering it delicately, pinched between his fingers.

"Officers," he said, "I am a delegate."

Park lifted the man's chin with the end of his riot baton. His fancy suit was fruity with tomato guts. Put his baton under the chin and lifted.

The guy was holding out a business card.

Park took it. Ju looking over his shoulder. There was a tiny lion holding a sword on the card's ivory face. Embossed in gold letters the card read:

DR. CHARLES WICKRAMSINGHE
DEPUTY MINISTER OF FINANCE AND PLANNING
THE DEMOCRATIC SOCIALIST REPUBLIC OF SRI LANKA

Park crumpled it in his fist and let it fall to the sawdust floor of the market. "Socialist what?" he said.

God, he was feeling frickin' great.

DR. CHARLES WICKRAMSINGHE

Intermission III

Three Hours Until the Meeting

When he imagined the names: the World Bank; the International Monetary Fund; the World Trade Organization. The Kennedy Round, the Uruguay Round. NAFTA, MAI, and the GATT.

When he imagined the economic ministers in headphones and suits sitting at long brown tables; voices translating Portuguese, Russian, Mandarin, negotiating the tax on French cheese; British beef imports; how many Toyotas will be assembled in Ohio.

When he imagined the great container ships cruising the seas, saw the steel hulls riding the ocean swells, the rough burlap of bagged coffee, the netted mounds of bananas; crates of strawberries grown fat under the summer sun of the southern hemisphere. When he imagined the container ships sailing from port to port, when he imagined the cables spanning the ocean floor, the twenty-four-hour financial markets, the satellites in orbit—why would someone want to stop this? It was free trade; it was global capitalism; it was the world.

Canceled? How could the meetings be canceled? It was catastrophic. It was impossible. He hadn't thought this ragtag army of malcontents could organize themselves long enough to get a cricket match going. Let alone shut down the most important global financial meetings of the decade. But they had. They had managed to cause enough confusion and chaos that the meetings were canceled. It was impossible.

And now here Charles found himself wandering around a bloody fish market.

Somewhere in his running he had gotten separated from the boy who had saved him, the boy in sandals and socks who was going to protect the Third World from the corporations of the world. And his running had taken him downhill, down Seattle's steep streets five blocks to Pike Place Market where, now, Charles, alone, studied the rows of fish on ice, fish on newsprint. He watched men in knee-high yellow boots heaving silver bodies from hand to hand. A man and woman working side by side, amiably removing the alien heads of jumbo shrimp.

Five minutes. This was all the time necessary to drop from the zenith of victory into the slough of despond. Five minutes, and now here he was, alone and staring in despair at bloody fish wrapped in butcher paper and blue plastic.

So focused was he on his own depression he didn't much notice the two cops or their armored vehicle. The officers were blocking the narrow aisle and Charles not really even paying attention. A bulky square-shouldered man with an unfortunate face. The man asked him who he was. The woman began to pat him down. Charles reached into his pocket for his passport and credentials, and that was the precise moment when the officers lifted him by the arms and threw him into the table of tomatoes.

He landed on his back. Tomatoes exploding all around him. Staining his jacket with juice and seeds. The tomato man crying in anguish and Charles in a state of complete shock thinking this was the very last. The very last humiliation this country would make him suffer.

They rolled him onto his face. He felt his arms pulled behind his back, and then a plastic zip cuff was looped around his wrists and cinched tight as any rope. Where his briefcase went, he didn't dare ask. When his meeting would take place he now knew would be never.

26

Strange lights appearing out of the poison cloud. Victor counted; he breathed; he forgot to count, he started over again. His body didn't belong to him. It belonged to the gas and the gas wasn't a gas. It was a drug. Divested of its context, seen without its surroundings, the massive tear gas cloud appeared almost innocent. Something neutral and harmless which didn't care one way or the other about your purpose like a low cloud humming along the ground on a misty day, wetting the grass, your socks, your pants with damp drops of dew.

But then it touched your face and your skin began to sizzle.

Do they add something to the gas, Victor wanted to know, to make you paranoid, a chemical to induce panic when inhaled, wherever it is manufactured, the underground labs of Virginia military, maybe that is where it was conceived, but no, this was concocted where? A little lab with glass and bright light, titer and teacher and trickle, a little lab and the green lawns and what did they do on college campuses in the heady 1960s? They protested and burned and organized and wept while inside the brown brick buildings on a glorious sunny day a nice professor with a beard and a salary sufficient to pay for a duplex for his loving wife and pretty kids perfected CS gas, originally discovered in the 1920s, sure, but perfected to drop on the North Vietnamese. But is that what he thought about? No, it was an academic exercise divested of meaning or consequence because what he makes is what he makes and he focuses on the task and not where it will land in the world. He pays little or no thought to what his work will do once loosed into the great brown-yellow elsewhere. Why care about something he can't control? Why care about something he maybe suspects will only bring troubling thoughts, bad sleep, an irreconcilable dilemma. My family for a North Vietnamese family? Does this make any sense? Is this a real dilemma? Of course I answer no. Of course I know somewhere in the back of my brain that what I use my intelligence and talent and training to perfect then travels a long path through the world that ends in choking searing pain for human beings halfway across the planet, daughters and mothers and sons and dads. I perfected this. But it is my work to perfect it, not to produce it.

How can we blame him, Victor wanted to know—the nice professor with a beard? He wasn't the one who dropped it on the North Vietnamese. How can we really blame the pilot that piloted the plane, or the navigator, or the bombardier. They didn't make the war. Blame the politicians who sent us in? Why bother? They are the most alienated of all, their work to make decisions for millions of people who are known to them only as polling statistics, a crowd of faces come election time, a map of Vietnam come killing time, a cluster of red dots which represents something which must be destroyed. They have the most difficult job of all—to somehow connect that splash of red to the human life it somehow denotes. An awfully tall order to imbue the mindless statistic with the humanity it represents, the village, the rice, the longing for life, the familiar worried glance to the sky to see if rain is coming and it is not rain or cloud that you

184

find there but American B-52s in formation. The terror and the strangeness of this alien bug blotting your sky and causing your children to cry in fear, your chickens to run in fear, but where will they go, back and forth in their pen, and the pigs to scream in fear, and the humans to run in fear, but where will they go, nowhere to go, of course, to escape the destruction that is coming, unless they mean to escape the confines of being Vietnamese. The bombs falling are their ticket to refugee status, the sucking engine whine the signal of their exile from the world where grass is grass and a bird in a tree something to love without thought because it means home.

No more birds, no more grass, alien life in exile, how could we ever ask anyone to fully inhabit the human life of someone so distant? We cannot ask this man to see where his product will go, how far it will travel, all the way to the shores of Vietnam, to the forests and paddies and roads. Hanoi—what the hell is that supposed to mean? We cannot ask him to know or to control the passage of time, how that war will end, and his gas still moving through the world, not yet done with its journey. We cannot ask this man to see the destination of his work, the consequence of what he uses his love and time and life to make. Cannot ask him to see the tear gas falling in the streets of Seattle, billowing around the bodies of peaceful protesters, cannot ask him there in 1964, perfecting CS gas in his lab, to hear the coughing it produces in Victor's body in 1999, to hear the wheezing or the awful scratching, to feel Victor's eyes burning in his head, cannot ask him as he fiddles, measuring and testing, ask him to hear above his humming the future screams or the stomping feet, cannot ask him to imagine the human courage required to sit in this cloud of poison gas and not move, to allow it to swirl and gather at your feet, to slide inside your clothes, to kiss your skin with its cracked fever lips, to lick at your face with its burning tongue. No, we cannot ask him to do that. He is alienated from his work. He is perfecting tear gas. He rides his bike to work. He gets terrible headaches. His youngest daughter does not speak. Rent is due.

The granulated mist drifting down like a poisoned spring rain.

Five feet in front of Victor the cops were going after Edie. Edie who had sat down in place of the Doctor. The Doctor whom they'd dragged away by the hair. She was chanting, her arms linked at the elbow to the people on either side of her. Victor watching a fat cop hit her in the face with the pepper spray. The way her chest was heaving as she struggled to breathe made him feel sick and angry, and angry wasn't really the word, and afraid all over again. He looked at John Henry, but John Henry was lost in the chant.

WE ARE WINNING
WE ARE WINNING
WE ARE WINNING

The cops stepped back to consult in a group. They gestured and talked and glanced at Edie writhing in pain. They decided something and one man went to his truck and returned with a medical kit.

Edie wasn't screaming. Her body rocked back and forth in silence where she sat.

The cops rummaged inside the medical kit and then approached again. This time they had Q-tips and gauze. They dipped the Q-tips in pepper spray. They rubbed delicately around her streaming eyes. One cop tried to pry open her eyelids, but her head was whipping violently from side to side and he couldn't get a hold. He stepped over the arms and stood behind her. He put her gray head between his legs and squeezed with his knees. With one hand on her forehead, and the other lifting her chin, he held her still.

They wore white latex gloves to protect their hands from the pepper spray and Victor watched as the man who had brought the medical kit from his truck worked the Q-tips under Edie's eyelid. Her body trembled between the man's knees. The man inserted the Q-tip into the other eye and ran it around as if trying to clear some obstruction and Victor wasn't angry anymore. There was no room left for anger.

The cops stood back again to see what would happen. They looked like some weird version of bedside nurses. Stepped back as if maybe a little curious to see what would happen when you applied pepper spray with a Q-tip under the eyelids of a seated woman whose head was held tight between a man's armored knees.

One cop snapped his white glove and said something which made another cop chuckle and nod.

What happened was Edie began vomiting. Still she wouldn't scream. Just handfuls of white vomit spilling from her mouth.

The cops pulled at her arms, but still she wouldn't let go. They seemed a little confused. They tipped the bottle over, soaked the gauze with the pepper spray, then wiped the gauze around her foam-covered mouth.

They ran the Q-tips up her nose.

Their latex gloves ministering to her body with heat and pain. They rubbed and poked and prodded. Then they stepped back, curious to see what would happen.

Victor fighting the tears and begging her to let go.

Please, Edie.

One cop absently twisted the gauze above her head, squeezing the excess pepper spray into her open mouth.

Victor didn't understand it. What force inside her allowed her to endure that kind of pain? What inner reserve of strength? What was possibly going on inside this woman that gave her the strength to sit silently and not scream?

She was throwing up from the pain. What inner force?

Love?

Faith?

Conviction?

Vomiting and convulsing and gasping for breath and still not releasing and still not screaming and Victor watching her and choking back the sobs that wanted to leap from his throat. He wouldn't cry. He would witness. He would be brave.

Please, Edie. Jesus, please, just let go.

Was it love, and then what kind of love was that—love for the action, love for lockdown, some sort of love for the earth and her six billion human fellows? Was her belief in justice enough? Compassion has its limits. It only went so deep, right? Victor thought this pain went all the way down. Whatever it was, Victor found he wasn't angry anymore. He watched as she rocked back and forth and the cops in their latex gloves stood by curious and talking, absentmindedly pulling on her arms, and he wasn't scared and he wasn't angry even as his own chest hitched and heaved.

Finally, it was enough. Edie released her arms and her seated body pitched sideways to the ground. The cops were pulling her wrists behind her back and cuffing her even as she continued to throw up on her peasant blouse and Victor no longer felt the need to fight the tears. He let them come.

He tried a little whisper and his face went hot, a little breath of a chant to beat back the morning air.

The people

188

John Henry's eyes crumpling at the edges where the skin gathered in folds. John Henry cracking a smile behind his paint-splattered bandanna. He looked over and dropped Victor a wink.

The second time Victor's voice was just above a whisper. A sort of croaking carried away by the breeze.

The people united

John Henry's broken mud-clod voice, chanting His red beard and crooked teeth. His chunky black glasses. Can another man's belief sustain you in your fear? Is a friend—nothing more than a friend, a real and true friend—enough?

The third time his voice cracked.

The people united will never—

He felt it in his chest, a growling vibration rising through his ribs, his larynx, his full voice, the rumbling of his vocal cords, the sound climbing through his throat.

The wind died and the smoke descended and Edie's body was mercifully swallowed back into the gray. A kid went skateboarding through the smoke in a torn shirt and suspenders. The cans followed him with a whisper down the street. Victor's goggles fogging with tears, and no, afraid was not the word for what he now felt, his voice exploding into the air as if by suicide bomb. John Henry's fingers reaching for his in the awkward pipe. John Henry barking, his own voice raised in strength to match Victor's, and Victor roaring now, his voice like thunder growing in his belly and spilling from his mouth, their voices sharing the same words, raised into the air proclaiming their belief, their togetherness.

THE PEOPLE UNITED
WILL NEVER BE
DIVIDED

THE PEOPLE UNITED
WILL NEVER BE
DIVIDED

THE PEOPLE UNITED
WILL NEVER BE
DIVIDED

27

For five hours now the tear gas had been falling. The streets swarmed with smoke and John Henry coughed and chanted and grimaced behind his bandanna, watching the cops as they stalked and fired.

For five hours now they had been going at it. They hit people in the face. They smashed hands and wrists, left purple-yellow bruises on shoulders and ribs and backs like odd constellations of pain to be examined by worried friends in the days to come. This was how badly the cops wanted to clear the streets and take their city back.

They tore away bandannas and gas masks, sprayed pepper spray into people's naked mouths. Unarmed peaceful protesters chanting in the street—the police dragged them away by their hair. Five hours of physical misery in all its varied forms, a torturing so intense the hours seemed like days. They were hungry and soaking and cold down to their bones. The gas was sticking to their clothes and skin. Everything burned.

For five hours now they had been assaulted by tear gas, been hit by pepper spray and clubs, and still they remained.

And still they would not leave.

They would not stop until they had accomplished what their

hearts had demanded they do and John Henry knew they were going to win no matter what it took.

They had stayed and controlled the intersection. Despite the police's best efforts, no more than a handful of delegates had made it to the convention center. The opening ceremonies had been canceled. The news passed from mouth to mouth, but he didn't need the human chain to know. No, John Henry could tell from the tilt of the cops' heads as they paraded back and forth, the way they huddled in small groups hurriedly talking, the way they strode through the crowd, the anger with which they struck. Every gesture and motion signaled their desperation and frustration. They had never encountered it before, either in the streets or in their dreams of the street: people that would not submit. People unafraid of their violence. Brave people who would not leave.

John Henry was speechless with glad-hearted joy. They had stayed. They had stayed and they were winning. He felt his heart swell with pride as he said, "Victor, how you doing, son?"

No reply from Victor. Pure human pride in the flock and nobody more deserving than Victor. Nobody for whom John Henry felt more pride and admiration than Victor. Look at him there. His hair which had been in two tight braids was now frayed and loose. His back rigid. It was as though he was absorbing the horrors of the day through the medium of his seated body. Flaked white spit had gathered at the edges of Victor's mouth. And his eyes, man. John Henry saw something building in the kid's eyes and he could not have been prouder of this young man right here than if he were the boy's own father. He hadn't been trained a lick, had entered through no gate save his courage. Knew not the power of sitting. Knew not how the rage which became a sorrow can become a kind of joy.

John Henry said, "How you doing, son?"

Victor didn't respond.

"Victor?"

And John Henry couldn't have been prouder of him than if he was his own son, but had the boy's fear turned to anger? Was he strong enough to allow the anger to become a sorrow which had the power to transform? Could he open himself to it—the suffering which redeemed?

King materialized out of the fog. To John Henry, she was radiant. The events of the day seemed to have spun her quick through her many selves until they had become fused and polished and whole. Her hair was atop her head and knotted. She shook it loose as she peeled off her gas mask. Her brown dreadlocks, her green eyes bright. Blood streaked her simple shirt, splattered against the white. She was alive and frantic and tired and talking, her hands everywhere on him, checking was he good, was he hurt, and the tiredness was in her eyes and the life was in her face and the frantic was in her voice and John Henry thought he had never seen a woman more beautiful than at this very moment. She knelt before him and touched his face.

"King," he said, "where have you been?"

She touched his shoulders. His chest. His sides. Back to his face. Squeezed both his shoulders, ran her hand along his face, adjusted his glasses on his nose.

"John Henry, please. We need to go."

John Henry saying, "We're not going anywhere. We're winning."

King speaking so quiet John Henry could barely hear her. "Do you really believe that? That we're winning?"

"King," he said, "we are talking here of the human reservoir that has struggled for five hundred years to achieve the impossible. The rights of all people to live in simple dignity, neither oppressed nor anesthetized. What are our personal concerns compared to this? We're not going anywhere.'

"Did you see what happened to Edie?" she said.

He nodded.

"They're targeting medics," she said.

He nodded again and she gathered her hands between her knees as if she didn't know quite where to put them.

"John Henry, I can't get arrested."

She sounded panicky, voice trembling, completely unlike herself. King was one of the most levelheaded women he had ever met—she played fast and loose with plans, sure, subverted their process sometimes, but she was brilliant and brave. She had a quick temper, sure, and he had been burned more than once in the five years he had known her, but in the chaos of a street battle she was stone-cold ice. This was a woman he would trust with his life.

"Tell me why."

She just shook her head. "I can't."

"King, are we talking about Vail? Again?"

She said nothing and John Henry imagined he could see into her lovely bile-filled interiors, her internal spaces, the places where she went alone to dream. John Henry saw it as an abandoned church—a cathedral, really, graffitied and high broken windows with pigeons sliding in and out, pigeons cooing in the archways, pigeons moving through shafts of light and shadow in the vestibule, a loose-timbered space, high-vaulted and desolate, and King lying on the floor passed out. King lying on the floor in John Henry's ruined church, head resting on his piled books, staring into the high dusty air, looking into the unreachable depths eighty feet up. There she was lonely and discontented and gazing. Content, perhaps, in the upper distances with the words rolling through her mind. Lying there, passed out drunk and waiting for what exactly to come flapping through her life?

"No, John Henry," she said, so quietly he could barely hear her, "we are not talking about Vail."

"What then? Tell me."

"John Henry." So quietly was he sure she was even speaking? "I shouldn't be here, John Henry." She was almost crying. Her green eyes filling with fear. "I can't get arrested, John Henry. I'm sorry. I'm so sorry. But I can't get arrested."

She was shaking. The calmest woman he knew, yes, but one who had a temper like a tornado. And now she was near panic. He had never seen her like this. What had changed? What had happened? He wanted to ask and then stopped. Stopped and stopped and stopped.

If she couldn't get arrested, she really meant it. Fuck, he knew that much. He didn't argue much with King when she got going, and if she couldn't get arrested, John Henry didn't want to think about what that might mean.

What else she might have done.

"John Henry, please trust me."

He nodded, thinking he really did *not* want to know.

"I'm staying," he said.

28

The way King was kneeling and looking at John Henry, Victor felt a certain pause in his life. A moment which opened and seemed large enough between heartbeats to contain every moment in his life up until that moment and Victor had what could only be called an insight. One of those sudden flashes of knowledge about a person that arrives wholly formed and is so surprising, whimming up from what unconscious antennae, that you know without asking that it must be true.

King was scared.

Maybe not on the surface, surrounded as she was by her brothers and sisters fifty thousand strong, her cadre of companions committed to the struggle. But no, he heard it in her voice. She knelt in front of John Henry and spoke and despite her demeanor what was it in her voice? What was it that made him think at the eye of the slowly turning hurricane that was her self, she was near panic? On the deepest level, this woman was terrified.

"You think we're going to lose," Victor said.

King turned to him. She made her mouth into a smile and rested a hand on his shoulder.

"I don't think we're going to lose, Victor."

"Yes, you do. And you're afraid."

"Listen," she said gently, and what was it in her voice that made him feel like he was the biggest fool the world had ever known. "Listen, Victor, nobody expects you to do this untrained. Everybody here will understand if you want out. You just need to tell us because we would have to replace you. Are you scared? Do you need out?"

"No, no, no. I'm good. I want to be here with you guys. I mean I get it now. I think I know why we're here."

"Fine," she said, and started to stand up. "Good."

"But listen," he said. King knelt back down in front of them. Looked at him with eyes so green he understood how you could drown in someone and never want to come back. And why did he say it? Because he wanted to prove to her he wasn't a fool? Because he wanted her to stay? Because he wanted her to kneel here forever and touch his face the way she had knelt and touched John Henry?

"It's all right," he said. "It's not wrong to be afraid."

She smiled. "Victor. I'm not afraid. I'm committed. This is what committed looks like."

"No, you're afraid," Victor said. "I get it. I understand. I was afraid, too. But now I'm not. Watching Edie I knew. We have to stay. We have to win. And if they beat us, I understand that now, too. And I accept that. We're going to win."

She smiled again, but there was something cold in her eyes that he didn't like at all. An ice in her voice as she said, "I know, Victor."

"You don't have to be ashamed to be afraid, King. You just have to own it."

She paused and he thought for a second she was going to slap him.

"Don't tell me what I have to own."

"King, we can't leave. It doesn't matter if we're afraid. We have

198

to stay. You have to feel the fear. You have to own it. Make it yours."

She exploded. Went from calm to furious as quick as turning a coin on your finger. There she was, right in his face, screaming at him.

"Don't you tell me what I have to fucking own!"

Victor cringing from the force of her anger.

She was spitting in his face while John Henry said, "King. Quit yelling at the boy."

"Are you fucking hearing me, Victor?"

And Victor saying, "Okay, okay, okay. I hear you." Because where was there to go? Nowhere. He was in lockdown.

"I am committed! Am I getting through, you straight-ass motherfucker? Committed!"

"King, goddamn it, quit screaming at that boy!"

"Don't you *dare* tell me what I have to *own*. I own what I own! And what I have done—"

Suddenly she put a wrist to her mouth. Took a deep slashing breath.

Victor saying, "No, no, no." Still leaning as far back as the chained-in pipes would allow.

She inhaled deeply again, her voice on the far edge of tears or no tears. "No, Victor." And now she did touch him. Held his face between her hands and looked at him. Her eyes were wide, eyelashes sequined with tears.

"You don't have to back away from me," she said.

"Where would I go?"

She laughed and ran a sleeve across her nose. Snuffled once loud and long.

"That's right," she said, trying to smile. "Where would you go? You're stuck with me. Big bad King."

She snuffled again and hawked from deep in her throat. She leaned over their knees and discreetly spat a yellow mess on the concrete at their feet and in that motion all was gone. It was as if she had sucked and spat the regret right from her chest. When she turned back she was all business.

"I'm sorry, Victor. I shouldn't have lost my temper. I shouldn't have put you in lockdown is what it comes down to. That was my mistake. I pushed you."

And John Henry saying, "King."

And Victor saying, "No. Nobody pushed me."

"And I'm sorry for that. But now I'm taking you out. Nonviolence is communication. Nonviolence is admitting your mistakes."

And Victor saying, "No, no, no." While King turned and said into her radio, "I need one for lockdown in front of the Sheraton."

And Victor saying, "No. I want to be here. This is where I belong. With you and John Henry."

Feeling something he did not want to feel, feeling the thing he went to bed feeling, the thing he woke up feeling, the thing he felt at his tent beneath the highway when he moved gravel from one spot to another with that stupid broom.

29

Bishop atop the steps of the Sheraton, beside the flagpole, looked at the mess of people gathering around the hotel and he looked up at the city towers and the apartment blocks and thought of the way people do people in what they call daily life. All the calls and all the years. Domestics and murders. Gunpoint theft from the store where you buy your cigarettes and milk. Apartments where he found babies taking care of babies and roaches in the beds looking at him like they owned the place. Maybe they did own it because there sure as hell wasn't any adult sort of figure around who might be a bill payer of light and food.

Here came the PeaceKeeper growling in low gear. He had called it back from Pike Place Market where the idiot Mayor had sent it. God knows why. The PeaceKeeper climbing the steps of the Sheraton. Bumping over the low steps. Down below any semblance of order was gone. His line had broken and he saw clumps of black in the crowd like lumps of cancer in a radiated lung, the backs of his troops' hooded forms chopping through the crowd. Batons swinging freely. He watched as one cop swore and delivered a sideways kick that barely missed a black kid's skull, the cop's boot landing instead squarely between the boy's birdlike shoulder blades.

Sometimes the job wore on you. Riding the ride and thinking about your history with people and persons. Thinking of your various failures to be the man you were supposed to be. Thinking of the way people do and the numbness that wants to shrink-wrap your heart and stick it in the freezer and where does it come from and what are you supposed to do once it is there? How to be free of it?

If he was being honest what he wanted most was to follow his son into the wild blue fuck-all.

Because life seemed what?

Simple there.

He remembered a party when they were first married, something one of her painter friends had thrown, and when they walked in, he in jeans and a brown corduroy coat, she in a short black dress with thin straps like dark string across her brown skin, and not just one but every head had turned. He could almost feel the conversation come to a stop. But she liked the attention and he did, too. He liked looking across the room at her talking to a man, some man, any man, or men, these artists, students, and such, and him a young cop on the rise, and what did he have to worry about, she loved him, and he liked to watch the men as they watched her, and she aglow with the story, she there, too. Then a gulp from her drink and a glance across the room at him as if to say, You know this story, this one that I'm telling and this other one, too, this one that I'm acting, here in front of you, the party, you know this story, it's so old, and who's that anyway you're talking to, a redhead? well then, back to my story, but later, tonight, in bed, it will be you and me and not these fools, no, and not that one either.

It was not always her, people gathered around him, too. The confidence of his quiet manner which drew them in. The way he listened and didn't jabber on. He had the air of someone you could talk to. Air your doubts in a private setting. Ask him what he really thought. This was a man whose opinion was not influenced by the mob, a man familiar, it seemed, with the darker corners of the human soul, a man capable of both fairness and forgiveness.

But fuck, right now, he wanted to be somewhere nobody knew his name; somewhere nobody looked to him for answers, somewhere nobody expected him to know what to do. He wanted to be in a place that smelled of diesel exhaust, sweetly rotting fruit, meat cooking on a grill.

He wanted to walk streets whose names he didn't know and couldn't pronounce. Wanted to be somewhere nobody knew his preferred brand of breakfast cereal and boxer short. Not an American male, aged fifty-nine, widower to a wife of long patient looks, father to a disappeared son, police chief of a medium-sized American city tasked with corralling fifty thousand citizens in the street. The Chief. No, he didn't want it. Just an American. That's what he wanted. To be in a place where he was just an American— even if he was hated, or an invading force, or an expatriate, or a coward, he didn't care.

You get a call on domestic violence and you arrive to find the man beat his girl until she couldn't see. You ride along with the ambo to the trauma unit and the woman who can barely see, you ask does she want to press charges and she says, "You don't know. None of you know the way that man loves me."

Bishop didn't want to know. Sometimes the world was too much. Too much blood and too much violence and too much gone-out-of-your-head-crazy to include in the human experience. You had to let it slip from your consideration of human life on the planet Earth. Didn't count. Except it did. No way to reckon it

203

except the world was dark. The world wasn't hard. It was awful. The Cold War was over and the Darkness had begun. The one where some people were scared to ever fall, the so-called middle class; and the others, fallen already, were squeezed beyond measure. And policing? Well the days of community policing were over. The world was a bottleful of sparkling darkness and cops the ones charged with keeping the cork in while the rich shook and shook.

But what were you going to do? Resign? Quit? Bishop was the Chief of Police, not the President. No, you made your notes and you shook your head and you did your best while the coldness slipped in, while the vise jaws squeezed shut. Tutted your tongue and when your shift was done you had a few beers and a shot and one of the other cops said something low, something funny and sad and twisted that let you laugh away the craziness of what you had to do and see. He laughed. They all laughed. Because the closing of the eyes was not something he wanted and the remaining human was.

Bishop descending the steps to meet the PeaceKeeper where it now sat rumbling halfway up the Sheraton plaza. Bishop's radio erupting in chatter as he climbed onto the running board.

Bishop Bishop Bishop.

Tom-four-two.

Bishop Bishop Bishop.

Horses. The horses—

Down below black-clad demonstrators dragged a dumpster into the street and, after some arguing and effort, pushed it up and over onto its side. They soaked it with gasoline and lit it.

Someone tossed a Coke bottle filled with gasoline and the dumpster erupted.

They were burning paper and sticks and garbage. The signs

that earlier in the day had carried another people's hopes for a better world. They broke the signs over their bent knees. They threw the pieces into the fire, whooping with a crazed delirium.

Blue flames licked at the wood. Charred and damp soot rose into the air and the way the flames seemed to eat the paper and the way the kids danced around the flames, jeering and celebrating, he just wanted to climb that thick rope of smoke up and on out of here.

A boy standing on top of the dumpster with his fist held righteous in the air.

A group of five flannel-clad demonstrators kicking trash cans into the street. The contents of a briefcase went flying into the flames.

Bishop's tanned face and the high color on his cheeks. His blue eyes gone small in his head. This was the face of a man trying to summit a peak about to grab his chest and pitch forward into the ice, never to move again, that's how much he disbelieved what was before his eyes.

An object whizzing for his head. Bishop ducked and a bottle bounced and rolled down the hood of the PeaceKeeper, unbroken. Disbelief like high-altitude death rattling in his chest because how and when had he ever believed this city was *his*?

He watched the kid silently raise a fist and felt a blinding sense of bafflement and defeat. Who knew what circulated in his mind, this boy, who perhaps imagined himself in a stadium in Mexico City, the winner of a gold medal in the 1968 Olympics, standing not on a dumpster but on the highest podium, his best friend beside him wearing the ribbon and the bronze, tens of thousands of spectators watching them—and he was not white but black, Tommie Smith with John Carlos, barefoot on the podium, the gold medal around his neck as "The Star-Spangled Banner" played to the assembled crowd; his hand a fist of solidarity and strength raised to the indifferent world, a black glove raised straight from the shoulder.

"Look at that fucking kid," the cop next to him on the running board of the 'Keeper said. The officer that earlier in the day he had busted from his horse. Officer Park. He was here on the PeaceKeeper beside Bishop, and how the hell did he end up here, who knew, that was exactly the kind of day it was. The peaceful protesters long gone and the citizens run amok, rioting and rampaging and he had once nearly broken his son's arm, done everything but force march him to the door and kick him out in the world. Burned his mother's books in front of the boy. Jesus god almighty, how could he have ever explained it wasn't the books which inspired the rage, it was loss. Nothing but loss and confusion and fear.

And it wasn't that Bishop had only scheduled nine hundred officers. No, his mistake, today, he thought was very simple. He had been too kind. He had allowed himself to trust these people. Kids spitting in the streets. These weren't peaceful protesters. These weren't decent people. These were punks and trash. He had mistakenly respected the truth of their position, treated them with a mercy they did not deserve. He had failed to see the true nature of the situation. All-out war in the streets of the city he was sworn to protect. War. And he was losing.

"Hey," he said blandly to Park, "take that kid out."

Park turned and raised his shotgun. Turned to his left and raised the gun and found the kid atop the dumpster in one fluid motion. Park shot in a direct line. The kid was across the intersection, a good sixty feet out, and yet the rubber bullet flew straight and true and took the kid in the stomach and dropped him in the street like he'd taken a punch to the gut. He went down like a

206

bag of fertilizer, tumbling into the street, loose-limbed with the dumbest fucking look of surprise.

The daily meanness. The absolute petty nature of the day-to-day. It was like everyone's eyes had gone hard. Not his fellow cops. The people. Women and men, mothers and fathers and brothers and sisters. They weren't criminals. They were people with no light left anywhere on their person.

He didn't know what was worse, really, taking down a couple of rioting citizens or having to roll out to the suburbs and smile into plastic faces whose eyes had gone gray as ash. People out there talked, oh yes, they hung bright colors on their words of this and that, pretty bold ribbons of kindness and concern, but he looked in their eyes, poor folks and rich alike, especially rich, and it wasn't nothing coming out but the dead hot light of I don't give a crap, just keep it out of my yard.

The necessary numbness, the cold core of watchfulness, and the problem of remaining a person yourself, a person who cares. A person who feels. A person who does not hate.

And then, as it sometimes happens, this man of good faith was given a gift. There was his mistake standing in the crowd. Standing there in black with a white T-shirt rolled to the shoulders and her hair piled atop her head. A black gas mask covered her face, but he knew who it was. The girl from this morning. He saw her singular presence, the singular mistake that started it all. Dear God, thank you. And he thought, I will fix this. Praise the Lord in his infinite goodness, and forgive me if I was wrong. But I will fix this. I see my mistake and there she is and I will wipe this mistake from the books.

I will get this day back on track.

A dignity they did not deserve—that was my mistake.

Look, there she is, he thought, and the anger seemed not the point at all anymore. "Thank you," he said because the sight of her—his mistake standing there in the crowd—had filled his heart with a simple gladness. With a deep-welled gratitude.

If he couldn't have his son, at least he could have his city back.

30

Victor was out. John Henry was out. They were both of them out of lockdown and Victor was still standing there rubbing his shoulders and wrists, feeling a surprising mixture of relief and pride, while John Henry stood arguing with King about something Victor didn't understand. He didn't mind. People weren't pissed at him. In fact, just the opposite. They were gathered around him massaging his shoulders and legs. Men and women congratulating him. Looking at him in a way nobody had ever looked at him before. It was surprising how good it felt to be out. How good it felt to suddenly realize he wasn't out; he was in. He had passed some test he hadn't even known he was taking.

Standing there just feeling good when his father came stepping through the crowd like a nightmare come to life. A black poncho billowing around him like a shroud.

In his right hand, his father held a small can of pepper spray the size of a tube of toothpaste. His thumb resting on the trigger. He was looking at King and headed straight for her. He had the strangest look on his face, a look of such anger Victor wanted to run, wanted to heed instinct and flat out disappear, but that's not what he did.

What he did was he lifted his feet to move—to step in front of his father—but his legs, weak from the hours of sitting in lock-down, buckled beneath him. He took one step and collapsed like a puppet suddenly without strings. A body falling toward the storm cloud that was his father.

"Hey," Victor shouted as he fell. "Hey now! She's a medic."

The Chief didn't even hesitate. Didn't even look. Just let loose with the spray, and Victor falling, calling out, caught the spray in the face as he tumbled toward the ground. John Henry realizing what was happening in the same moment, in the air then, too. Trying to catch him, and his father, did his father just pepper-spray him? What did Victor expect? It was an automatic reaction of muscle memory and speed. But did he recognize me? I don't know. I don't know. He is a cop right now, not your father. But did he know it was me?

Victor's eyes exploded. His whole face attacked by a wall of heat. He was on his hands and knees, blinded, hands reaching out for something, anything, and there seemed to be a pile of bodies. Everything was arms and clothes and legs. His eyes like hot coals in the cave of his sockets. He wanted to tear them out. He couldn't see. His hands in front of him, the fucking pain, you are not prepared for it, the fucking suddenness of the heat, the intensity. Everything was pain and fallen bodies. He felt the armored boots of a cop. Pulling himself to his feet, his hands claws grabbing at the plastic of his father's poncho. Twisting away the pain. Victor tried to call out, tried to let his father know that it was his son. But his throat was a wall of flame, no sound but the animal body crying out its pain.

Everything seemed to be moving slowly. He could hear with an almost supernatural clarity. His father grunted, surprised by this body groping at his feet. Victor could hear him breathing, a sound so familiar it just cracked him at the core, his father snoring in the other room, his father's grunts lifting a bag of mulch for the garden, and oh god, who knew there was so much pain possible in the world? Victor heard his own hands twisting in the poncho, heard his hands grabbing at the plastic. He heard the scrape of his father's boots on the pavement. He heard the creaking of his gear. And he wanted to say, Dad, Dad, it's me, but his throat was closing down. He wanted to say, Dad, I have so much to tell you.

Dad, I'm here. Dad, stop.

Dad, I'm home.

The unbearable briefness of moments. The moment, in some ways, he had returned for, and here he was, mute. His throat was closing. He let go of his father's poncho to claw helplessly at his own neck. Then, from the air above his head, he heard the thin high whisper of a baton. The baton of an officer who was protecting the Chief. The Chief being pulled away.

Dad, did you know it was me?

The baton collided with Victor's body at the base of his neck. His head rocked back. Flung into the air, he heard the silence of the pavement waiting for his heavy idiot's head.

And who was there to greet him in the darkness?

His mother, her feather earrings swinging to and fro and her arms outstretched?

No.

His father, off-duty wearing sweats and reading the paper at the kitchen table?

No. Not him either.

The American girl in Bolivia begging change with her bowl and her dog, the girl he had wanted to kick in the head?

Yes. There she was. The girl to whom Victor had given his last twenty dollars, the girl he had sat down next to on the oil-stained curb and together watched the passing traffic. The girl he had talked with until the lights of the buses were the only lights left sweeping through the darkened station, the girl whose body and dog he had slept between later that night in a dingy hostel with a brothel making the noises a brothel makes in the rooms above them.

His body connected solid with the ground. His head hit the pavement and grew dark as though punctured and leaking light, and Victor curled warm with her body at his back, and him drifting like a leaf on the breeze of the dog's easy sleeping breath, his arm slung around its neck. A small moment of peace in what had been a long and stupid road. A family of sorts.

Of course, when he woke in the morning, everything was gone. Girl. Dog. His backpack and all its contents. His heart and all that might have once cared because, yes, he had finally learned it for himself. Care too much and the world will kill you cold.

31

King stood and watched as John Henry dragged Victor's limp body through the intersection, his arms locked firmly around the boy's chest. She had a sort of daydreamy feeling, this detached feeling you get when you see a car crash happening as you walk down the street. A slowing down of time as if she were somehow smaller than herself, standing just an inch to the left or right of her own body.

"John Henry," she said.

Was it a story she could tell? How they had traveled for three days from Guadalajara, riding in the back of bouncing pickups with other migrants heading to the border, changing trucks in small towns, the small clustered houses where they took on food and water and gasoline, and she wanted to talk but the men were silent, and the closer they got the more difficult the journey, more difficult than she had ever imagined because the silence and the guilt and the fear, and because always, the growing knowledge of her own willful ignorance—her anger and arrogance. What had made her think this would be easy?

John Henry cradling Victor's body in the circle of his arms.

John Henry saying, "I know it hurts."

John Henry saying, "King, I could use your help over here."

Could she tell him how near the end of the third day, late in the afternoon, Ignacio banged on the cab of the pickup, and they stopped.

"We get down here," he said.

She looked around in surprise. Barren desert. The sun dipping toward a rag of mountains between sky and earth and nothing but scrub grass and powdered bone dirt in between.

"Here?" she said.

"Here."

"But this is nowhere."

Could she tell him how they arrived at the river at nightfall? Ignacio and his son and her, three dark figures with their hands held flat above their eyes as if to shade the sun, three dark silhouettes like paper dolls cut from sky, staring across a river at the United States.

Could she tell him about the river? How it was a cold black rush carrying branches and the odd piece of trash: a Styrofoam cup, a torn bag attached to a branching stick, flotsam spinning circles on the eddying current. An ominous sort of silence to the thing.

Could she tell him how she stripped down to her bra and underwear on the bank as the boy stole shy glances? How she hadn't showered or bathed in three weeks and her skin felt gritty with worn-in dirt, how her clothes and pack went into the trash bag, how she was thinking of the weight of the gun, thinking of the panic in Guadalajara in which she had bought it, and now that she was here, standing at the river, so close to home, she no longer wanted it—could she tell him she had never wanted it?

John Henry dragging Victor, King following. He deposited him on the curb on the far side of the Sheraton, leaned him against a newspaper box. John Henry lifted his arms over his head and stripped his sweater and pressed it to the back of Victor's bleeding head and laid him down. The Chief, it seemed, had lost his taste for violence. King didn't see him anywhere. He had sprayed the kid and then disappeared into the crowd, heading for the glassed lobby of the Sheraton looking like he was going to be sick. But King knew he would be back.

"John Henry, we got to go."

"Baby, I'm a little busy here."

She had told him about Vail, hoping arson was kind of sexy. A badge of honor and a proof of your commitment. Except not exactly. And maybe not among everyone. It wasn't exactly a non-violent technique, was it? Burning down a ski resort.

What about sighting a gun on a man's chest and squeezing the trigger with a cold slow breath? What about watching a man flop in the sand and bleed out a mile from the border? Would John Henry think that nonviolent?

Victor curled on the concrete in a fetal position, legs pulled in a fishhook, his chest rising and falling rhythmically. Gasping great lungfuls of air and pawing at his eyes.

King told him to quit it. She didn't have time for this.

Victor stopped touching his eyes and looked at her mulishly through the swollen slits. He coughed once, twice, whole chest heaving, and then went back to rubbing at his face with the heels of his hands.

She wanted to tell him. Wanted to tell John Henry how she reached into the zippered pocket of her pack there on the dark bank of the river and pulled out the gun and shells.

Wanted to tell him how Ignacio backed away, asked what she was doing, and she replied, "I don't want this anymore. I want to give it to you." Wanted very much to tell him how the man waved his hand, dismissing the idea, and said, "This is not a good

215

thing to have or give," and how much she agreed though she did not say.

Explosions rocked the intersection. Tear gas looping in the street. People running in twos and threes, bandannas pressed tight to their mouths as they ran.

John Henry saying, "Don't touch your eyes."

John Henry saying, "I know it hurts."

John Henry saying, "You're going to be all right."

That detached feeling in her body as if she were floating just above herself, just watching.

More than anything she wanted to confess, wanted to tell John Henry every detail she had never told a single soul. How she offered Ignacio the gun by the barrel. But how it was the boy who stepped forward instead and took it from her hand.

"Be careful," she said. "It's loaded."

The way the boy held it flat in his palm, testing the weight of it, then gripped it and lifted it and sighted across the river.

"Blam," he said.

The harsh warning tone in his father's voice when he said, "Give that back to her."

Wanted to tell John Henry the way the boy looked at his father curiously. How the gun remained extended at the end of his arm as he said again, "Blam."

Wanted to tell him, too, about that daydreamy feeling like she was watching a movie about what she was actually doing in the here and now. It was a confusing, scary feeling—becoming a piece of your personal history even as you lived it. As if she were already at home and here came her face edging across the TV screen, and look, there was John Henry cradling Victor's head in his lap and she heard his voice saying, "King, help me," but it sounded like it was coming from the distant end of a long narrow hall.

"I have to go, John Henry."

"King, please. I can't do this by myself."

Oh god, how she wanted to tell him. How the man and the boy waded into the water, then were out ahead of her, already lost in the dark. How the river gurgled coldly around her body, pulled at her bra, ran through her underwear, the coldness of it a shock she felt all the way to her spine, the current fast and hard, the sky as dark as a vault above her, the gun in the bag tied to her wrist and the current tugging, wanting it, it seemed. How she stroked with the other hand and gave good strong kicks with her legs, breathing evenly through her nose as her mother had once taught her, long ago in the murky waters of some backwoods lake.

Long, long ago. When she had been a girl she was no longer.

Could she tell him how her heart was a slow steady throbbing in her chest? How the dark shapes of trees finally appeared and she stumbled the last few feet to shore? How she pulled herself from the water and stood with her hands on her knees, panting and shaking, the garbage bag hanging heavy from her wrist? How surprised she had been by the rush of gratitude, the sudden deep relief she felt to feel American mud between her toes?

Out front of the line, three cops were hacking at the crowd, working as a team and moving into the block. Tear gas drifted acrid over the huddled heads as the cops clubbed and sprayed, as they dragged people, arms bent and cuffed, through the street to the waiting buses.

"John Henry," she said. "We—"

"I'm not leaving."

Could she tell him how she did not hear them and longed for their sound, not their talking but the sound of their swimming, the dipping arms, the errant splash as their legs broke the surface, the hissing vacuum of the river around their bodies, sucking them downstream?

How she heard nothing, only her labored breathing and the water sliding quietly along the shore? How she picked her way carefully through the brush, shivering and listening and hoping?

How a sudden blaze of light swept across her face, and she fell flat to the ground, instinctively buried her face in the dirt, seeing the pebbled dust, the rough bark of the pines, the low thorny scrub brush washed in a harsh white light?

How she had crawled on all fours toward the cover of bushes, thorns poking at her hands and elbows, still in her wet underwear?

How she stopped and rose up behind a dense clump of brush, a slick of conflicting emotions turning slowly inside her, the inner reaches of which she did not want to plumb because on top was not just the dumb animal gratitude of returning home, but that familiar foreign fear twisting around her insides like a coil of razor wire, icy to the touch.

Tear gas wafted around their ankles and climbed their legs. John Henry kneeling in the gutter, saying, "You're going to be all right, kid. You're going to be all right. Everything is going to be all right."

She heard the sound of a bank alarm. An electronic wailing that wouldn't quit. She heard grumblings of motorcycles and looked over her shoulder and saw cops navigating the crowd on black-and-white Harleys.

She was dreaming. She was in a dream. A woman praying a mixed-up Buddhist mantra going, "Jesus Lord Om God Help Us."

"Jesus Lord Om God Help Us."

"Jesus Lord Om God Help Us."

Could she tell him what she had seen from where she hid?

Ignacio and his son on their knees in the dirt, the older man with his belly and scarred arms, his son looking like the boy he was, shivering in his wet briefs, fifteen feet away or more, and still she could see the water dripping from their hair, the look of terror in their eyes.

A lawn chair sat empty in the clearing, a pickup parked off to the side, illuminating them in the stark glare of its headlights. An old man stood halfway between the truck and where they knelt. He held a shotgun in his gnarled hands. It was leveled at their chests.

Could she tell him how the blood was pounding in her ears? How the shape of the gun was distinct through the plastic of her garbage bag?

How the old man stepped out of the light, opened the door of the truck and leaned in, and she heard the squawk of a CB radio and how for a moment he was just a dark form fumbling in the cab, the shotgun leaning against the door, and the man and the boy motionless, their kneeling bodies throwing long shadows across the dirt to climb distorted into the trees?

John Henry trying to clear Victor's eyes.

"John Henry, I can't stay. I can't do this."

Could she tell him the way the boy looked at his father in absolute fear? How she saw the question on his face? How Ignacio made a motion with his head, barely perceptible, as if to say, no, wait, and the way the boy turned and his eyes flicked to where she was rustling in the bushes and their gazes met, and she saw the knowledge of the gun so clear in his look, and then the truck door slammed and the old man was walking back into the light?

She watched herself watching herself as John Henry struggled to open Victor's eyes, struggled to clear them with the Maalox solution from a water bottle, and she thought of John Henry and his alcoholic father. His stories of the factory where they had

219

worked the line together. John Henry and his father, slicing hogs together, stepping through the blood together, wiping their faces with gut-soaked gloves, and talking Work, and talking God, and his father telling him he loved him and he had to get himself out of this factory—this man now supporting the boy's head and trying to pour the milky solution that was meant to ease the burning.

John Henry.

A man who had been put to the test and come out on the other side a man of total nonviolence.

John Henry.

Who believed that suffering was redemptive. That suffering redeems us exactly at the moment when we invite it into our lives and endure it with love.

Of course she could not tell John Henry.

John Henry most of all whom she could never tell how she rose up from where she hid and inhaled and sighted and squeezed. How the gun did not tremble in the slightest.

John Henry, whom she could never tell that she thought it would be loud, the gunshot, a roaring that would never end, but that it was not loud at all.

"King, help me," he said.

She felt like she was watching a movie, felt a cold unreality in her chest that was like a rope drawing tight. The claustrophobia of nowhere left to run because her anger was a thing that had followed her all her life, not anger, but a wild rage that wanted to hurt everyone and everything she had ever loved, and she had torched that ski resort, and done worse besides—she had entered the country in the worst of ways, crossed the border baptized in the blood of an innocent man, and if not today, then one day soon, someone was going to make her pay.

"I have to go," she said to John Henry.

He stopped what he was doing to look at her.

"Then go, King," he said. "Help me or fucking go."

She turned from him feeling that quiet haywire stillness that prepares you for something awful and vast. She heard Victor cursing. She heard John Henry reassuring him. She took a step away from them both.

One step.

Two.

John Henry whom she would never tell about the sweet ache of violence and how it does not happen once, but loops in your body like a movie reel that is the sound of your breath and the roar of your own beating heart. John Henry most of all whom she would never tell how the shot was not loud at all, but was the most quick and final sound, a short sharp snap like a door slamming shut. Like the click and fall of a key tumbling a lock.

One.

Two.

Three strides and she was gone.

Look at her go. A running girl disappearing liquid down tear gas streets. While the man she loved knelt in the gutter, feet wreathed in smoke.

DR. CHARLES WICKRAMSINGHE

Intermission IV

One Hour Until the Meeting

The bus door swung open with a pneumatic hiss and a cop pushed Charles through and up the steps and the door shut behind him. He stood at the front, looking down the rows. No cops on the bus. They were busy with more important things. Still sixty, maybe seventy protesters crammed into the seats. Their hands were cuffed behind them. Their faces bruised. Bloodied. Clothes torn. There was the strong smell of tear gas. The smell of urine. Charles counted at least fifteen other buses, stretching for blocks in the industrial lots behind the convention center, all filled with people's faces at the windows, and he didn't know, but he assumed that meant it was some sort of jail.

One hour until his meeting with President Clinton, and the American police had just thrown him in jail. And there he stood at the front of the locked bus and looked at seventy protesters who stared back at him like they wanted to rip him limb from limb.

A ripple of fear washed over him. And yet, what distinguished him, what made presidents and prime ministers call him friend, was his desire to talk to anybody, his ability to engage with any person's experience and opinion. The willingness to plunge off the cliff of who we think we are. That blind leap into another view.

He looked up and down the rows. He cleared his throat.

"My name is Charles Wickramsinghe and I am the Deputy Minister of Finance and Planning in Sri Lanka. I am a delegate and I am here for the meetings that you are trying so hard to shut down."

A voice yelled from the back.

"That we did shut down!"

"Yes," Charles said, "that you did shut down. And now I am here, with you, and well—" He paused. "And now I am here and I would like to hear your objections."

There was a deep silence. He heard the wind throwing sand against the sides of the bus. And then they erupted in a great cheer, and suddenly they were up from their seats, grinning and cheering, having broken free of the plasti-cuffs and yet continuing to sit here while the hours wore on, and then they were helping him into a seat.

In groups of twos and threes they came to speak.

They told him about the Rainforest Alliance and the Ruckus Society, about the United Auto Workers and the Longshoremen.

They talked calmly, knowledgeably about the WTO, about Monsanto, about intellectual property rights, about pharmaceutical companies who wanted to stop the manufacturing of generic AIDS drugs in Africa which were saving millions of lives.

They talked about unfair American corn subsidies, explained how cheap American corn destroyed the Mexican agricultural economy, put Mexican farmers out of work, sent them from their farms in the hills to the capital, and when there wasn't work in the capital, pushed people farther north, across the border.

And they were not saying something he had just discovered, but there was something that mattered, some necessary feeling that needed to be spoken aloud, and maybe it was nothing more than finally here was someone that would understand, and if not understand, here was a man that would listen and consider.

They told him about the IMF, about the World Bank, about Third World debt. Did you know, they said, Nigeria pays more every year on the interest of their debt than they do on education and health? Did you know that because of debt repayments most Third World countries pay more to the First World countries than they receive?

Did you know Monsanto—a huge chemical company—was now marketing itself as an agricultural company, as a company that made food? Did you know they sell farmers seeds that make plants which don't produce new seeds? Did you know the farmers then have to buy new seeds from Monsanto every year? Telling him about the trade war between the European Union and the U.S. over hormone-treated beef. The Europeans didn't want to eat it; the U.S. wanted them to eat it and took them to court, to the WTO, which said, yes, the Europeans must import the hormone-treated beef. To stop it was an unfair trade restriction.

The seventy protesters in detention aboard this bus—the seventy John and Jane Does, intent still on practicing civil disobedience, and jamming up the jails—Charles looked at their faces as they talked. They were the faces of that part of the American character that believed not in American destiny, but in the promise of America itself, that same promise with which they had once welcomed dusty hardworking immigrants to their shores.

They were the last of the believers and Dr. Charles Wickramsinghe, seventy years old and the Deputy Minister of Finance and Planning for Sri Lanka, who was born in a British colony where the frocked nuns laughed at his mother and smacked his hand with a ruler, Charles Wickramsinghe, who had owned a dog in his undergraduate days at the Royal College Colombo, a slat-ribbed stray he'd taken in and named on some lighthearted whim Alfred, Lord Tennyson—Charles Wickramsinghe was surprised to feel a widening respect. A respect with more than a pinch of regret. Because how wrong had he been? To think they knew nothing. To dismiss them. All these thoughtful young people striding toward the gates of capitalism—they had taken Gandhi's hunger strike and arrived at this. And as wrong as they were, as mixed up and incomplete their understanding of the economic issues, he had to admit it was protest and it was outrage and it was completely peaceful—the machetes and machine guns nowhere to be seen.

Two months ago Charles had done an interview with *Time* magazine. They were doing a feature on debt relief in the developing world. The Jubilee campaign for the Millennium. They had found him. Sri Lanka's little story. One man and his staff struggling to make gains in the world economy against the backdrop of a twenty-year civil war. Good copy. He had met the reporter in London, a luncheon at the London School of Economics. She wanted to know about the long run of five years. What did he hope to accomplish. What will entry into the WTO do for a small island nation like Sri Lanka. What do the developing countries want, she asked, as if he could speak for 150 of Earth's 190 nations. As if they wanted anything different than the rest of the world.

Refrigerators, he wanted to say. TVs and SUVs.

But Charles had a deep duty to believe in the system, and a reluctance to speak rudely to reporters. So he spoke of trade liberalization. Opening Sri Lanka's markets to the products and investment of the West. Of modernizing.

He could not speak of forcing Sri Lankan farmers to compete on the international market with multinational corporations who grew rice on 5,000-acre factory complexes in California and Texas. So instead he said, "What we need is to grow up. To develop. Our fishermen—can you believe it? They still fish from wooden boats.

Those without a boat—and there are many, believe me—put a wooden post in the water and they fish standing *there* as if they were a *stork*, a sarong-wrapped bird fishing from a pole."

The reporter chuckled.

"Roads, dams, bridges, great hydroelectric turbines turning in the night. Rice. Yes, we grow rice, but the rice farmers are worse even than the fishermen if that's possible. Completely *backward*. Farming as their fathers did. Farming as they have for decades, for *centuries*.

"Traditional, backward, undeveloped, not of the modern world. It does make for a lovely postcard," he said, "I'll give you that. The terraced fields, the bright green of the paddy. A farmer in a colorful sarong, holding a hoe and looking toward the camera as if he were a museum piece, ankle-deep in mud. But do you know what we count as our greatest export?"

She shook her head.

"Servants. Our most successful product so far has been our daughters. We send our daughters to the Middle East where they work as maids."

He said, "What kind of country are we? Who are we? We are postcards and maids. We are children who must grow up. Join the global economy. Modernize."

Modernization. What did that even mean? Were there a people in the world who were not modern? Was Sri Lanka not modern? He liked what Gandhi himself had said when asked what he thought about Western civilization.

"I think it would be a good idea."

And what of Gandhi? What would he say to the reporter? To the media? To these earnest souls gathered here in this makeshift jail? The man who broke British rule by refusing their cloth, their salt. We will make our own and be free, and so they did, and so

229

they were. This man, the moral courage. The damned genius of it. Breaking an empire by refusing their goods. By spinning your own cloth. By marching to the sea to collect your own salt. And who could deny it—they had changed the hierarchy of the world. And yet, what was required now was not a leader like Gandhi, not a man of unbending principle and courage. No, what was needed was a duty-bound minister capable of compromise. Gandhi would not compromise. Going on a hunger strike to protest unfair trade restrictions. Can you imagine? Nowadays they would let him starve. No, what preceded success was not moral courage but moral compromise. That dubious promise of the riches that trade would bring—Charles believed it. He had to believe it. Development. Modernization. The Western way. It might be a path of suffering, but what other path was there?

Gandhi was the man that freed a nation, but it was Nehru—a man of compromise—that built it. It was Gandhi who freed a people; but it was Nehru—a politician—who gave them jobs. Which one should he choose? His doubts weighed against his duty. You cannot have prosperity without a nation of your own. And yet, what good is freedom if you are shackled to your hunger by chains as thick as any ever worn by slaves?

The door swung inward with a hiss and a cop climbed the steps and after looking up and down the aisles pointed to Charles in his black suit jacket and white shirt stained red and said, "You. You're the delegate?"

A dagger of dread in his chest.

The police officer consulted a piece of paper in his hand.

"You, are you Charles Something Something from Sri Lanka?"

Charles nodded politely. "Yes, I am the Deputy Minister of Finance and Planning for the Democratic Socialist—"

"Right," said the officer. "Come with me."

32

As a younger happier man with long dark hair and an earnest smile, Bishop wore a beard, kept it neat and trim. His ma used to say, But Bill, you don't eat, you're so thin, don't those police feed you, and he rubbed his beard and grinned at his pops, who had his head buried in his plate who thought young Bill Jr. was wasting his life, but back then Bishop didn't know the feeling that when your son is wasting his life he is wasting *yours*, back then he didn't know that a son became a father, and he grinned at his own, loving the old man's grumbled incoherent unknowing. What a dinosaur!

But he was the dinosaur. The one out of touch with reality, out of contact with the world that lived around him.

Powerful explosions shook the windows of the buildings two blocks down, echoing and approaching through the narrow canyon of Sixth Avenue.

Bishop on the PeaceKeeper paused and turned to look.

Shredded groups unraveling through the streets. They weren't running but moving fast, bunching to talk and then scattering in loose clusters as another boom came rolling down the street behind them.

The sixties ended when Kent State. Ended when National Guardsmen opened fire on a college campus and killed four students. Do you think this was an accident or what? But whose fault? The men who pulled the trigger? Or the man who ordered them there with loaded rifles?

A no-parking sign lay in the street. Newspaper boxes stacked as a barricade in front of the Sheraton, crowds surging behind them, taunting the cops.

Bishop still astride the running board of the PeaceKeeper, directing the shots. Park was at his side taking out the targets. The rubber bullets flew. Another officer, a young Latina woman, stood on the other board, across the flat roof of the PeaceKeeper. The crowd was pressing against the vehicle and Bishop was thinking they would soon have to climb on top.

Maybe it was the bullet's fault. Poor bullet, just doing its job. Poor greased bullet punching holes in their pretty student bodies white as cream.

Another explosion. Bishop told them to aim high. A white-hot phosphorous flash that broke over their heads and rattled the windows in their metal frames.

And now here they came. A tired tattered band of protesters hurrying down the darkening street. They no longer had their signs. Another armored vehicle pushed them forward, out of the intersection, cops in wedge formation out front working their batons.

Bishop wanted to clean himself out, clear the bile, drop a nuclear bomb of astringent down his hatch, the rings of annihilation radiating from the hardened world-sick heart outward, flattening his doubt and disbelief like a concrete building gone to dust.

Because he had lost. Lost everything that mattered to him. Lost his wife, lost his city, lost his son. He had lost control of himself when it mattered most and now it was too late. Everything was lost.

It had come over the radio not ten minutes before. The Mayor had declared a civil emergency. The Governor had called in the National Guard.

And so Bishop would respond. It was his city. They were his people. And if he had to take away their rights to protect their rights that's exactly what he would do. Fuck the National Guard, and fuck the Mayor, too.

How do you win a battle against a force with endless reinforcements?

There was only one answer really.

He had declared the entire downtown core a protest-free zone. Then he told his officers to load their guns with rubber bullets and let them loose. He told them to use their batons and cuffs. They had run out of propelled tear gas for the moment, but he had whistled up the Sheriff's Office in Tacoma and told them to bring in more of everything, more gas, more pepper spray. They would clear these streets. He. Him, nobody else. Him, the Chief. He would fucking do that.

His radio saying

Bishop Bishop Bishop.

The chanting was dispersed, not chanting really, it had disintegrated into individual voices shouting, and Bishop listened to the layered scraps of noise. He watched the knots of people streaming past, groups of blue and green and red and yellow, their faces pinched and worried as they ducked their heads and ran-without-running.

A brightness above his head. He looked up and saw a tendril of smoke creeping around the corner of a building, high, eight, nine floors up. The sound seemed to begin there. There was another

233

white flash and then that great concussive boom which banged glass all down the street.

He listened to the noise because it was a strange sound and in the back of his brain it signaled something, but what? The violent explosive booms like the rumble of separate lightning shots that came bouncing off the buildings. It was a tumbleweed of jagged sound caroming off the steel and glass, and it sounded the way a city being bombed sounded in his imagination. The way the noise came turning over itself, separate explosions linked in an overlapping chain, the weird echoing roar of dogs barking in a tunnel.

Another explosion which set the windows of the building directly beside the PeaceKeeper clattering and he fought the instinct to just open the hatch of the 'Keeper and drop right in.

Truthfully, Bishop hadn't been right in years. Your son disappears as though dead and you are supposed to be all right? He felt like he hadn't been able to breathe, hadn't taken a single full breath, since the day Victor disappeared.

Instead of whatever one does in the course of a life, Bishop wandered the supermarket in a daze, lingering over the bright boxes, amazed and confused. He spent hours in the vegetable aisle, the soft mist gathering on his brass buttons, wetting the arms of his uniform as he examined the leafy greens, turned bok choy in his hands grown suddenly old.

Shivering in the freezer aisle talking to the carcasses of headless frozen birds.

When Victor left it broke something off inside him and sent it into the world. His boy in the world and Bishop's heart like a shadow following him around all his days.

All his son's strange unknowable days.

In the supermarket wondering how was it that his hands knew how to grieve and he did not.

In the supermarket Bishop stared at the bananas from Peru. He plucked one from the bunch, peeled and ate it, the light mush trapped between his teeth and tongue.

Something went missing, the weight that tied him to the ground. The world tilted and his son disappeared and he walked on floors that leaned and pitched, rooms turned upside down.

Grief and its decaying orbit. He felt like a rocket gathering speed, inescapably caught in gravity, spiraling closer and closer to home, to return and death. The cool comfort of Earth's dark seas.

In the market, he gathered apples in his arms. Rubbed dirty potatoes with a thumb. Hefted the weight of a cantaloupe in his palm. The sticker said Product of Mexico. He nestled the fruit to his chest and did a slow shuffling dance to the gods of global produce there in the fluorescent light. He turned the melon to his ear and listened for his son's voice.

Product of Mexico.

The sudden unfamiliarity of familiar things. Was that what he had heard? The secret language of the ordinary world? Was that what had called him?

At home Bishop opened the refrigerator and stared. Again that strange frozen light. He opened and stared and felt as if he were somehow living in that light. His life squeezed and processed in a plastic tub. Here it was, another sweet advertisement for the good life, and goddamn it, it was the good life. He ate a piece of cold chicken. He spooned pasta salad into his mouth. He drank a diet soda from the can and cursed his ungrateful son.

He ignited a handheld tear gas canister and threw it overhand into a knot of people around the PeaceKeeper.

The canister came winging back.

He ducked and pointed. Park turned and fired into the crowd.

33

Guatemala, Honduras, Nicaragua, El Salvador—the places in Central America Victor had come to love—where the governments had gone to war—not even gone to war, shit. No. Guatemala, where the government had started a soft war aimed at the hospitals and schools and families. Guatemala, where fathers and mothers and sons and daughters had been stolen and shot and tortured. Disappeared. Imagine a man taken from bed in the middle of the night—your husband, your brother, your *father*—the sounds of trucks in the street, the rifle butt on the door, they drag him across the room and out of the door by his hair, with a fistful of hair, and he's holding both hands above his head, both hands wrapped around the fist that drags him as if he had found a new way to pray when he is only holding tight to the fist to keep his hair from being pulled out completely, to lessen the pain that is not even beginning to make sense yet, the onrush of terror so complete it is a blank dark wall with one light shining, outlining a stain there, his terror complete and dark like a bag pulled over his head and that bulb which shines against the blank cinderblock wall, the only light in his terror is the thought to grab with both hands the fist which pulls him across the floor by his hair.

And the only thing remaining the unbearable silence which

follows as you look into the eyes of those that remain as if looking at the very future itself, the future which just now began as his feet bumped over the threshold of the door and the sound of the night started again as if nothing had happened. He is gone. And you never had a husband. You never had a father. You never had a son.

Two years ago, Victor had been picking lettuce in California. The Inland Empire, Watsonville, where he and forty thousand had gathered to protest. Gathered to protest, he heard his father laughing, and what is that supposed to mean?

He didn't have an answer to that. It was the phrase you used when someone asked What did you do in Watsonville? We gathered to protest. It was small talk. It was what you said to the neighbors, people that maybe understood, or didn't and called forth what empty image in their mind? Gathered to protest? A labor march?

Words mean things, Victor, and what do these words mean?

And what *did* Victor mean? Why had he gone? It wasn't something in the usual run of things, no, to walk away from work, to join a group, to mix with their bodies, their clothes and hair and sweat and conversations which he didn't understand, and he didn't know what it was at first, a sweet sort of overpowering perfume, and then realized it was the smell of other people, realizing with a smile and a shock that it was the smell of the food they made, the smell lingering in their clothes, it was the smell of their homes, walking together, what a beautiful intimate kind of crazy thing, and he laughed and imagined a whole family of people with food on plates gathered around the TV and he recognized the smell, and he knew the music from the TV, and he smiled, imagining himself part of a family, a visitor or a guest, or maybe a son, why not, sitting there with his brother, and his cousins, and his aunts and uncles, and his parents, all of them gathered around a TV, paper plates on their laps, eating and shouting the answers to *Who Wants to Be a Millionaire.*

Why did he go? He went because the people who worked in those lettuce fields were abused. He went because he worked, too, and he understood it, but he didn't have to live it and that was different.

But what does that mean, son? The people in those fields were abused. I work, too.

Victor didn't know. It was shorthand somehow. He couldn't think of how to explain what it was shorthand for. His father said I've seen dogs that were abused, I've seen horses that were abused, but what in the heck does it mean, those people were abused? And Victor wanted to say they are decent people, Dad, if only you could have been there. They are human beings of worth, as much as you or me, and he heard his father laughing and coughing, not because he disagreed they were good folks, but that phrase, human beings of worth. Was there not a single word he could say that had not been emptied of value?

What he wanted to say was there are workers in California, and they work in Watsonville in the fields of lettuce. They work for money like we all do. And these workers, these workers that are abused, that don't get paid enough, that work terrible hours, and make nothing, that are abused, that wash their feet and faces in ditches, that wash their little babies, if only you could have been there, Dad, and seen them washing their children's faces with ditchwater, scolding and talking as if this were the most normal thing in the world.

What we get used to. Do you understand? What we require of others so that we may live our lives of easy convenience. Dad, there are people who work all day every day for thirty years assembling the three wires that make a microwave timer beep. What are we supposed to think of this? How do they survive it? Why do we ask them to?

If you had met them, Dad, you would understand. If you had stood in that field, heads of lettuce stretching to the horizon, and the feeling, if you had met them, I'm not saying you would feel one way or the other, he wanted to say to his father, but if you had met them, shook their hand, and marched side by side with them, heard their voices, heard them laughing, and shared lunch with them, you used to like to laugh, Dad, remember, before Mom died? If you had eaten lunch with this family, seen the mother scolding her kids and laughing the way Mom used to yell at me and laugh, and the dark face of the father breaking into a smile as he offered me an orange soda—if you had drunk an orange soda from the bottle, warm from the bottle, but good, an orange soda on a sunny day in a lettuce field, and you arrived walking, and forty thousand people arrived on buses—this is what he wanted to say, if you had sat in the dirt and the heads of lettuce to the horizon. Lunch, Dad. This is what he wanted to say, if you had eaten a chicken salad sandwich wrapped in a paper napkin, and the mayonnaise leaking down the little girl's chin, and the father, his face was wrinkled, you know by the eyes? and he wore a mesh hat that said Budweiser on it, like the one you used to have, and he wore it kind of at an angle, not a fashion or anything, but just the angle it landed on his head when he took it off to wipe the sweat with his forearm and then snapped it back onto his head, and he put his hand on my back to say welcome, or thank you, I don't know, and the chicken salad sandwiches, and that orange soda warm and fizzy from the bottle that he opened with a bottle opener that was swinging from his belt. He wanted to say all this and more to his father three years since he had spoken to him. It was a feeling he had, as difficult to name or say where it came from or where it went as the fizzy mist of the orange soda. He wanted the words to describe all this and more to his dad. He wanted him here and by his side so he could say these are human beings. These are people and their lives are no different than ours. We are human beings. That woman could have been my mother. And they work hard, too hard, Dad, but they still remember how to laugh. Remember what it used to feel like?

Instead he said, "We went to protest. I walked into the lettuce and we gathered to protest. Those people work hard picking lettuce. Lettuce? Lettuce. They are not paid enough. They are treated badly. So we gathered to protest."

That's what he said to his father because the words to say otherwise simply weren't there.

He said, "I went, Dad, because it was the right thing to do."

Except he said none of this. Just mailed him a postcard of California grapes postmarked Salinas.

He looked at John Henry from where he sat propped against the newspaper box, his new friend, this white man with the red beard and the black glasses and the cowboy hat, and what Victor wanted to say, simply, was thank you.

He looked across the street, and there was the armored truck. Two cops atop it firing concussion grenades into the crowd. And there beside them, his father.

And Victor taking this in, looking at his father standing there on the running board of the PeaceKeeper, really looking at him. He saw the heaviness of the man's body, as if the bones were weighing him down. He looked at his back, at his shoulders and arms, at his father's *hands* and he knew. This was the desperation he had always felt. This was the blindness he had fought so hard to be free of.

Victor nodding and thinking, The world will kill you cold? Maybe it was worth it. He turned back to John Henry, thinking of all the man had done for him, and Victor, he decided it was all of it worth it. All of it worth the possibility that he might end up cold, worth the possibility that he might get hurt. He smiled at his friend and handed him back the bottle of Maalox and water and climbed to his feet. He steadied himself on John Henry's shoulder. And then he turned and stepped into the intersection. He pushed through the crowd and passed out of the mass and into a stretch of empty asphalt, a black stretch of road leading him from here straight to the PeaceKeeper. How it had taken him so long to realize, he didn't know. He walked toward the PeaceKeeper. He could end this entire thing right now, if he could only speak to his father.

And that's exactly what he was going to do. Go speak to the man.

Go speak to his father.

The Chief of Police.

242

34

King was running.

And then she wasn't.

Because the knowledge had come pounding up through her feet as she ran. There is no way to take back a bullet. King. The most perfect American girl with only love in her heart—she had killed a man of eighty-some years. Why not admit it? She had put a bullet between his belly and his Cracker Jack badge and she had looked in the mirror every day since and nowhere in all her years had she ever seen the person she would become hiding there inside her face.

No way to take back a bullet. No way to ever go back to John Henry.

She slowed to a walk. On a side street, away from the action, a sort of loose-limbed group carrying backpacks leaned against a dumpster in various postures of total boredom and how fucking stupid is this riot. In their oversized black hoods, they looked like some sort of Judgment Day cult, monks risen from the radioactive mud of a burnt-out city. They squatted and stood and leaned against the dumpster, looking as though they were waiting for the signal to come alive, the command no one else could hear. A few had gas masks. Some had crowbars.

Two of the black-hooded monks disengaged from the dumpster and approached a bank window. A group of protesters—middle-aged men and women—had decided to organize themselves against what they thought was an act of vandalism. They were going to protect the bank.

The two lines were yelling philosophies in each other's faces.

King had trained three hundred nonviolent revolutionaries in the desert, every one of them a good soul and King herself with only love for the millions of the Third World and she asked herself what was one man's death—border patrol agent or racist militia-man—against so many millions dead? She told herself the scales did not balance. One man's death didn't matter because there was the truck, and there was the CB, and she had dragged him among the dark trees to watch him die. It did matter and she knew it. The millions dead—they were exactly what made it matter. And yet there she had been, her, King, kneeling in the sand beside him, watching the odd sad way he clutched at the air as if there were something there in front of him which might save him if only he could catch ahold of it.

Two of the black-hooded youths casually kicked a newspaper stand into the street. And the violence of it, the anger toward a newspaper box—King slowed and stood watching.

"Stop!" one of the marchers said. "This is supposed to be—"

King noticed a crowbar leaning against a lamppost. She picked it up and tested the weight of it in her palm. It was extra long, a four-foot piece of metal designed for maximum wreckage. It felt good in her hand as she pushed through the crowd, using the handle to clear a way. This tall woman dressed in black pants and a white T-shirt splattered with blood as though a map of parts as yet unexplored, unconquerable lands far or near—the men and women looked at her face and then stepped aside because she was

244

maybe one of the lunatic blessed, a radical personage willing to give her life, possibly infected with the disease or despair of those she touched.

And she felt it like a cold block of ice lodged in her chest, leaking slow cold into her veins and she knew exactly what she was doing, this twenty-seven-year-old woman who wanted to shut down the WTO, who wanted to end the suffering which was the world without end, this twenty-seven-year-old woman, who wanted to remember, but could not, a time when she had still been a little girl tugging on her mom's hem in some innocent supermarket aisle.

And yet, no way to go back to the girl she'd once been. No way to go back to John Henry. No way to go back to the lie she had built.

She was a nonviolent revolutionary. She believed in the transcendence of suffering. The righteous power of pain, and yet no way to avoid prison of one kind or the other. The memories started coming. A small shudder in the drizzle and here it came, that familiar blinding comforting rage, the familiar anger sharp as any knife.

No way to undo the world where they lived in a shack made of loose boards, a family of six in a shack the size of a car on blocks, and in her life anytime she wanted she could sleep in an apartment where she turned hot water on and off and stepped from the shower and toweled dry thinking about what to eat for breakfast.

How easy to slip into that life where she had a closet for her clothes and a closet for food and how easy to believe this was somehow normal. That's what got King. Because where was the logic in the thing? The gun in her hand and the man's chest opening to the sweet smell of his blood among the sagebrush, a smell she would

245

never be able to forget, to unremember, like a handful of pennies on a sweaty summer's day. What could possibly connect that man's breathing beating conflicted life to this singularity of blood in the sand? How could a human life, a thing so layered and vast it was a world unto itself, be reduced so quickly and completely to a cold corpse beneath the trees?

In Mexico she had seen shipwrecked houses lit by candlelight. Houses of cardboard and tin. Scavenged wood. Night fell and here came the little flames. Light spilling from the warped boards like a flood of little hands to grab at her face, her shirt, her heart. And she remembered how she had squatted there on her haunches in that concrete truck stop in McAllen, Texas, hitching to Seattle, how she had leaned against a cinderblock wall, the cracked pavement and twilight. She remembered washing her hands and face in the metal washbasin of the restroom, the water going pink and brown, and then outside the arc lamps, orange flowers blooming in a pot on the barred windowsill, how she had bowed her head, while her chest heaved and the full weight of what she had done came trailing its fingers along the smooth cavern of her chest. She had huddled against that wall and wept and let it come, trying to remember it all passes. Even this.

The world and all its impossible wanting.

The bank window was a mirror and in the mirror she saw the green eyes of a coward. She hefted the weight of the crowbar. The green eyes of a girl who did not deserve anything but the burning to which the world had condemned her.

Arrest her? Let them arrest her. Prison was where she belonged.

NONVIOLENCE
NONVIOLENCE
NONVIOLENCE

They were chanting like an army of robots. The window in front of her beckoned. Something that looked like her face standing there watching her. She began swinging the head, getting the weight going. She heard wind pushing paper down the street, the rough whisper of the crowbar swinging in her callused hands. From far off, she heard voices, but they were distant decaying whispers as though she were at the bottom of a well.

The shot and the way he blindly reached, arm pointing and falling back. The airy bubbles of blood that sent his last breaths into the world.

The bar paused at the top of the arc.

In the mirror of the window she saw her own reflected face staring back at her.

When she was thirteen she had watched the Brixton riots on TV. She didn't know what it was at the time but her mother's boyfriend, who had hooked up an illegal cable box, didn't go to work for a week, and they sat on the couch, drinking beers forbidden by her mother, and watched London burn. Sat on the couch next to each other while the hot summer sun baked the yard where tires collapsed and gathered rain, but it was cool and dark in the trailer and they were drinking beers and the beers so cold. Fresh from the fridge where he pulled and cracked and wiped a lip of white foam and grinned.

So cold her teeth hurt in that good kind of way.

All those people so angry and he didn't have an answer for what made them that way, just said, "The cops shot someone's mom," and then drank and grinned and she didn't need to ask because it was written into his face and his body and the way he moved through this stupid trailer and this stupid town, she would burn it down, too.

Sitting on the couch watching people burn and loot and smash, the gasoline vapors of whatever thing she was had found their image in the world and she moved from the couch to the floor, this thirteen-year-old girl in front of the TV with her cutoffs and her long white legs curled beneath her like earrings of silver or steel. She felt the heat baking her face and the gasoline wetting her hair and she looked into their faces and the thing that was inside her cried out in recognition. Half-drunk on the floor and her mother's boyfriend doing something in his jeans behind her and calling her name.

A faraway shouting, a rhythmic chanting, a siren singing somewhere up there in the daylight above the well.

She brought the crowbar down, swinging hard. It crashed into the window with a rolling, sickly, solid boom. Her reflected chest split with spiderwebs. She raised it again, swinging, and let it fall, driving it into the window with all her force. She felt the solid weight, the crush of tempered metal on glass, as the clawhead leapt into the window. She took two steps back. There was nothing in her mind save the window and the bar and her wish to utterly annihilate that fractured beautiful green-eyed fool looking back at her.

No thoughts in her mind, just a cold mechanical rage. The window imploded. Glass laminate raining across the potted plants, the wooden desks, the smooth stone floor.

There was a gaping hole in the window, a ragged crater at the center of her chest. The line of people who were protecting the bank window moved back in alarm.

A wailing started on the far corner. A human wailing.

In some part of her heart she wished it were a cop. But it was not.

She turned to see a young girl kneeling on the corner, maybe sixteen or seventeen, blood running down her face. She was crying.

248

"Please come help us," she said. "The cops are going crazy. They're beating a man in the street."

King was beside her and did not want to be.

The girl was crying and having a hard time just making sentences. And King, what did she care? She knew she needed to leave. The girl was on her knees in the street. At the foot of a traffic light saying, "We didn't do anything. And they just went crazy. Please. Please come help us. We need more people. We didn't do anything." And then she was crying again and King couldn't understand what she was saying because the girl was sobbing in her arms and King was holding her and waiting for her brain to tell her feet to move. They weren't going to just start moving on their own.

Move, she told them.

The black-hooded monks headed for another target and King standing stupidly in the street, holding the bleeding girl, while she stood waiting for her brain or her feet or her heart to make a move while the cops came a-marching and the explosions rocked over their heads and a girl sobbed beneath a traffic light, which was going from red to green to yellow and back to red again and somewhere a siren like birds singing over the sea.

35

Officer Tim Park lived in a one-bedroom studio in Ballard where he slept on a futon that turned into a bed, or was it a bed that turned into a futon, he didn't know and it didn't matter because he rarely slept, and when he did, barely managed to shed his uniform before falling heavy to a sleeping bag, exhaustion being the price for the relief of dreamless sleep.

Most nights he drank and then crashed, the TV throwing light across his face, and the futon, and the near-empty apartment where the only thing he had hung on the wall was a set of photos he'd brought with him from Oklahoma in heavy frames and glass. They showed the Alfred P. Murrah Federal Building in black and white.

Before and after.

He didn't like the photos; they bothered him, the face of the building blown half open, insides gaping. You could look right into the blasted interior. The contents of offices—charred desks, overturned chairs, phones still connected—just hanging in empty space like something torn out by the roots. Shredded and burnt office paper drifting like confetti.

He had been there that day, of course, one of the first responders, but still those photos looked to him like something utterly foreign. Something he could not relate to, even though he had been there, like pictures he'd seen on the news of places like Venezuela or the Philippines when an entire hillside gave way and the people and their cooking stoves and their dogs and their TVs and their kids went sliding into the mud-slicked abyss. More than anything the photos reminded him of the moon, and he often stood there alone, home after a shift, the lights off, stood there alone just looking; 168 people died in that blast, more than 600 injured, stood there alone in the darkness with a beer in his hand and his shirt unbuttoned. And if his hand went to the scar, if his fingertips softly traced the smooth flesh, idled along the density of that patch of wealed skin where no hair grew, did he notice? Did he notice his own hand touching his face as he contemplated his photos in total bewilderment?

He wanted to know: How did they allow that to happen? And every day since. How did they allow that to happen?

Not here. Because here he was taking care of that. On top of the PeaceKeeper tracking the crowd over the barrel of his shotgun loaded with rubber bullet shells and laying the violent ones down.

The crowd was furious. Objects, small objects, were flying over his head, ball bearings and golf balls and water bottles. He was standing on top of the 'Keeper and Ju was keeping them back with the baton, but they were at his feet, screaming. A plastic bottle bounced off his helmet and how the fuck were they going to get out of here?

He heard Ju on the other side of the 'Keeper, cursing, saying, "What the heck was that? A soup can? Was that what they just hit me with? A freaking can of soup?"

Not thinking how are we going to get out of here. Not thinking because he didn't have time to think, what is a choice and what is not because here he was standing atop the PeaceKeeper, while the crowd surged and screamed, and down below him on the front hood was the Chief himself. The Chief, who right this very moment was swinging with his baton, unaware that the very same kid that Park had nearly busted this morning for selling weed was headed right toward him. That skinny black kid with the braids and the olive green jacket. There he was making his way through the crowd, headed straight for the Chief. The kid with the strangest, weirdest sort of grin on his face. He looked happy. And the Chief—did the Chief even see the kid? No time to ask. The kid looked nuts and Park lifted his shotgun and placed the barrel on a line that connected him, Officer Timothy Park and his weapon, to the black kid in the street with the crazy-ass grin. He would protect his Chief. Because that's what a good cop did. A good sane rational cop who understood how things worked. He closed one eye and cocked his head to the barrel. Sighted on the kid, who the closer he got to the Chief, the nuttier he looked. He was about twenty feet out now. Dang, Park thought as he sighted and took a breath, preparing to squeeze the trigger on the downward slope of his exhale, kid is so crazy it looks like he wants to hug the old man.

What a fucking world.

36

Bishop knew he had not necessarily been the best father. He had raised his adopted son as though he were his own. More than his own child. He had loved Victor, when he was young, as though he were a living part of the man himself. And yet he was not tender, exactly. No, he raised his son to be the man he knew he would need to be. To have done different would have been a disservice to the boy. A mercy he could not afford.

He had grown up poor, Victor, and this the boy did not seem to regret or resent. He never said his mother should have provided him more. She should have bought him and fed him and given him more, because she did feed him, feed her son, and she did love him, love her son, and if he didn't have the fashionable clothes, Suzanne had said he didn't need to be another asshole in two-hundred-dollar sneakers.

But then Suzanne died and Bishop bought his son the shoes, the shoes that were for assholes and the shoes that were on his hero's flying feet, but Victor left them in the box wrapped in paper. It was a gesture of love and defiance, was how Bishop saw it, and then his boy disappeared and maybe, Bishop thought, he should never have bought him the shoes. Maybe he didn't know a goddamn thing about his son.

How can you protect your children if they don't want to be protected? How can you protect your children if the thing from which they need protection is you?

Bishop had once stumbled on him, surprised his son in his room with his head buried in the orange box, inhaling the odor of rubber and new leather and imagining what?

When he raised his head from the box and saw his dad standing in the doorway, the thing he wanted to know was did he think the world was a good place?

Did Bill Bishop think the world was a good place?

For whom, dear son?

And yet they were happy for a time, the three of them. Fifty-nine years old and it had been a good life. He had a wife he loved, a happy home, a good kid with good grades heading to a good college when that day came. And then Suzanne was gone and everything gone with her—his son, his family, his belief that the world made some kind of sense, that justice prevailed. She left and the gravity from beyond just pulled him inside out. Left his guts hanging in the wind.

His silences engulfed him. And into that silence he threw his son.

Victor came to him one evening, a little less than a year after her death, some sort of ticket clutched in his trembling hand. "Dad, I'm not going to college," he said.

"And why is that?"

"I'm going to Guatemala."

"And why is that?"

"I don't know exactly."

"And what do you hope to find there?"

"I don't know."

"Is this about me burning your mother's books?"

256

"No."

He was a month past his sixteenth birthday. He was a child and a fool. But what were you going to say? Bishop sensed that he had already lost him; failed to protect him in some crucial sense. But it was exactly this knowledge he could not allow himself to see or speak. This traveling—it was merely a boy's bluff against his father. A more sophisticated version of the play Victor had enacted at fourteen following his mother's death: running away from home every three weeks with the regularity of clockwork. Various sheriffs picked him up in his hovels of rebellion and brought him back: hitchhiking on the I-90; burgling a house on the outskirts of the UW campus; in the Great Northern train yard, trying to jump a freight. He never escaped a radius of more than thirty miles, and they always brought him back home.

He wanted to say, Victor, go to college.

He wanted to say, Son, the world is not hard. It is awful.

But how could he, a white man, truly prepare his son for that bleak knowledge which was coming? White man. Black son. Bishop hardly thought in these terms. But he knew. The world would judge Victor harshly. It was a narrow road he would have to walk. Even with all his advantages, still there was little margin for error. One mistake could cost him everything. Bishop *knew*. Christ, he was a cop. There is less room for forgiveness, son. Keep your hands in plain sight, son. Don't make a sudden move, son. Don't wear those baggy jeans, son. And no matter what, no matter what, no matter what the officer says to you, do not respond in anger. Ever. Do not lose control. Just do whatever they tell you to do, no matter how humiliating.

And did he say this to his son? Which was worse? To tell him. The necessity of telling him. To ruin that innocence. To prepare him for a future which, god willing, would not come to pass. Or

257

to *not* tell him, and by not telling him ensure that that future did indeed come to pass?

Bishop remembered it so clearly. Victor standing beside the stainless steel refrigerator and holding a plane ticket and staring at his father as if he were a person he had never seen before. A strange man who had put on glasses and taken up residence in his home. Or perhaps it was more accurate to say Victor was looking at him as though seeing him for the first time.

And what did Bishop say?

He adjusted his glasses and went back to his paper and said, "Well, who's stopping you, son?"

Victor would have to learn his own lessons.

"Your mother would be very disappointed."

Bishop's radio babbling.

Gasoline

Bishop

Kerosene and ninjas.

Gasoline. Stolen gasoline.

Bishop Bishop Bishop

Snipers and kerosene.

Bishop pointing and Park firing. Another protester went down in a heap. He switched the radio off and felt an odd immediate relief. Thank fucking god.

A protester stepped from the crowd and a space seemed to clear. A burning dumpster was behind him, and in the flickering light Bishop saw bars of shadow across his body and he looked something like his son might have looked waking up from a nap, thirty pounds lighter and covered in oil-flecked grit. Flames huge behind him.

His face hidden in the hood of an olive green jacket. He was yelling something at the PeaceKeeper. The crowd was chanting. Surging toward the hotel.

Rain in the air and no small number of memories suddenly pressing in on him, ghosts rising through the smoke, the creak and haul of riot, and Bishop seeing none of it. Seeing only the white shoes polished to a shine. All week he had watched the faces of the city pass. How many he seemed to recognize! And from each familiar face bloomed a memory, a shock of emotion that buzzed around his skull. All week he had walked and wandered, he had watched and waited for that one face to pass—Victor.

And now here he came. His son.

His physical appearance so markedly changed from when Bishop had last seen him. A boy become a man. But what he encountered there in the darkness of the clamor, what he saw, was not the sun-kissed world traveler he had perhaps imagined his son would look like. No, what he saw was a skinny man destroyed by the day, bedraggled, with eyes nearly shut and two loose braids and a pair of Air Jordans on his feet which had always seemed out of proportion, too big for his body at sixteen, but which Bishop realized weren't too big for him at all anymore.

The very same shoes. The very same son. He had grown into his feet. Into his skin. The son who had lifted his head from a shoe box at the age of fifteen and said, "Dad, do you think the world is a good place?" The son who, one year later, had disappeared into the world and Bishop wishing every day since for him to come back. The son who was now nineteen and it made him want to weep. When had his son gotten so tall?

Bishop heard the sound of the shot before he realized what it was.

Didn't know what he was seeing as he watched Victor crumple in the street like a paper kite.

And then he realized. He took two steps across the running board and grabbed Park by the vest. Another explosion rocked the intersection. Bishop swung him around just as the man was about to fire his weapon again. Swung him around until they were face to shocked, surprised face. You have to take a side, and in that moment it could never have been any more clear. The police fired on Victor, fired on his son, and Bishop chose his side. He knew exactly to whom he belonged. Whose body. Whose hands. Whose breath and beating heart.

Looking into the man's eyes. Seeing the fear there. Asking himself, What about an unarmed nineteen-year-old scares an armed police officer?

37

King saw Victor twenty feet from the PeaceKeeper when the shot took him in the chest. The daydreamy feeling was gone, shattered. She felt a certain clarity in the deepening dusk as she climbed the hill to Sixth and Pine. The smell of burning diesel drifted down the street. It was a sort of antiseptic, this familiar smell of combustible fuel and trash. It took her back to Central America, to Chiapas, to Mexico—diesel fumes and the sweet pungent odor of fruit and sweat. Bus-seat stuffing and a leak in the roof and a sweat-soaked shirt hung on a line. Big-leafed trees in the backyard. The way the first drops of rain raised craters in the roadside dust; the veneer of oil collected from passing cars, taxis, Toyota trucks, the rumbling multi-ton buses with their wheels the height of a child, their swinging crosses to guard against the low mean spirits of the night.

She saw the rubber bullet crush Victor in the chest. His arms snapped back and he went down, legs tangled, his down jacket leaking feathers in a great burst of white.

She saw Victor go down and she saw, tracing the rubber bullet's path backward to the PeaceKeeper, the asshole cop from this morning who made the shot.

And then the cops descended because you do not try to

approach the PeaceKeeper, you do not threaten a police officer by walking toward him, and she saw Victor, curled and cramped and surrounded by armed angry cops. His face looking up among the dark anonymity of the assembled riot gear.

Four of the cops stood back. As if joined by one brain, one beating heart, they stepped forward together and their batons descended.

King knew she would remember, drifting toward sleep some day far removed, the solid thump the wood made falling upon him. It was the sound of the true heartbeat of the world, and once it had been heard, there was no way to stop hearing it. Thump-thump. Thump-thump. And what was it in that long and prolonged instant—what was it that told her this pain would go on forever? What was happening there was no erasing. There would be no apologies, no forgetting, no reconciliations. Just the opening to the pain that is your friend dead or shot or starved or beaten. Disappeared into the place where the disappeared die. She saw six cops standing over him and there was something in the way their fists rose and fell that made her heart want to stop. Like a clock that had run out of time. King could see it in every crunch and shuddering shock. Something in the way they stood over the boy working their sticks. Heard it in every hoarse burst of air. Something in the way they raised their batons, feet spread for balance as if gathering strength from hip and leg. The way they paused before swinging as if measuring the blows.

And King knew exactly what John Henry would say. John Henry would say look at how they are forced to hit him. We have won. Look at what they are forced to do to save themselves.

And tell me is what they protect worth a man's life? Free trade? This is something we all want and need? Why must they beat a man in the street if the answer is yes?

Victor was bleeding now and King heard the wet slap of the clubs on flesh. She thought nonviolence. She thought I will witness this. Victor scared like an animal on the pavement, his hands covering his head, and she said to herself, I will witness this. I will witness this and I will remember this and wasn't this exactly what John Henry said would happen?

Yes, it was. But it wasn't supposed to be Victor. And who, John Henry might have said, had guided him to this moment? Tell me, King, who put Victor in lockdown?

They rolled him onto his back. Two cops bent and pried his arms from his face. You could glimpse some clue of it in their arms and shoulders. The force behind their blows, the desperation of their fury, the angry and frightened look in their eyes—it was the ancient terror of a police whose mission it was to control people who were unafraid of their violence.

If you are not afraid of dying.

She saw a kid dancing with a can of lighter fluid ablaze and Jimi Hendrix playing "The Star-Spangled Banner" on someone's battered boom box, and there was a time when she thought she knew the feeling that had brought them here, these people who were now in the street joyfully burning the city. She had thought she understood it on some level, what brought them out, what thrill there was. No, not thrill.

Just say it.

If you are not afraid of dying, then what freedom you fucking feel. What freedom there is to burn and wreck. To stand in the middle of a city street, a street with the lights to go and the lights to stop and the taxis passing and the buses passing and the limos passing, and the lights that told you when to go and when you had to stand there on the corner looking helpless and lost; the cops and the cameras and the people with their lives lived behind

263

walls that you see in the eyes and what a stupendous devastating freedom to stand in the middle of a street like this and torch the motherfucker. What a cold excitement in the chest to break a barricade and burn a dumpster. To put a crowbar, yes, through a bank window.

That intoxication of ignition, the sweet smell of fuel, the way the paper rose in the heated air light as tissue, burnt and torn messages rising to a god you did not believe in—yes, there had been a time when she thought she understood this.

The world doesn't give you what you want?

Burn it down.

Now, watching their bodies taking the blows, she saw it for what it was.

Because where have you arrived when you take your piece of pavement, your glass bottle, your stone, to go to war with a modern military? When all you have left is your body, or the body of your son, and that is what you throw in the street. That is your final roadblock to occupation.

Jesus Christ, look at them. Attempting to take a city with nothing more than their bodies and whatever currents might run inside.

No, revolution was not glamorous. Revolution was a sacrifice. A desperation. The last insane leap to some future where you might have the room to breathe. Except there was nothing there when you landed but a wall running east to west.

Or was it the most clearheaded sanity—this last leap? The final decision you would have the power to make. Which would it be? Hurry now, the tanks are rolling in the street, the troops are at your door. Time to choose. Slavery or suicide? Surrender or fight?

But this time, no. She would not let her rage overcome her. Neither her despair. She would not meet violence with violence.

She believed in the transcendent power of love, the overwhelming force of nonviolence, and it was love that had saved her long ago when the anger had burned her to nothing. Love that showed her another person to be, love that taught her how to recognize the rage and not be consumed by it.

Victor. Did she have enough love to include Victor?

Victor, who was now covered up on the pavement, leaking blood, while four cops stood above him beating his prone body with batons and measuring their blows as if what they needed to control the situation was more pain.

If only they could apply more pain.

A woman on the edge making soul-struck cries with every blow.

The way they measured the shots. The way those motherfuckers stood and lifted and paused and *measured*. The way they paused and calculated before driving their batons into his back. The way they stepped back to make room for the others who came rushing to join as if it were a form of sport.

How bright blood is when it leaves the body. How quickly it pools on the pavement. How it comes streaming out from the tiniest hole, comes out so fast it's as if it was waiting to leap out of your body since you were born and bawling in your mother's arms.

What is the function of the heart, if not to convince the blood to stay moving within the limits where it belongs, to stay at home.

Stay at home, stay at home, stay at home.

But restless thing that it is, your blood, it leaps into the world.

And the thing seemed prolonged, the seconds stretching out into eternity as they stood in a group and hammered at his face, smashed Victor where he lay huddled on the pavement, and King watching and witnessing and then she was running again. But not away. Running toward it this time. Running toward it as surely and swiftly as she once moved her arms in that small backwoods pond where her mother had taught her how to swim. The crowd chanting.

WHAT DOES DEMOCRACY LOOK LIKE???
THIS IS WHAT DEMOCRACY LOOKS LIKE!

There was nothing in her mind save the batons falling and her body running. She could have been anywhere. Any dust-choked square on earth. Any running girl, running to save a friend. Look at her go. Headed straight for that fucking armored truck and the mangled motherfucker from this morning. The asshole who made the shot that took him down.

WHAT DOES DEMOCRACY LOOK LIKE???
THIS IS WHAT DEMOCRACY LOOKS LIKE!

She dodged three officers, took two steps, one foot grabbed the front bumper of the armored vehicle and then she lifted into the air. The few scattered cops who were protecting the PeaceKeeper moved back in alarm. And then she was flying up toward the hood of the thing and there could have been nothing more surprising than what she saw before her.

The cop with the fucked-up face was not on the hood. He had suddenly disappeared with the Chief and who she saw in his place was a brown-skinned woman with a gun. Her body heavy with armor. King thinking, How did that happen, as she landed and saw her own body mirrored there. A body braced and armed.

WHAT DOES DEMOCRACY LOOK LIKE???
THIS IS WHAT DEMOCRACY LOOKS LIKE!

She saw her own boots and her own legs and her own face mirrored in the boots and legs and face of this cop. Her hands. The long fingers. The chewed-to-the-nub fingertips. Yes, a mirror of her own scared and trembling hands. Except this cop was holding a gun.

And King was not.

38

The first baton went straight to the head, a stereophonic boom that seemed to blow out his ears. Victor tried to crawl away, but someone kicked him and flipped him on his back and then stepped onto his flailing hand. Time seemed to slow. He felt the boot pinning his upturned palm to the pavement, felt the pinch of gravel against his skin, and he felt the beginning of a knowledge. They were working on his body, but he was just a hand turned to the sky. He felt where the tread was worn and thin, felt where the sharp edges dug into his fingers as the cop bore down, felt in his palm every impress and contour of the hard rubber sole. It was as if his hand were the centering essence of his fluid being, he felt it wholly as if he were not a man and a body, but only a hand cradling a boot, open to receive a sky swollen with cloud.

He was both boot and hand. Black boot and brown man's hand. His hand, skin the color of strong tea, the hard knobby knuckles pressed to the pavement. The warm pulse of blood in the veins, the lined white palm with his creased fortunes and folds. He looked at the storm clouds, blackness within blackness, and he felt something sliding from him.

Cops coming a-running to join in the fun.

The cop lifted his foot, releasing the pressure for a moment, and

269

then smashed the boot down hard to stomp Victor's hand where it lay on the pavement.

The sound was the crush of shovel on gravel that was the bones in his hand shattering.

Victor screamed. He couldn't help it. He pulled his destroyed hand to his chest and felt it coming over him fast now, an ache inside his chest that he had felt forever and never named. He didn't want to die. Simple things this young man loved. The color of the leaves in bright morning, how the green seemed lit from within and the sky so endlessly blue. The smell of woodsmoke high in the mountains. The mottled brown-gray of a river in flood. An open window and whatever sounds might drift through. The song of the world, taxicabs, laughter, birds. Just one bird washing herself in the rain gutter beneath his open window. The quality of attention, to idly watch a bird flutter and preen, to hear the soft whirr of her wings, to hear her whistle.

He did not want to leave this place yet, this planet of mountains and seas, the human body, the blood-heat of a hand pressed against your own. He felt a terrible sadness sweeping over him. There was something about meeting her, perhaps not apparent at first, but which revealed itself slowly, the way that a bell will strike and the awareness of it comes after the fact of the ringing, so too it came over you gradually while spending an afternoon with her digging in the veggie garden, or perhaps you spent your summer Saturdays from grade school on up working down in Beacon Hill, constructing those simple wooden frame houses that had not existed before her arrival, yet which were after such a part of the neighborhood, such a part of the character of the neighborhood and what the neighborhood thought of itself, that it could be said that perhaps she had not organized the men and women and materials, not cleared the lots, not spent every Saturday there with hammer and nails in her dark hands, but instead had arrived with the wooden frames already intact and existing fully built and had only set them down along the avenue in the same manner that she had arrived in Seattle with her young son and climbed the steps to their room and set down their suitcases.

Victor's mother.

Perhaps you spent a cold and shivering morning opening the soup line, from the time you were eight on up, in the early morning hours before the first school bell, fed the men who would spend all morning, perhaps all day, shivering in their thin clothes from warmer weathers and waiting for a job to come by in the form of a pickup truck and a wave and a whistle. Not so different from the whistle of her own childhood, she had once said to him, the steam-kettle shriek that had called his grandfather to the factory. Maybe you spent a cold morning with her offering these men hot soup and rolls, so that they would have some food in their stomach to sustain the wait, something even to sustain the work were they lucky enough to get it.

Maybe it was a hundred cold mornings you spent with her. Even a thousand would not have been enough.

Maybe you were with her one of these many cold mornings with the steam rising from the pots, and it would have come over you slowly, as you passed the hard rounds of day-old bread, as you listened to the way she spoke with the men there, noticed the way they joked with her as a friend without any trace, large or small, of self-consciousness or shame or even deference, the way the men were grateful for the hot food yet accepted it only as one might pass a plate down a family table. God bless the beautiful necessity of food and flesh. And a certain funny feeling stealing over you because how do you see your mother as a person separate from yourself, a person necessary to other people, and loved, and yet Victor had, he had seen and understood that if tomorrow the order were reversed and these men, warmly clothed, handing the food to his mother, to himself, then it would be unchanged. He had seen and known, yes, this boy, with the uncanny sense that were it he in his thin clothes, shivering, blowing the steam from the soup, wondering about work but talking about other things, then all eyes would still be clear, there would still be the low murmur of a joke in the thin air and the food still passed from hand to hand with a nod and a word of gratitude, and whether he knew its name or not, this was all of life that Victor really would ever need to know. All of them, finally, eating, his mother, this black woman with earrings of hawk feathers, and Victor slurping soup from his bowl in the cold morning, talking and nodding with the men, and they treated him, too, as one of them, as a boy, but someone worthy of talking to, and Victor chewing and listening, eyes bright, and when had he ever in his life felt so at home as in this moment, among these men, and his mother's guidance that allowed him to see it, that allowed him to be, and it finally clear to him that he was in the presence of something which he did not completely understand but which he knew to be great.

When that is taken from you, there can be no giving it back. No getting back to where you might once have been. God knows he had tried. Had traveled the world up and down and not come upon it again, the feeling of standing there in the cold mornings, and his life with some purpose. And it was as simple as this. Feeding a few hungry men before they went to work. That was all, and it was both the largest, most important thing to be done, and the smallest, and Victor didn't want to go. Not yet. All the people he would never meet. To sit and talk, to waste time together, to eat beans from a bowl, to pass nothing more than a few cans of beer, to watch their faces as they laughed. He felt the baton blows

272

raining over his body like fistfuls of packed dirt and felt for the first time how nearly unbearable the power of human life, the unbelievable fragility—there were times with people, touching them hand to shoulder, walking, singing, the human voice, there were times when he was with people that he could hardly stop himself from crumbling, just falling to pieces. What was that? Not sadness. Goddamn this place. It had been with him forever and did he just now know? Why now should he know just how much he loved this dark fucked-up place. A baton smashed his mouth bloody and he thought I don't want to go. I don't want to die. I will join you, one day, but please just one more day here, one more hour with these people. I just started. Let me see one more face. One more moment in this place. How fucked-up it is. But I don't want to leave.

He felt a tooth work loose. He felt the batons battering him like hail, a shot to the kidneys that exploded like a star. He choked back a laugh that wanted to become a sob. He was glad to have done what he had done. To have wandered the world. To have loved his mother while she was alive. Even to have joined the people here today, it was nothing, so insignificant, but he had raised his voice to a good and true human pitch, that was what he had done, but now he knew all along it had been this. This had been the plan. To stomp the breath from his belly until he breathed no more. They wanted to erase him and all that he was from the face of the earth.

And he was going to let them.

39

Ju saw the girl coming before the girl even knew she was coming.

When Park and the Chief had gone spinning off the side of the PeaceKeeper, Ju had climbed down to the hood. She was alone, but she felt calm. The kids were shouting stuff up into her face, but she wasn't worried, no, she was holding them back with the baton leveled at their chests and looking around, and waiting for some help. Not wildly looking, because it was important to remain calm, to retain the appearance of calm.

Ju wanted to remember they were human, these screaming mouth shapes beneath her, but she already had everything, both arms and face and the way you stand and how you respond to stress and the way you carry yourself, engaged in trying to hold them back.

Because that is what it meant to do the job. To be a well-trained police officer and not an angry hippie punk protester with a face full of metal and the privilege of getting pissed off whenever you felt like it.

Beneath her armor sweat was sliding down her back, gathering in the crack of her ass. Her hands were clammy without her gloves. She was armed, of course, with her pepper spray and her service weapon in a positive retention clip, but her bullets she preferred in her clip and her clip on her belt. The weight and heft of violence—an officer with a gun on the hip—were under ordinary circumstances enough to calm and quell. It was how you carried it—the ineffable it-ness of you in the world. The threat of force, the ability to dispense death and immediate pain—this she preferred over that force unleashed.

If she had had time to think, she would have thought there will be time to think about all this later. Time aplenty to contemplate and look at the day from different angles. Time enough to consider her actions and what had led to what and how it had all come undone. Time to let the guilt or shame or pride take up residence in head and gut, but later, because now she was a police officer in this city by the sea, this shining beacon of democracy and freedom and there was a threat.

She had watched as Park fired and his rubber bullet took the kid in the chest and he went down. Four officers swarmed him, but then she lost sight of the melee because more officers were running to surround the pile and now she watched as this wild horse of a girl broke from the mass, dodged the three officers in front of the PeaceKeeper, adjusted direction and picked up speed, pointed toward Ju like a bullet with her name stamped on the side.

It all registered in a flash. She didn't need to think about it. That's what it meant to be good police. And later. She would think about what all this meant later, at home, a week from now, watching TV, or in the bar with Park, because right now she was a cop and there was danger approaching. The girl was coming on hard. The girl was already in the air and climbing the distance like a series of steps and she was about five seconds from Ju when Ju reached for a rubber bullet to drop in the chamber and discovered she was out.

Time was moving slowly. This was how it worked. She was processing information. She was making decisions. She was trained.

She knew what to do. The girl's face was a contorted mask of rage. But not her. Not Julia. No anger in her, no she was calm, she was reacting calmly, she was in control even if she felt the buzz of stretched nerves as she reached for a rubber bullet and found she had none left. Things were happening slow and fast. She was trained. She was responding to a threat to her life and body. She was making decisions.

Because the girl was leaping, the girl was in the air, and she looked aglow with flame. This was not peaceful protest. This was grief in all its loss and fury. This was the world coming to kick down your door. To steal your family.

Ju unholstered her sidearm.

Then the girl landed on the hood of the PeaceKeeper, and Ju raised her department-issue .38 and still the girl was coming and she fired.

The bullet took her high in the shoulder, the dark blood flowering like a bruise and how funny, how weird and funny that she didn't know about it yet even as the force of the bullet took her high above the heart. Ju raised her gun and fired and the girl stopped in mid-stride, trapped on the trajectory of the bullet like laundry hanging on a line, her face pure surprise.

Things moving slowly, very slowly, the noise narrowed to a tunnel, the chanting a whisper, the roar a soft sighing. Nothing but the shot and the girl.

It would repeat later in Ju's mind on a loop she could replay at will, the shot, the shoulder, the dark blood, her arms pinwheeling, and the falling. Later Ju would think of the way it stopped her, the force of her violence, the way it threw the girl's body in the street like something you kick, and it wasn't really worth kicking in the first place, but now, now there was a hand on her leg, and she turned to see Park at the bottom of the PeaceKeeper.

Park's hand on her leg. Park climbing up onto the PeaceKeeper at the sound of the shot. Park's hand on her leg to help himself up and she was turning and there he was, her partner, a look in his face that she had never seen, saying, "Ju, what happened?"

"I went live."

His face looking frightened and human.

"You did what?"

"Live. I went fucking live."

She would think about it later, when she had time to think about it, what his face had looked like in that moment and what she had felt, she would remember and piece it together. Frightened and human. So scared. She was a trained police and what had she done? She wanted to tell Park she had done what she was trained to do. She had protected herself and her fellow officers. In the face of a clear threat, she had laid it down.

Look, there it was. Dirtying the street with its greasy blood.

The threat.

DR. CHARLES WICKRAMSINGHE

Intermission V

One Hour Late for the Meeting

A broad man in a tidy blue suit escorted him to the private elevator. He swiped a key card and the doors swished open pleasantly. They stepped inside. He swiped the card again, entered a few digits, a string of ten, and the doors shushed closed and they began to rise. The walls were made of glass. After two floors they were looking out into the night. The street looked like a battleground after a marauding army had passed through. Bodies everywhere. People passing and lying and sitting and the revolving blue and red lights of the police. The elevator rose with a barely audible hum. The sensation of motion was slight, a scant pressing of the feet to the floor as the elevator raced skyward.

Four floors down was the street. Charles recognized it as Sixth Avenue. The site of his confrontation with the protesters. How long ago that now seemed. Another life. Another man.

The elevator rose above the smoke like a plane finally clearing the clouds. Moving swiftly and surely. Up. Up. Up. The lights of the downtown area fell away. The windows of office buildings were lit and became clear. And then they too blurred in perspective as the elevator rose and the vista opened beneath them. The lights of the city, the famous lights of the city burning beneath them, white and yellow and red, but mostly orange like scattered embers of a city laid to waste.

The elevator rose and rose. Rose above the buildings and then some more. The hotel itself seemed to be shrinking to a point. The elevator's trajectory bending backward and up, a curving of the metallic spine headed toward the top. The elevator man or security man or whoever he was drummed his fingers against the back wall. He offered Charles a stick of gum, which he refused. Why did he feel as if he were a prisoner at execution, riding to the gallows?

The elevator slowed and stopped. The pressure in his belly eased. The security elevator man put the gum in his pocket and gave him a little friendly nudge with his elbow. "Go ahead, sir. They're waiting for you."

* * *

Then he was in the clatter of the dining room, soft music overhead, dim lighting, the cool recycled air of the air conditioner, delegates of various nations huddled in groups of two or three, animated economic discussion, the light tinkling of ice in glass as they complained and argued in loud voices. Evidently they hadn't appreciated being trapped inside their hotel all day. Across from Charles sat two of his oldest friends, Sir Edward Bancroft, Teddy to those that knew him, one half of the pair that made his only friends during those lonely years at Cambridge. Sir Teddy, in his tan suit and blue tie, in a wheelchair to which he'd been confined as long as Charles had known him. Sir Teddy. The Director-General of the World Trade Organization.

The other friend was Martin Oswego. Martin was from the Ivory Coast, the West African nation, and he, like Charles, had been a scholarship boy from a former colony.

Look at them now, financial ministers at the highest levels of power, drinking double martinis in a fancy American hotel.

Five minutes. In five minutes he had gone around the world. From victory to ignoble despair. And now skyrocketing back from despair to happiness, realizing all in an instant who had called for him, whose power had pulled him from that bus, given him a fresh change of clothes, a new suit which was a perfect fit, whose power and influence had snuck him through the employee entrance to the Sheraton in the loading dock, and sent him all the way up here to this hall in the sky.

"I was arrested, Teddy. They put me in jail."

And here came Sir Teddy's booming laugh.

"I know, Charley. You certainly did make a fucking mess of things."

And here at the heart of everything, in the holy sanctuary of the Sheraton dining room—delegates only please—was the Director-General of the WTO laughing and saying fuck like he was a cowboy in a saloon, and not a single person surprised by the man's manners.

"They canceled the meetings, Teddy. Those children. They canceled our meetings."

"The meetings aren't canceled," Teddy said. "They were just delayed, that's all. We'll have our meetings tomorrow. Or the next day. Or next month. Fucking kids."

"But Teddy, how can they be delayed? I had a meeting with—"

Sir Teddy cut him off with a chuckle deep in his chest. He patted the padded arm of his chair.

"I know who you had a meeting with, Charley. Sneaky bastard, good for you. But Charley, you didn't miss your meeting. Clinton isn't coming."

A crushing wave of nausea passed over him.

"Clinton's not coming?"

"No, Charley. Secret Service said it wouldn't be safe."

"But Teddy—"

Teddy wasn't listening.

"Did you hear Fidel sent a delegation?" Laughing, shaking his head good-naturedly. "Can you bloody imagine? The Cubans? Here? What, trading cigars and rum?" He laughed. A great basso rumbling boom-boom-boom.

"You have to give it to the old man," Teddy said. "He's got a pair on him, eh? Jesus, god, the Cubans. Can you imagine it? You know, though," he said, leaning in close, "I would have loved to talk with him. Fidel! What a leader!"

* * *

Charles drained the rest of his drink and raised his hand for another. His steak sat forlornly cooling on his plate, hardly touched. He had taken one bite—the blood rushing into his mouth—and nearly retched. In his increasingly inebriated state he tasted in its marbled veins of fat only his own frustrated hopes, his singed and bloody ambition.

Sir Teddy made a joke and Charles forced himself to laugh. Watching the casual manners of his friend, the friendliness riding softly above the authority, Charles had instantly realized his own position all these years, all those meetings with all those presidents and prime ministers. He was a small fish. A big joke. The banana-and-elephant man. What the fuck did Tony Blair care about him?

He gagged down this newly discovered knowledge with a gulp of gin and vermouth. The olive loosed from its pick, bounced its way down his throat. Coughing, coughing, coughing. Choking on his helplessness. Martin leaned over and whacked him on the back

284

and before Charles could switch to something safer, another martini—a double—arrived in his hand as if by incantation or curse.

Something niggling at the edges of his brain, something that had more to it than his rising drunkenness, and his inability, his goddamn timidity in the face of Sir Teddy. Sitting right here and Charles had not the courage to ask him for the favor he needed. Charles found himself drifting. He found himself remembering, he could not say why, Tennyson. His dog. That stray scraggly mutt from his days at Cambridge, the scrawny mutt he had found on the street and fed and brought back to his bedsit, the dog easing his loneliness, his foreignness. He named him Tennyson, and Tennyson trusted him. Lived with him for weeks, loved to run along the river in the Backs, barking at the punting fools rowing between the locks. But what had happened to Tennyson? Charles thought of the day it was discovered he was keeping Tennyson in his room, and told in no uncertain terms that he must get rid of the dog if he was to remain in Cambridge lodgings. Well, he had nowhere else to live—impossible—and didn't know anybody in the whole of England who might possibly take in the stray dog he so foolishly loved. He now remembered, for the first time in many years, possibly for the first time since the day itself, taking Tennyson to the shelter where a white-coated technician had rubbed Tennyson's head and then stuck a needle in his leg and Charles holding his dog in his arms and telling him it would be all right, old Tennyson, shaggy-haired Tennyson, the light draining from his eyes, the sweet dog from the street whose head sagged in Charles's arms while Charles stood there and told him it would be all right.

Charles pushed away his drink. He lifted his fork and picked at three asparagus spears, limp beneath a murky hollandaise. Oh, he was a coward and a fool. Even Tennyson must have known that.

"Teddy," he said, interrupting whatever the fuck the man had been talking about, "I was supposed to meet with President Clinton."

"Yes, I know, Charles. And as I said, he will arrive later tonight or not at all."

"I have to have this, Teddy."

Teddy eyeing Charles, and sipping his drink. He smiled again though his manner had utterly changed. Gone was the casual authority of a man entertaining his friends with stories of their ill-spent youth. Here sat the Director-General, the real Sir Edward Bancroft, clothed in the folded robes of his true self, all those centuries of power and wealth. Martin sat meekly beside him, quiet, it seemed, now that there seemed to be an argument brewing.

"Listen, Charles," Teddy said, "I am not unaware of Asian history. African history. The history of colonialism throughout the world. But that's *old stuff.* The millennium is upon us. You and I, we're the positive people. The people who believe in change, in progress, in moving forward. Getting past fucking *history.*"

Charles clutching his steak knife beside the plate.

"We are here," Teddy said, "to negotiate the terms of world trade. One hundred and thirty-five nations to discuss, in clear and open meetings, the rules by how we will all play the game."

His voice took on an edge, a note of exhaustion. "Those children, out there"—he flung his arm expansively toward the room, a gesture which seemed to include in its sweep the street, the city, possibly the entire globe.

"Those *children* may believe different. That we are trading away democracy, the environment, labor laws. That we are starting a new American empire. For whom? Global corporations?"

He looked down at his hands, then met Charles's eyes directly. "Can I be honest with you, Charley?"

"Please stop calling me Charley."

That small smile appeared and disappeared.

"Dr. Wickramsinghe, I don't mean to insult, but what do we have in Sri Lanka? We have a small island nation the size of what, Belgium, that has been at war with itself since 1983. A sixteen-year civil war which shows no sign of abating. A tiny poor nation. What do you possibly have to offer anyone besides warmed-over wage slaves and more of the same?"

"Textile factories—"

"Producing what? Undershirts and shawls? Blouses and briefs? Even if you did have a meeting today, why would it be with President Clinton? It wouldn't be with Clinton."

He stopped and smiled. Rolled gently back from the table in his chair. Charles realized with a shock he did not appear to be drunk in the least.

"It was never going to be with Clinton. Jesus. It would be with some mid-level bureaucrat who, despite his fifty other meetings with B-list countries today, would pretend to be interested in Sri Lanka's tea and rubber trade. Your textiles!"

"Teddy, don't go."

"Our man from the Treasury, who may once have had high dreams of his own about changing the world, would probably talk about the importance of privatizing the telecom business, privatizing the water and electricity, grumble about distortions to the market, the inefficiencies of state bureaucracies."

Charles was silent. He was afraid to even move lest Teddy leave him entirely behind. How many meetings had he had that were, in fact, *exactly* like this? Teddy had just described his last five years of meetings.

"And you know what, Charley? You might sign some small agreement. Big to you, of course. Giving away all your state enterprises. Selling off your water and electricity and communications. And do you know what that would be?"

Charles couldn't possibly begin to answer. He looked at Teddy no longer eating, his chair angled toward Charles. Martin, too, no longer eating, watching the two of them in shock and disappointment.

"That, Dr. Wickramsinghe, is how you play the fucking game."

Teddy raised his hand and motioned to a staffer who had been sitting, waiting, at another table. The young woman politely made her way to their table and bent to Sir Teddy and Teddy spoke into her ear and she nodded, looked at Charles, and then walked from the restaurant.

Teddy cleared his throat. "Listen, we support development. But there are some serious problems with the Sri Lankan way of life. I can assure you there will be no entry into the WTO for Sri Lanka, nor any free trade agreements with the U.S., unless you enact some serious reforms. Tighten your fucking belt. I believe we have made it very clear that your grossly overfunded health and education will have to go."

Charles straightened. "The Democratic Socialist Republic of Sri Lanka," he said, "has one of the highest literacy rates in the world. We pride ourselves on our education."

"That is commendable."

"We could not cut our education programs."

"You would have to."

"The people would not accept it."

"Dr. Wickramsinghe," Teddy said. He was calm and mocking and amused, his voice doing a fair imitation of Charles's own baritone intonation. "Is the *Democratic Socialist Republic of Sri Lanka* a country where the economic decisions that affect the nation's future are made by the *people*?"

The young staffer returned and offered Teddy a sheaf of folders, which he took and tossed on the table.

"But we are willing to work with you if you are willing to work with us. Here are the terms of the agreement, which include, as I've said, the proposed budget cuts. Sign and you begin Sri Lanka's entry to the WTO. It's as easy as that, my friend." He smiled, open and full now. "Of course, as the lead negotiator on this deal, there would be a significant bonus for you personally."

Charles looked at Teddy carefully, at the band of fat beneath his chin, at his wheelchair, at his rueful grin, and Charles thought of the house he would buy in the hills of southern England, the small touches his granddaughter would add, flowers on the windowsill, embroidered curtains. He thought of the walks he would take alone in his retirement, down the chalk cliffs to the shore, the sound of the crashing waves and the cold gritty sand between his toes, gulls wheeling and crying above in an English sky of English clouds, the perfect peace he had long dreamed of.

He thought of great slat-ribbed Tennyson, his mongrel dog racing him beside the water of the river Cam, tongue lolling like a madman, tail going like a whip. The happiness of that stupid dog. Tennyson's inability to see the end whose coming was inevitable. You can only rise so high, Tennyson, before someone like me, someone that loves you, is forced to cut you down. Charles looked out the window. The scene was now completely enveloped in fog and cloud. Nothing to see. Nothing to feel. A hotel wrapped in gauze.

Teddy rolled back from the table and turned. "You take your time," he said. "Take a moment to figure it out. Politics, Charles, is not for idealists. It is the art of the possible. You would do well to remember that. Maybe Martin here will offer some advice."

And then he was gone, making his way in the wheelchair to

the other tables. Charles looked at Martin, who earlier this year, Charles knew, had negotiated a third round of loans from the IMF. Charles saw for the first time how much the years had aged his friend. It was his eyes really that held the weight of all those years, all those compromises, and watching him now, Charles knew just what it had all cost him. He had the eyes of a man who has just been told his house burned down with his wife and children inside. Sad eyes that looked like they would never recover from the shock, had maybe not even yet allowed themselves to register the full weight of the news.

Martin smiled at him and gently patted his hand. "It will be all right, Charley. You'll get used to it." But Charles didn't hear words of comfort. He heard, in fact, the echo of what he himself had said to poor old Tennyson all those years ago on the veterinarian's steel table moments before they put the needle in him that laid him out forever.

Charles looked at Martin, saw the sky behind him, the cloud cover thick and gray. He heard the low chatter of the room, ice chiming in the glasses like little bells, the explosive laughter of Teddy banging above the heads. No, he thought, nothing is going to be all right.

40

All across the world they watched the TV. In their living rooms and dens. Gathering outside the café. Dozens in the street watching through the window. Their hands going to their mouths.

On the screen, they were running in the streets. They were jumping in the streets. They were running and screaming in the streets.

The TV news. Hurricane winds tossing the reporter's hair, waves crashing behind her. A city in flames behind her. A war behind her. Everything always behind her.

When the Wall fell. The way people swarmed over the concrete. The way they took hammers and crowbars to it. Tore at it with their bare hands. Swarming. They wanted to hold a piece of history in their hands, to take it home with them. To hold it in their hands like a book. To put it on a shelf.

The reporter on top of her hotel in Baghdad, the rocket fire falling like stars to earth. Or incandescent earth rising in missile-shaped pieces through the Iraqi night.

What was it, '91, '92?

They called it the Gulf War.

On the TV black-hooded protesters threw a newspaper box into the window of a Starbucks.

The footage was on a loop. They smashed the window. They smashed it again.

Smash. Smash. Smash. They smashed the window. They smashed it again.

41

What the TV did not show:

The convoy of twenty trucks rumbling through the streets, tarp-covered and flat green, headlights cutting weird and spooky shapes in the night. The eight hundred souls aboard, rocking and jostling, heads down, contemplating the bayonet, thinking this was the weirdest of missions, a convoy of twenty National Guard trucks rolling through an American city, American soldiers going armed into the American night, the loose edge of the tarp flapping in the running breeze.

The TV didn't show Park in plainclothes humping two duffel bags down Sixth. Replacement tear gas canisters flown in from some sheriff's office in eastern Washington rattling inside. Park's straining arms, his sneakers, the sweat wetting his face and soaking through his softball league T-shirt. Ju shot somebody? Why did Ju shoot somebody? You were there. I was there. Did Ju shoot somebody? Did the Chief try to throw you off the truck? What in the heck happened?

He wasn't interested in what happened. Or how. Only what was to happen. What was coming. He didn't think about the past. He didn't dwell.

He slowed at a knot of protesters gathered on a corner. They were blocking the street, unintentionally, or intentionally he thought as the faces turned toward him, the people clocking his clothes, the way he walked, the department-issue black duffels and his buzz cut. His disfigured face. A bulky blond man with a dried smear of blood across his forehead stopped Park with an arm to his chest.

"What you got there, my man?"

Park could feel then the loose emotion in the street, the anger, how it wanted to coalesce around him in his half-baked undercover getup and tear him apart.

The big guy looking at him skeptically and hands beginning to take the duffel bags from him when he stopped and said, "Don't I know you from somewhere?"

"No," said Park.

"No, I do. On the TV maybe? You play ball?"

"No."

"The weather or something?"

"No."

"I'm sure of it," the big guy said. He tilted his head and regarded Park. "Holy shit," he said. "You're that cop from Oklahoma City."

"A fucking cop?!" said a guy in a black leather jacket. "Fuck that."

"This guy saved thirty-five lives or something. Dragged kids out of there. I remember I saw him on the *Today* show or something."

"Yeah? How the hell do you know that it's him?"

"Check his face, shitbird."

Park standing there, sweating while the small crowd of late-night vigilantes studied him. "You don't end up with a face like that for nothing. Let the man through."

"What do you mean let him through? He's a cop."

"Fuck yes, he's a cop. The guy's a goddamn hero. Let him through."

The TV didn't show Dr. Charles Wickramsinghe slumped in the sky bar of the Sheraton hotel, head buried in his arms.

"Martin, listen, how many of the African ministers are you in touch with?"

The two men—one brown, one black, one tall, one short—sitting at an abandoned table littered with plates and glasses and a folder with a pen atop that sat on the white linen in front of Charles's arms and head.

"Martin, tell me, how many of the African ministers are you in touch with?"

Martin cursing under his breath. Charles suddenly sitting up.

"How many, man?"

"All of them I suppose."

"And do they trust you?"

At this Martin paused again. He regarded Charles for a moment and then said, "Yes, they do."

"Good. We need to get them together."

"What are you planning to do with that?" Martin gestured toward the folder with his eyes.

The TV didn't show their conversation, these two economic ministers of small Third World nations, Charles talking, Martin nodding, the two of them suddenly laughing, nor the new light which gathered in their faces as they stood up, nor the embrace they shared there in the restaurant that had a solidity to it which had not been present in some forty years, these oldest of friends, these newly minted comrades. Charles clapped Martin on the back and together they made their way to the elevator.

Charles hit the street, holding the folder and thinking he wasn't just going to refuse their offer. No, he was going to shut down the entire round of meetings and make sure they didn't start until they started on fair terms. Just as he had once flown the world gathering signatures, now he was going to gather people. He was going to gather enough of the African ministers, the Latin American ministers, the Asian ministers, and together they were going to make the meetings fair and transparent. Environmental regulations. Labor laws. These would be included, or the meetings would not continue. What was it he had heard in the street so many times today? Fair trade, not free trade. Well the big boys—the *developed* countries—couldn't have either, if none of the former colonies agreed to participate. No factories for their clothes, no mines for their minerals, no markets for their subsidized rice and corn. Nobody to trade with, if that's what you wanted to call it. Charles was going to make sure they didn't go another round. He straightened his suit and stepped from the back door of the Sheraton. He looked down the block to where those city buses were parked. But first he was going to get some people out of jail.

John Henry had watched the bullet throw King in the street like a doll made of rags and sticks. Her legs kicked out from the force of the blow, and he watched her, King, his friend and lover, bent into a geometric construction of body he would have never thought possible and John Henry thinking of the anti-nuke demo where they had first met, thinking about the desert, about the gate guards, and the scientists, and the regular staff. The janitor that wore a blue zip suit and a radiation badge and made, like, seven bucks an hour. Quiet John Henry and rage-filled King, how many years ago, and the janitor that brought them water there in the desert, tipping it to their mouths because they could not use their arms; telling them how everyone was talking about these eight crazy people chained together in front of the facility, how nobody in the entire place knew what to do—geniuses and generals alike—and John Henry remembering how King's face had burned, how they had sat together for five days without food; how their lips had cracked and split as they grinned in dusty lockdown, how the janitor who watched from behind the chain-link fence had started crying and could not stop until he had left the confines of the fence and brought them the little plastic pail of water, turning it to their swollen mouths in the heat and the light.

But that was not what John Henry remembered most. What he remembered most was that man telling him how they had looked like corpses out there. How they scared him. How he looked at them, eight sitting corpses turning to mummies in the desert heat, and knew that he would never work in this facility again. How he could not continue, not after seeing their bodies like that. And how King leaned from the truck, leaned into the desert air, and kissed the man gently on the cheek and said, "Thank you."

John Henry thinking how King was unafraid of fire because made of fire herself. And the lights of the ambulance trying to push its way through the intersection. And the stretcher which they slid beneath her and dropped the wheels, the stretcher to roll her to the vehicle when it could not make its way through the crowd.

And John Henry moving now, too, moving toward the PeaceKeeper. The noise of the people that remained rising to a nearly unbearable pitch. My people. Moving toward the cops stationed there, toward the black patch of paving that stood at their feet. My people. And John Henry knew he could not save King, already taken away on that stretcher, and he could not save Victor, who was still on the ground surrounded by angry sweating cops and their batons, Victor a small thing lost in that circle of rage, so John Henry knelt. Kneeling because he could not save King, praying because he could not save Victor. Lying down in front of the PeaceKeeper because if he could not save them, then he could join them.

John Henry stretched out, his head against the cool concrete, his single human body at the foot of the cops, his body on the ground in front of their slow-rolling machine. And they could move him, they could beat him, they could spray him or gas him or cuff him or kick him, but for now, for this one moment, as long as it lasted, he would lie right here on the city's bloodied ground—one man alone—and he would breathe and not be moved.

Out of the chaos, he heard a groan. Not a sound of pain, but something familiar, a sound from his childhood, from a million dinners with his family and his father, it was the easy familiar groan his father made lowering himself to his chair, and John Henry looked up to find an older black man easing himself down onto the pavement, creaking and groaning, yes, as he lowered his body to the ground, his hand raised to his wife, who was on one knee, and then, too, lowering herself to the pavement beside the two of them.

Their three bodies stretched side by side on the pavement. Breathing evenly. The man reaching for John Henry's hand. His dusty dry fingers so surprisingly strong.

The TV didn't show Bishop in the swarm of cops, trying to throw them off with little success. Didn't show his face or his body or

298

his baton which he would not use. Pulling at men with his hands, nothing but his hands, while they hammered at his son.

And the TV didn't show Ju atop the PeaceKeeper. Her tired feet, or the familiar ache in her lower back, or how she wanted nothing more than to go home and see her sister's kids, let them play xylophone on her tired spine, except that they were in Guatemala, four thousand miles to the south, on the wrong side of two borders, and here she was geared up for civil war and she had just shot someone, discharged her weapon in the course of duty, which was legal and allowable and exactly what she was trained to do, except she had realized as soon as the gun fired and she saw the woman's body crumpling in the street that legal or not she wanted nothing to do with it. That wasn't the job.

But then, time went a little funny and when she looked in the street, she didn't see the girl. What she saw were bodies. Bodies upon bodies lined side by side. More lying down with every passing moment. People lying in the street like corpses, head to toe, and arm to arm. Bodies clothed in blue and red and green. From her vantage point there atop the PeaceKeeper, what Ju saw were human bodies lying in the street as far as the eye could see. A line of corpses from here to the horizon line. The smoke drifting lazily over them, bright where it passed beneath the streetlamps. The black buildings reflecting faces without names, bodies whose families would never know, and soon the priest would come, soon the words would be said which closed one door forever and opened another. Soon the mothers would come, clutching photos to their chests, come to look one last time for what they knew was here but could not find. Then, finally, the cupped hand throwing dirt. The sharp grunt of the shovel in stony soil. Then the grass. Then the cold morning dew which did not care. Then the daisies growing in white bunches from their bellies, flowers in yellow from the new earth of their eyes and hands and mouths.

Twenty feet away the sounds floating from the circle of cops. The boy a bloodied thing beneath them. And the Chief in the pile, trying to pull cops from the circle. Ju stepped down from the PeaceKeeper. Her legs were shaking. She was going to do what she should have done since this whole thing started. What she should have done all those years ago when rage ran loose in the streets of L.A. and the cops spurred it on. What she should have done and what she had always wanted to do. She was going to stop it.

She lifted her foot and placed it carefully. She began to walk among the breathing, steaming dead. Began to walk toward that sound, picking her way among the bodies, walking toward that ring of men who were grunting and growling like dogs on a deer. Because how do you stop a pack of men who have been wounded in the fight, who have scented blood on their adversary and are closing in for the kill? How do you stop a pack of dogs who have lost their minds in fear and rage? You remember that they are not dogs, but men. Frightened and angry human beings.

The TV didn't show the hospitals or schools or prisons. The smell of ammonia and blood, that certain sterile smell King associated with death in modern corridors. The clinical light which dimmed, or the pain which ripped through her shoulder as King tried to lift her right hand and found it handcuffed to the gurney, the pain which went all the way inside her muscles and liver and kidney as if she had been sliced open from head to toe and then roughly cut into as many pieces as each organ would allow.

The TV didn't show her being whisked through the twilight city by efficient forces beyond her control, handcuffed in an ambulance while the sirens cried and the cars pulled to the shoulder so they could pass, and King thinking, all she had done, and all she had become, and every rule and code she had broken, and everything she had believed and burned. How many of her friends, beaten, broken, in jail serving sentences for trying to break the spell? Everything she had tried to live and failed.

The ambulance and the EMT and King suddenly tearing at the tubes, using her free hand to rip at the IV lines in her arm, to tear at the tube that wound down her throat. The sudden rush of activity in the small space which was filled with his moving body and the warning tones which monitored her life and her head bucking and the lines whipping back and forth as she tore them free and the medic's weight against her body, trying to hold her down, and King croaking into his face, "Let me fucking die.

"Please just let me die."

The man who took her hand in his, not an effort of restraint, but holding her hand and looking into her face, and in his eyes she saw not the state, not institutionalized evil, not modern medicine and all its chemical compromises, not the death of human connection, not a servant of that state which built prisons for you at every turn, no, what she saw in his eyes, in his face, was nothing more than simple human concern, the sudden affection of one human being for another.

And she had broken everything she had ever built, smashed it to pieces, and even still she had watched Victor beaten, and watched a man bleed to death in the sand, and the light of a single candle glowing from inside their homes of salvaged wood and tin and she with her home of food and electricity and there was a warmth coming from his eyes as he held her hand and said, "You're going to live."

She felt the warmth and smoothness of his palm encircling hers as he said, "It's going to hurt like hell, darling, but you're going to live."

That wasn't what the TV showed. It didn't show him holding her hand or the siren wailing or the machines beeping or the singing of the tires on the asphalt as they raced her to the hospital and it didn't show all she knew or all she believed and it didn't show how she might in some way live in this world the way it was.

42

This is what the TV showed:

An airplane.

A big white thing eating light. A white and blue Boeing 747 customized in the USA to ferry its precious cargo from shore to shore, flying high above dangerous seas. Recognizable to all who watched with its bald hump behind the nose and its glassy eyes and a white moveable stairway pushed to its side where was embossed the great official seal. The camera framed the oblong portal that was the door. And there standing on the threshold at the top of the stairs, pausing before descending to the tarmac and whatever waited beyond, the TV showed a man. There he was with his beautiful smile in the door of *Air Force One*, his white hair spectral like a halo. The President of the United States of America.

And this is what the TV showed: The President waving for all the world to see. The President standing at the door of an airplane, waving and grinning his reassuring grin. The President of the United States giving the world who watched a big thumbs-up.

Below him on the TV a scrolling banner read:

VIOLENT PROTESTERS CLASH WITH POLICE.

And then the TV cut to a commercial of a family eating hamburgers in their car.

They looked so happy.

Epilogue

The darkness came in slow and gentle and the wind as it rose carried the smell of bays and beacon lights, the sound of a mast rope snapping against metal, voices calling low across the water.

Evening fell on the estuaries and inlets and bays. It caught a great blue heron in perfect silhouette and it snuck among the twilight feathers of an egret standing brilliant white among the marshy reeds. Dusk settled on the ferries and the yachts and the small boats rocking on the waves, caressed the men and women sliding on the deck in their yellow slickers, their hands and faces bright dabs of light in the deepening dark.

Quietly, it fell in the surrounding country, on the garlic fields and the apple orchards and the fallow fields planted in winter rye where it was broken only occasionally by the light of a swinging lamp or the sweep of head beams running in a field. A small fire smoking in the cold.

The rush of night reached the city and seemed to settle for a moment atop the buildings, paused and built among the concrete helipads, the radio towers and their blinkered red lights, the colonies of parabolic antennas gathered there like a forest of white-dished ears listening to mystics muttering in the sky. It settled and then seemed to step from the flat-topped roof of the city like a woman stepping from a parapet into empty space and her body, plummeting like a falling needle, piercing the thin skin of ice and then disappearing, and the night now a river in flood cascading down the steel and glass facades of the office towers and insurance buildings, the multinational banks, its darkness curling and sliding, puddling in the street, beginning to gather around the huddled figures at Sixth and Pine. The prone body of Victor. His father, the Chief, who had fought his way through. And here in the lamplit black a man holding his son. Here in the neon night a woman who had done the right thing, who had stopped her fellow officers from beating an innocent man—she was being led away in cuffs. But Victor didn't know about any of that. He only saw his father's face here above him. Saw him through the haze of blood. And had he ever really looked at his father's face? His father holding him, gently. Had his father ever really held him?

"Beautiful, isn't it?" Victor said.

And his father's breathing was slow, his voice shaky as he said, "What's that, Vic?"

"The sky."

It was from Victor's vantage point, there in the shelter of his father's arms, a low cloudy canvas made of gray and the reflected orange of the city's lights. But his father didn't look. Instead he said, "Vic, you hang on. Okay?"

"Sometimes I wish it weren't."

"Weren't what, Vic?"

"So fucking beautiful."

And there was nothing to say to that because it was true. Sometimes he wished it weren't. And Victor reaching for his father's hand. With his one good hand reaching up for his father's hand, feeling the roughness of his skin where it sat upon his chest curled into a fist.

306

With his one good hand, Victor took hold of his father's fist and uncurled the callused fingers, one by one. One by one by one by one.

And he wanted to say, I found what I was looking for, Dad. Here we are. Here it is in my hand. And that feeling beyond the rage, beyond the sorrow, the one I always felt and couldn't name? I know its name now, Dad, that emptiness in my chest.

Victor heard himself breathing and felt the blood everywhere on his face. He wanted to say all this and more to his father, but the most wonderful sensation was taking over his body. He could not resist its sweetness. It felt as though the entire crowd was climbing inside his body, as though they had scaled the ladder of his spine, and taken residence in the various parts of his body, heels clacking on each bone-white rung as if climbing the steps of an apartment building that now belonged to them.

People coming and going and climbing the steps to their own apartments, people loving and complaining, people entering and putting their shopping down and putting their keys down and entering the bedroom where they removed their shoes and sat on the bed for a moment and massaged their feet, looking at the wall and imagining what? He felt them taking residence in his body. His body teemed with life and dreams, the apartments growing and stacking, his awareness expanding with each shallow breath. And here was one last apartment, lit by the glow of a shaded lamp. His mother, how long dead, lived here. She was waiting for him like always, with dinner on the table, watching him with bright glassy eyes, head rested in her hand, and her eyes slipping shut, a light snore drifting from her throat, sitting there, his mother, in her robe and slippers, the slippers he bought with his savings, his savings from the community garden where he carried lemonade for the men and women, well, truthfully the slippers he stole from

307

the department store at the mall because his mother's slippers were worn out from the daily friction of feet and floor, but that was all right, because there was his mother, he felt her there, living and waiting peacefully inside him, for whenever he cared to get up off his butt and join her, waiting for him by the lamp, waiting for her son to finally come home so that they could sit down together and eat.

And here in the darkness a father holding his son. The night caressed their cradled forms, snuck beneath their clothes, pooled in the whorled flesh of their ears, and Bishop felt not relief, not anger or shame, but fear. Bishop was suddenly afraid. Because his son was looking at him, not alarmed, not as if Bishop were a coward or a bully or a liar, just looking at him calmly, a small smile beginning to light Victor's battered face, coming from his eyes that could hardly open. And something about that look as if he understood exactly what his father had done, how blind he had been, before and before and before that, too, understood perhaps not the facts but the feeling, the sadness and fear that had been wrapped around his father's heart, squeezing his throat and his courage and his life, and how did his son know?

How could he *know*?

And yet there he was, his son, looking and smiling through his half-opened eyes, not a look of concern, but as if he understood in some way, the sometime knowledge of what this is, the knowledge of the whole ugly beautiful thing, the knowledge of the courage it takes to move into fear and to fuck up and to go on living, knowing that sometimes it is two people alone and some small kindness between them that is not even called family, or forgiveness, but might be what some, on the good days, call love.

Acknowledgments

Writing can be a lonely art, but (fortunately) no book is ever truly a solitary undertaking. I consider myself incredibly lucky to have made such friends and family along the way; compadres all over the world, *mil gracias*.

I want to thank:

My mom, in Florida, for your patience and love, and for always picking up the phone. The time we got to spend together while I was writing this, all the meals shared and the cross-island walks—all of it was truly a gift.

My father in Pennsylvania, for your integrity, your commitment to justice, and your love, for your couch and your cooking, for all of the million kitchen conversations, I am so deeply grateful.

P. J. Mark and Marya Spence, at Janklow & Nesbit, for taking a risk, for taking the time, for your incredible insight and your unwavering support. It wouldn't have been possible without you.

Lee Boudreaux—your belief, your brilliance, your friendship and fire.

The incredible team at Lee Boudreaux Books and Little, Brown and Company, Reagan Arthur, Keith Hayes, Peggy Freudenthal, Miriam Parker, Carina Guiterman, Julie Ertl, and, most especially, rock star publicist Nicole Dewey, who is simply the best in the biz. I'm lucky.

The Hunter College MFA, my people, for telling the truth, and kicking my butt, Peter Carey, Colum McCann, Claire Messud, Nathan Englander, and Patrick McGrath. For all the conversations and all the books and all the early reads, Bill Cheng, Scott Cheshire, Kaitlyn Greenidge, Brianne Kennedy, Carmiel Banasky, Alex Gilvarry, Noa Jones, Liz Moore, Jessica Soffer, Anna Bierhaus, Victoria Brown, Lauren Holmes, Phil Klay, Vanessa Manko, Jason Porter, Jeffrey Rotter, and, most especially, Tennessee Jones, who read this manuscript more times than I can count.

Ellis Freeman at the London Film School, who rearranged my brain and showed me the way, thank you.

For your continued friendship and love of what we do, from the University of Houston Creative Writing Program, Chitra Divakaruni, Emily Fox Gordon, Coert Voorhees, Matthew Siegel, Giuseppe Taurino, Oindrila Mukherjee, Nina McConigley, and Tiphanie Yanique.

This book was a long time in the making and over the years there were many countries, many homes, and many friends who gave me shelter in the storm. Forgive me if I've forgotten to name a few. You know who you are.

In Culebra, Aibonito, Oakland, and elsewhere, Dr. Héctor Sáez. Thank you, my friend. In the West Village and Woodstock, Peter Hirsch and Cusi Cram. For your friendship, energy, and the incredible gift of four months in Sifnos, Greece, Elaine Moore Hirsch. In New Orleans, Dan Packard. For the house in Hobart, many thanks to Will Packard. For the best pasta in Montreal, Mylène Bayard. In Woodstock, Noa Jones and Eva Huie. For her reads near and far, Shivani Manghnani. At the Center for Fiction, Gordon Lish, Robb Todd, and May-Lan Tan. For putting gas in the car and money in the bank, Jesse Placky, owner of Condorcam. In Purulhá and DUMBO, Isabel Carrío. In Seattle, Peter Mountford, Dean Spade, and my cousin Calen Yellowrobe. In Santiago, Puerto Varas, and Maitencillos, Chile, Francisca Cifuentes, Anthony Esposito, and Derek "Che" Way. Living the dream, brother.

My deepest gratitude to the Hunter College Alumni Scholarship & Welfare Fund for their support; Susan Hertog, whose generosity makes possible the Hunter College Hertog Fellowship; the Bread Loaf Writers' Conference; the Norman Mailer Writers Colony; the Asian American Writers' Workshop; and the Elaine M. Hirsch residency in Sifnos, Greece.

For insight as to what actually happened during those five days in Seattle, I'm indebted to the following books, films, and audio recordings:

Direct Action: An Ethnography, David Graeber

The Battle of Seattle: The Story Behind and Beyond the WTO Demonstrations, Janet Thomas

Webs of Power: Notes from the Global Uprising, Starhawk

Five Days That Shook the World, Alexander Cockburn, Jeffrey St. Clair, Allan Sekula

The Battle of the Story of the Battle of Seattle, Rebecca Solnit, David Solnit

Breaking Rank: A Top Cop's Exposé of the Dark Side of American Policing, Norm Stamper

Blue Blood, Edward Conlon

This Is What Democracy Looks Like, Independent Media Center and Big Noise Films

Breaking the Spell, dir. by Tim Lewis, Tim Ream, and Sir Chuck A. Rock

Trade Off, Shaya Mercer at Eatwell Media

N30: *Who Guards the Guardians?* Christopher DeLaurenti

N30: *Live at the WTO Protest November 30, 1999,* Christopher DeLaurenti

WTO 1999 Seattle Protest Excerpts, Public Radio Exchange and Miles Eddy (an enormous thanks to Miles Eddy, who also provided me with over two hours of raw audio from the protests, recorded by him and Justine Cooper)

For access to their archives of written, visual, and audio material, many thanks to WTO History Project at the University of Washington, the Seattle Police Department, and the City of Seattle.

And of course to the 50,000 and beyond who made it happen. As Arundhati Roy writes, 'Another world is not only possible, she is on her way. On a quiet day I can hear her breathing.'